UNDERCARD

UNDER CARD

★ ★ ★ ★ ★ ★

DAVID ALBERTYN

SPIDERLINE

Published in Canada in 2019 by House of Anansi Press Inc.
www.houseofanansi.com

House of Anansi Press is committed to protecting our natural environment.
As part of our efforts, the interior of this book is printed on paper that contains 100%
post-consumer recycled fibres, is acid-free, and is processed chlorine-free.

23 22 21 20 19   1 2 3 4 5

Library and Archives Canada Cataloguing in Publication

Albertyn, David, 1983–, author
Undercard / David Albertyn.

Issued in print and electronic formats.
ISBN 978-1-4870-0480-4 (softcover).—ISBN 978-1-4870-0481-1
(EPUB).—ISBN 978-1-4870-0482-8 (Kindle)

I. Title.

PS8601.L3352U53 2019   C813'.6   C2018-901842-9
C2018-901843-7

Book design: Alysia Shewchuk

 Canada Council **Conseil des Arts**
for the Arts **du Canada**

*We acknowledge for their financial support of our publishing program
the Canada Council for the Arts, the Ontario Arts Council, and the Government of Canada.*

Printed and bound in Canada

MIX
Paper from
responsible sources
FSC® C004071

P.M.

★★★★★★

★ ★

1

12:34 p.m.

THE AIR REEKS of sweat, crushed leather, blood. Dust rises like charged particles. Muscles ripple and punches snap in this secluded Las Vegas gym, as fighters sharpen their skills before their make-or-break moments in the casino.

There are none sharper than Antoine Deco. He confines his gaze to the target before him. One focus, on the bag and in the ring. One focus for the last twenty years.

Antoine stands back, wipes the sweat from his eyes, sees the young reporter watching him. A nobody. Else he wouldn't be here waiting to interview him, a fighter in the undercard. He'd be with the big boys, grovelling before Gibbons and Suarez.

Antoine prefers it this way. Unseen, underestimated, overlooked — the pain he felt growing up is now his secret weapon. He crushes his gloved fist into the bag. Throws a series of combinations. Alejandro, his trainer, grunts, trying to hold the bag in place. *Smack.* Antoine's fist leaves an imprint. His feet are light, rested; his lungs deep, pliant, pushed beyond the brink more times than he cares to remember. *Smack*. Leather on leather, his gloves on the bag. The only sound sweeter is the padded thud of his fist on an opponent's face. No, the crack of an opponent's nose. No, the gurgle of a—

He draws back. Sweat running from his nose like blood. Mouth-breathing like an animal. Not yet. So much to get done first.

He throws his last punch and turns to the reporter. The *hijo de puta* looks impatient. Fuck him, I didn't ask for an interview.

Alejandro hands him a towel, which Antoine mashes against his face. He swipes it over his shoulders, arms, and chest, loops it around his neck, and nods to the journalist. Let's get this over with.

They sit on black metal folding chairs in front of a back wall, far from the bags and the ring, beside the benches and weights. Antoine sprays water into his mouth, swishes it before he swallows.

"I've always wondered," the journalist begins, his tone convivial, as if they are friends, "what kind of a name is Deco?"

"A fake one," Antoine says. "My father picked it when he came to this country."

"I see. And where did he come from?"

Antoine stares at the journalist. This man with his little notebook and his silver pen, poised to publish the secrets of his life; this man who looks about the same age as him;

this man who is so — Antoine searches for the word — so *normal*. He spots a wedding band on the man's ring finger. Wonders how the young wife would feel if he cut the finger off and kept the ring. "He never told me. Somewhere south of here. Obviously."

The journalist shifts in his seat. Antoine can sense what the man has been hoping for. Redemption tale. Sob-story orphan turns gangbanger turns inmate turns pro athlete. Grateful to God, grateful to boxing, grateful to everyone.

But it's me he's got. Antoine Deco. Grateful to no one.

"Most rankings put you in the top fifteen in the world as a middleweight. Kolya Konitsyn is ranked in the top five. A win tonight would be a major step toward a shot at the title."

"Is that a question?"

"What would winning tonight mean to you and your career?"

He almost smiles, imagining this reporter tomorrow. The man will be kicking himself when he discovers what Antoine has done and all he asked for were clichés.

"I'll tell you the truth," Antoine says, leaning in. "Win or lose, I'm not looking beyond tonight."

"You take it one fight at a time?"

"No. I'm all about the long-term."

"Just not tonight?"

"Tonight's the destination. Only thing left is execution."

The man eyes him uncertainly. "You, um...after some early defeats in your career, you haven't lost a fight in over

two years. You've skyrocketed up the rankings. What—
what do you attribute this rise to?"

Antoine's gaze takes on a malignant glint. "Technique
and athleticism. What else would I attribute it to?"

"Prison, maybe? Everyone says you're a different fighter
since you got out. You haven't lost since. What's the — is
there — a connection?"

Antoine listens to the shuffling of feet and the slapping
of leather on leather. He hears the commands of trainers
to their charges, and the grunts of those charges as they
execute the commands.

"Not in the way you're thinking. It didn't make me
stronger or teach me to value each moment or whatever
bullshit people think prison does to you. That's not how
you rehabilitate people. Prison forced me to train myself."
Antoine smiles. "I'm a good trainer."

"So you wouldn't call yourself 'rehabilitated'?"

He wants gossip, Antoine thinks. No better than a
snitch. "I wouldn't call anyone 'rehabilitated.' Even those
who never went in. Except—"

"Except who?"

Antoine grimaces. Rises from his seat, his back hard
and straight like a board. "Interview's over."

"Wait . . . hold on . . . you said I had till one — we've
still got five minutes. Who do you think doesn't need
rehabilitation?"

Antoine looks down at the journalist, eyes dark. "Got
things to do. Tonight is the fight of my life, after all."

★ ★ ★ ★ ★ ★ ★ ★ ★ ★ ★ ★ ★ ★ ★ ★ ★ ★ ★

2

1:11 p.m.

ONE STEP ONTO the thirsty yellow grass of Auntie Trudy's long backyard and he almost turns around. Too late. He's been spotted.

"Look at you! Prince Shaw home at last," Auntie Trudy gushes. She rounds a food-laden table on the flower-bedecked back porch. The entire cookout, fifty or so people, turn to face him. "Free at last! Free at last! Thank God Almighty...our boy is free at last!" she cries at the top of her voice, as if she is the embodiment of Dr. King and not just quoting him.

Tyron takes a step back, and Tara, his cousin, pushes his shoulder from behind. "You can handle it," she says. "It can't be worse than the Taliban."

He gives her a dubious look.

Auntie Trudy rushes toward him, huffing in her rose-tinted dress. "And just *look* at you!" She wraps her strong arms around him, more of a tackle than a hug. "More handsome than ever. Our own war hero. We missed you, Tyron."

7

She stares deep into his eyes and he has to look away. He doesn't deserve it. This devotion. This love. And from a woman who isn't even blood, even if he does call her Auntie.

"We missed you," she says. "This city needs a Shaw in it."

"Come on, Auntie Trudy. You're making me blush."

"Well, blush then, 'cause I ain't stopping."

He can't help but smile. He swallows her in his arms and lifts her off the ground. He plants a kiss on her cheek, and now she's the one blushing and speechless.

From two yards down a pit bull alternates between barking and moaning for affection, and beyond, the vast desert sky. From one desert to another, he thinks. A life lived in dust and sand.

There are other people coming up to him now, congratulating him, welcoming him home. His head begins to spin. It doesn't help that despite his protests Auntie Trudy keeps shoving plates full of barbecued chicken, devilled eggs, and mashed sweet potatoes into his hands. But he cannot deny that all this feels exceptionally good. He has been gone for such a long time. Gone to such awful places. Gone to do such terrible things.

People ask him about Iraq and Afghanistan, about the Marines, about himself. They ask what he plans to do now that he's back, and all he can do is shrug.

And then they ask if he's heard about Keenan Quinn.

"Did you hear about the trial?"

"You hear he got off?"

"You hear about the protest tomorrow?"

"You lived with him and his family, right? Back in the day?"

"You still talking to that killer?"

"You lost your woman to him, huh?"

"You going to ask him why he took another Black youth from us?"

Yes, Tyron has heard about Officer Keenan Quinn. "The whole city's about to boil over because of him," said Tara on the drive from the airport yesterday. "And right before the Gibbons-Suarez super fight, with the entire country's eyes on us. I'm worried about what might go down, Tyron."

From the moment he heard the story, Tyron has struggled to reconcile the memory of his best friend from childhood with that of a white cop who shot and killed an unarmed Black teenager, a boy named Reggie Harrison. Keenan isn't the type—*wasn't* the type—to do something like that. Keenan was never a racist. They'd practically been brothers.

"YOU HEAR ABOUT your boy from back in the day?"

"Yes, I heard about Keenan," Tyron snaps at Ricky Laurent, the latest to corner him.

"Nah, man, not Keenan. Your *other* boy from back in the day. The Mexican kid."

Mexican kid? At first Tyron draws a blank. "Antoine?"

"Yeah, yeah, Antoine 'Dex' Deco. You hear about him?"

Tyron's eyes narrow as if he's staring down the sights of his assault rifle. He has not heard Antoine's name in years. All he can say in the wake of his surprise is, "I'm not sure if he's Mexican."

"Whatever. *Latin* kid. He's fighting tonight."

"What do you mean, 'He's fighting tonight'?"

"Uh, dude, maybe you heard it's the fight of the decade tonight at the Reef. You hear that? Well, your foster brother is in the damn undercard." Ricky laughs at the absurdity of it. "How's that for a welcome home?"

"You're kidding me."

"Have I ever kidded you before?"

"Just every time I've ever spoken to you."

"This is a first, then. I'm not kidding. Your buddy is fighting in the undercard to the Gibbons-Suarez super fight. The world is going to be watching and every celebrity you can think of is going to be there."

"But how? Last I heard, Antoine was in prison."

"Man, you have been gone a long time. He got out a few years ago, and ever since then he's been tearing shit up. He wins tonight, he'll be on his way to a title fight. Don't you got social media?"

Tyron shakes his head. "I don't like to be distracted when I'm over there."

"Safer that way, huh? Stay focused on survival."

Survival? If only that was all Tyron had to think about

back there. For him, total immersion in a world of suicide bombings and beheadings, in lining up a human being and pulling the trigger, was easier than constant reminders that another world existed. "Something like that."

He tries to shut those thoughts out of his head and return to the present. He is only partially successful. Antoine, he thinks. He was the worst of the three of us. Keenan and me beat him in the ring all the time. "How'd he get so good? Antoine, I mean."

"Hey man, sports is your area of expertise. All I know is the hottest women in this city, in this country — and by extension . . . *the world* — are gonna be ringside tonight. And what's this?" Ricky tugs on his shoulder. "My main man, back in town just one day, happens to be boys with the guy who's gonna win . . . well, not the main event, but at least one of the fucking fights! That should get us into some kind of after-party. I don't need A-list groupies; B-list's good enough for me."

"Now you really are joking."

"I've never been more serious in my life."

Tyron can't help but snicker. "Yeah, that sounds about right."

Ricky turns, holding out his arms to Tara, who looks fit in her tank and denim shorts, her muscles toned from her days on the track. She joins them with a paper plate filled with garden salad and corn. Her face oval and smooth, her hair short and untreated, she stares at Ricky's outstretched arms until he reluctantly lowers them.

"What are you guys talking about?" she asks, as she digs into her food with a plastic fork.

"Ricky was just asking me to hit up Antoine Deco for tickets to the boxing match tonight so he can work celebrities."

"C'mon man — 'work celebrities.' I'm just a boxing enthusiast, Tara. I was actually hoping we could bring you along. Better yet, Ty's probably jetlagged, doesn't want to go out tonight — that's cool — just you and me could go." When she doesn't respond, Ricky pumps his fist into his palm with a loud slap and says, "Beautiful, it's a date. Looking forward to it, Tara."

Tara gathers her breath, winding up for a long rebuke, but decides it isn't worth her time and simply says no, then walks away to join a larger group.

"Smooth."

Ricky's eyes are still on her. "Is she single?"

"No."

"No? Really? I thought she split with —"

"No to your actual question. You can't go out with her."

"Why you would wanna deprive your own flesh and blood of a catch like me, I just don't get. So, how about them tickets?"

"Yeah, it's a real mystery. I don't know, man. How am I supposed to ask Antoine for tickets? I haven't spoken to him in years, Ricky. I'm supposed to just show up at the casino on the biggest day of his life and ask him for a favour?"

"You a genius, dog. You really are. You know that? That's a great idea. Way better than mine."

"What was your idea?"

"Get you on board and let you figure out the rest. I guess this *was* my idea."

Tyron gives a low chuckle. "I'll think about it."

He sets his cup of water down and works his way across the yard, trying to thank everybody for showing up to welcome him home.

"That boy is still so foolish," Tara says to him when he takes a break beside her. He follows her gaze and sees it's aimed at Ricky.

"I wouldn't know," he says.

"You having a good time?"

"It's all right. Thanks."

"You know, I asked Naomi to come."

Tyron spins on her. "You invited Naomi?"

"Don't look at me like that."

"Why would you do that?"

"Because she's a friend of mine. And because she's a friend of yours too."

"I wouldn't call her my friend."

"Okay, she's the love of your life. Is that better?"

He doesn't correct her this time, just sets his jaw like he's about to quarterdeck a grunt.

"Relax, she's not coming."

He refrains from sighing. "It's too much for me, all this. I'm not ready to see her."

"You know, that's exactly the reason she gave for not coming: 'It'd be too much for Ty.'" Tara adds with a smirk, "Does she know you or what?"

"Funny. So, you and her are tight now?"

"We both coach at UNLV. Bumped into each other there about a year ago. We been hanging out ever since."

"She's coaching? She don't play ball no more?"

"Retired a few years ago."

He didn't expect that. All Naomi ever wanted was to play pro ball. "She and Keenan still married?"

It annoys him how much Tara's eyes sparkle. "Technically."

"What does that mean?"

"You'll have to ask her."

Tyron exhales in exasperation. There is another question he wants to ask, but he's afraid of the answer. Do they have children? He decides to leave that bomb untouched. "I thought I might never hear about Naomi, Keenan, and Antoine ever again. I come back and they're on everyone's lips."

Tara shrugs. "Your old crew is making moves. Some good, some bad, some just...moves. It's how things go sometimes."

He nods at her in agreement, but in truth he is distracted. Over the crowd, Marlon Joseph, at the back of the yard, is trying to catch his eye, beckoning to him with his bald, glistening, chiselled head. As Tyron's youth football coach, Marlon was terrifying: intense, imposing, six feet, two inches tall, iron-hard slabs of muscle. As his parents' friend, he was awe-inspiring: quoting Marx and Malcolm X, always with a book in his hands. Tyron is unsure how he feels about him now, but he respects the man enough to obey his summons. He excuses himself from Tara, then sidesteps a large group.

"Ty, Ty, get over here," says one of the women in the group.

Slowing but not stopping, he works his way through well-wishers clasping his hand, patting his back, and finds himself before Marlon. He puts his large hand into Marlon's even meatier one. Marlon's goatee is grey, the sole betrayer of his age.

"Good to have you back, young brother."

Tyron almost says, "Good to be back," but falsehoods are distasteful to his lips, and he is not yet sure if it is good to be back. "People keep telling me how proud my parents would be if...you know...they were still around."

"People remember what your parents did for our community," Marlon says. "They were special people. And they *would* be proud."

The words hit him hard, coming from Marlon.

"You coming to the rally tomorrow?" Marlon asks.

"I don't know yet," Tyron says. He's only recently learned of the march planned for the next morning, in protest of Keenan's not guilty verdict.

Marlon nods. "What are you going to do now that you're back?"

"Everyone's been asking me that. Getting home seemed like a fantasy. Anything beyond was just too far away."

"It's like that with prison. You have all these ideas, but can't see anything beyond those bars opening. How old are you now?"

"Thirty-two."

"Important time. But what time isn't important? Still, if you aren't married yet and don't got kids, you got options like a young man. You know what I think?"

"What's that, Marlon?"

"I think it's fate. You getting back here now, just as that cop gets off. He being your old friend and all."

"Fate?"

"Yeah, fate. We need a Shaw more than ever, Tyron. You don't know what to do with your life, I'll tell you what to do. Take up the mantle of your parents. Teaching, community organizing, activism. Continue their legacy. It's what you were born to do, young brother."

Tyron holds Marlon's stare as long as he can, then looks out at the sweeping desert sky. He draws in a breath of hot, dry air. I need to be somewhere humid, he thinks. Somewhere wet and green. The only wetness in the desert is blood.

He turns back to Marlon and says, "Continuing their legacy starts with me going to that rally?"

"That's right."

"You know the Quinns took me in after my parents passed."

"I know."

"I'm a Marine, Marlon. Loyalty is everything to me."

"And if that loyalty to a murderer conflicts with loyalty to your community, what do you do then?"

"In that case, I stay on the sidelines."

"So you aren't coming tomorrow?"

Tyron gives a quick shake of his head.

"Think on it," Marlon says. "A miscarriage of justice like this can't stand, no matter who the perpetrator is." He puts a hand on Tyron's shoulder and somehow grows even more serious. "Black Lives Matter is just getting started. Things are happening, son. At last, they're happening. We need you in on this. People respect and believe in you. Sports star, war hero, and most of all, the only child of Terrence and Viola Shaw. You can inspire us. Not just young people, all of us. Me included. We need you, young brother. Promise me you'll think on it."

Tyron clasps Marlon's hand and they embrace.

Walking back across the dry lawn, Tyron recalls when the general pinned those medals on his dress blues. But those medals didn't come with the well of unease deepening within him.

★ ★

3

2:18 p.m.

THE DEEP SEA greens and dark blues of the Reef Resort and Casino make Keenan feel submerged, like he's been transported to the lost city of Atlantis — if Atlantis had slot machines. He wishes he was actually submerged, actually at the bottom of the ocean, staring up at actual luminescent coral and not this knockoff crap protruding from the ground, the walls, the ceiling.

Not the worst way to go, once the lungs close up. The pain would be brutal, but there has to be some kind of serenity at the end, he thinks.

He walks past a nightclub and a shark tank on his way to the escalators, scratching at his beard, the fake black beard he glued on an hour ago. He can't even show his face in public anymore, the smooth fair skin or light red stubble too recognizable from the media coverage of his trial. People get out of his way — they know he's cursed, even if they don't know his true identity. He crosses another row of slot machines to a set of elevators, the doors polished to a sheen. His reflection stares back uncomfortably.

The Reef cap pulled low to cover his red hair, the aviator shades hiding his blue eyes, that stupid black beard on his face—he looks like a stalker. What woman would look twice at this chump, except to make sure he isn't following her? At least this dope looks Italian and not like he just stepped off a boat from Dublin. The doors slide open and he's split in half like a bad film edit.

He exits on the fourth floor and walks down a couple of carpeted hallways to a metal door that reads EMPLOYEES ONLY, taps his keycard to unlock it, and heads down more hallways to a series of offices with executive assistants staffing desks out front. He explains who he is and is told to go straight into the office of the casino's director of security, Raymond Monk. Keenan is expected.

At the door Keenan hesitates, poised to knock. He is grateful to his father's old friend and former partner for getting him this job, yet an old feeling returns to him, a forgotten disquiet associated with this man. Keenan's father, Craig, used to say that Raymond Monk was the kind of guy who couldn't wait for a fight. In their narco days he would crack skulls without a second thought. Keenan has seen the man only a handful of times as an adult, and it was cool every time, but always some wariness from childhood lingered.

"It's open," Monk calls out when he knocks.

Inside, Keenan smirks: even Monk's office has an underwater vibe. A long fish tank atop the mini-bar and cabinets; the plush carpet patterned in wavy, watery hues of green and blue; the walls a dark, almost black-blue, suggesting the office has sunk into a chasm on the ocean floor—did they never think they were overdoing it? Women seem to like this kind of shit, though. In Keenan's experience the Reef is the best place in the city to pick up. Just have to avoid the sex workers. But Keenan can spot a hooker with his eyes closed. And he's never had to pay for it.

Not anymore, though. Maybe he will have to start paying for it; who's going to want to sleep with the most hated man in Las Vegas? A disgraced cop. A murderer. Even his wife doesn't want him anymore.

"Keenan," Monk says, rising from his desk. "You're late."

Keenan checks his watch. "I thought I was early."

Monk laughs. "I'm just fucking with you. Like my digs?"

The large office has a desk, a small conference table, chic metal chairs with black leather upholstery, filing cabinets, bookshelves, a safe; no windows, though. Keenan wouldn't like to work in an office with no windows. "It's great. Big."

Monk smugly folds his arms and bounces his head down like he's Mussolini. Close-cropped grey hair atop his heavy, carved bones, Monk has the kind of face that could break knuckles without losing any of its rugged appeal.

"Take a seat."

Keenan approaches and shakes Monk's hand. Keenan looms over him; the man must be a couple inches under six feet, though he has the arms and shoulders of a brawler. Monk's grip is so tight that Keenan's hand aches, and he is forced to squeeze back like they are in some kind of competition. Overcompensation? Is that what Keenan recalls of this man?

They sit on either side of the desk and Monk pours them each a scotch. "I tell you, Keenan, this whole situation is a blessing in disguise. Getting kicked out of Metro, I mean. The private side is the shit. If I had to do it over, I would've left the force sooner."

Keenan clears his throat, and says with some effort, "I resigned. But I see your point."

"You resigned or they *forced* you to resign?"

A flash of what his life as a police officer would have looked like after the trial brings a lump to his throat. The moment that boy dropped, Keenan knew he could never police these streets again. And that was before he found out the shooting had been recorded on someone's phone. "I resigned. But maybe I saved some people headaches."

He accepts the scotch. They clink glasses. Keenan isn't used to drinking in the early afternoon, but who gives a shit anymore?

"Christ, this country has turned soft. To think they brought charges against you for that. The homeboys should know by now: you run, you get a cap in your ass. It's natural selection. Clear out the dumbasses, we might get somewhere." Monk takes a long, slow sip of the amber liquid. "Hell, but what do I know? It got you working for me, right?"

Keenan has the urge to argue with Monk in some small way, to dissociate himself from Monk's rhetoric, but when he attempts to do so in the most subtle, conciliatory manner, his body recoils. He drinks his whisky, because it is the only acceptable thing to do in the moment. He always obeyed his instincts without a second thought; now he doubts everything, every action, desire, decision. Keenan is afraid. He can no longer trust his natural inclinations. But what difference would it make to speak up anyway? He knows he'll be lumped in with people like Monk regardless of anything he says—forever seen as "one of them" thanks to one atrocious error in judgement.

Monk leans back in his chair and puts his black alligator cowboy boots up on the desk. "When the time is right I'll introduce you to Mr. Bashinsky. Wait for this shit to settle down first." He slides his boots off the desk and leans forward in his chair, surprisingly earnest now. "He's a special man, Bashinsky. A visionary. The best casino owner this town has ever seen. Make a good impression on him and it'll change your life. It sure changed mine." He downs his drink and pours another one, motions Keenan to follow his lead.

"Excuse me, Detective Monk, but—"

"I haven't been a detective for a long time, junior. You want to be formal, it's Director Monk. But you were a kid back when I first met you, Keenan. Remember that? You would tell me about all your little girlfriends. 'The little player,' we called you."

Keenan doesn't remember any of this.

"Call me Ray. Your dad and me go back so long it should

probably be Uncle Ray. Get over here on Uncle Ray's knee, boy," he orders, slapping his thigh and laughing.

Keenan stares at Monk. "That's pretty creepy, sir."

"Ray."

"Pretty creepy, Uncle Ray."

Monk's face breaks into a grin and he hits the table. "Give me your fucking glass."

Keenan does as he's told. "My shift starts at three." He checks his watch. "That's in half an hour."

"Your point?" Monk hands back the glass, full of whisky.

"You want me showing up drunk on my first day?"

"I do if your boss is the one getting you drunk. Then you should drink all he gives you, show that you know how to take orders."

Keenan takes a huge gulp to show just how good he is at taking orders. Too good, he thinks.

They finish their drinks and, the bottle empty, switch to bourbon for the next round.

"The shit your old man and me got up to when we were undercover..." Monk whistles. "But no son wants to hear those kinds of stories about his old man. Am I right?"

"Right. Last thing I need is more of my dad's cop stories. A hundred times is usually enough."

"Ha. That's your old man right on."

The alcohol is getting to Keenan, his tongue suddenly looser, his worries less important. He has been drinking a fair bit lately; he isn't used to being hated. Setting his drink down, he unconsciously reaches for his wedding band. He rotates it around his ring finger, his mind drifting to his wife, Naomi. He grimaces and wonders once again if he should just leave this city and all his problems in it. Or go a step further and lay his problems to rest for good.

"Disguise ain't bad," Monk says. "When the dust has cleared and you meet Mr. Bashinsky, you can stop wearing it."

Keenan nods. "I want to thank you again for giving me this job. I don't know what I would've done if you hadn't."

"Don't mention it. It don't cover half of what I owe your old man. And we needed extra people for the fight anyway. Huge night for us. You a boxing fan?"

"When there's a big fight. I boxed as a kid. I trained with Antoine Deco, actually."

Keenan can feel the change in Monk: sparks leap off him. Monk looks down, unclenches his hand like he just realized how tightly he was gripping his glass tumbler. Keenan stares at him, wondering what Antoine could've done to precipitate such a change in this man. Although Antoine does tend to have that kind of effect on people.

Monk leans back, feigns a smile. "I knew that, actually. Your pops told me. Deco's come a long way. Further than any of us imagined."

"You can say that again," Keenan says.

"You might bump into him tonight. You'll be ferrying fighters back and forth."

"Cool," Keenan says, even though he has no interest in

seeing Antoine ever again. "So Gibbons and Suarez will be a big one, huh?"

"There's no fight bigger. Gibbons and Suarez have been ducking each other for years. At last the money got too much for them to keep saying no. Pussies. I never ducked a fight my whole life."

"You're a brave man." Keenan regrets saying this immediately. He runs his tongue over the inside of his teeth, absorbing the pungent aftertaste of the bourbon, hoping Monk missed the sarcasm.

"Want to see how brave I am?"

"No."

"We can throw down if that's what you want."

"No, Uncle Ray."

Monk laughs and they clink glasses for the final time.

★ ★

4

3:02 p.m.

THE BUZZER SOUNDS, deafening, drowning out the parents cheering in the stands. Her point guard hands the ball to the ref. Her girls grin at each other. Another victory.

As Naomi Wilks crosses the gym floor to shake hands with the opposing coach, she reflects that she might be better on the sidelines than she was on the court.

"Great game. Good luck for the rest of the season," she says to her counterpart, a middle-aged woman in a tracksuit. Naomi, meanwhile, wears a charcoal pantsuit, in the manner of her old pro and college coaches: got to look professional on game day.

"I can't believe how much your players have improved," the coach says. "Seriously, great work."

Naomi smiles. "Thank you."

She high-fives the opposing players, and has an encouraging word for each of them: strong performance; solid D; the shot was dropping, nice job. Then she walks back to the sidelines in her flat, non-marking, dress shoes. They patter on the hardwood, so different from the spongy bounce of her old ball shoes and the squeak they made when she changed direction.

At the bench, her team gathers around her. "You balled out," she says to each of the delighted fifteen- and sixteen-year-olds as she high-fives their hands. "You balled out!" She switches from high-fives to shoulder bumps, and the girls love this, jumping up to collide their shoulders with their towering coach, who leans in gently. At her size and strength, she would knock the girls over if she put her full weight into it. Then she starts dabbing before each shoulder bump and the girls lose their minds. Why an arbitrary dance move elicits such excitement from these kids she doesn't understand, but it pleases her to hear their laughter.

Some of the parents come down from the bleachers to thank her. "It's so special for them to have you," one mother says after the girls have left for the change room. "To see you and to know that you've done it, it inspires them."

Naomi stares at the woman, thinking it ironic to hear someone say that she's "done it" compared to what she thinks of her WNBA career. It wasn't a failure, not by any means — she even won two championships with the Mercury — but she was always a bench player and never came close to achieving what she thought she would. "Thank you," she says, lips stretching into a wide smile.

She congratulates the parents on their daughters' performance, excuses herself, and joins her team in the locker room. "You're getting better individually and you're getting better as a team," she says to their flushed, expectant faces. "This is how we move forward. All of us, me included, finding ways to improve on our own, and finding ways to work better together. You're doing exactly that. I'm proud of you. I'm proud of all of you. Team on three."

She reaches out her hand and the girls pile theirs overtop.

"One — two — three — *team!*"

Naomi is happy in that moment. Truly happy. But later, driving home beneath a bright, beating sun, melancholy drifts over her. Sitting at a red light, she looks at the tired faces in the cars around her, and wonders if hers looks as glum. Hard to imagine after the elation she just felt, although a glance at herself in the rear-view mirror is not promising. The light turns; she navigates the Saturday afternoon traffic.

She cannot hang on to it, that sense of community; it evaporates as soon as she's left the gym. She wonders if something is wrong with her, for her emotions to swing so far in so short a time. Or if something is wrong with the society she lives in, for her to feel this alone this often.

She won't find any solace at home, she knows that much. Keenan's too depressed these days to appreciate anything of hers, not that he would anyway. Keenan could be fun when it was his scene, but he was never the type to take a backseat to something of hers. Not that she wants to share anything with him now. He's been acquitted; he's

not going to prison. And she did her duty, stood by him
when he needed her, even if he didn't deserve it. She still
hasn't asked him how he could have done such a thing,
killed an innocent, unarmed person. It doesn't matter now
anyway, what's done is done; she's just waiting for the dust
to settle before she tells him it's over.

She pulls into her driveway and looks at her phone. A
text from one of her personal training clients asking if
she's available Monday morning, and another from her
friend Tara Haynesworth.

Hey girl you missed a great cookout. Ty misses you! And
you know he looks better than ever ;)

Tyron. Naomi wishes she hadn't gotten so excited
when Tara told her he was coming home. She'd wanted
her feelings for Ty to leave with him when he joined the
damn military — of all the things he could've done to
break them up . . . Another woman? She would've killed
him, but at least it wouldn't have been so unexpected. She
knows she's not ideal: too talkative, too tall, too muscu-
lar, too emotional, too much, just in general too much.
She always expected him to leave her for someone else,
the way girls were falling all over him wherever he went.
But he never even noticed them. And what did he end up
choosing over her? A pair of wars. A pair of wars over a
life with her. Thanks, Ty. Nice confidence boost.

Naomi drops the phone in her purse and heads inside.
It's a two-storey suburban house, perfect for a growing family, but empty and a little eerie for a couple on

their own. At least it gives them the space to avoid each other. She walks into the kitchen, dumps her purse on the counter, and runs a glass of water from the tap. Drains half of it at once.

So quiet, she thinks, looking over the kitchen and den, unchanged since they moved in four years ago — renovations aren't exactly on her radar.

She grabs her phone and punches in Tara's name. Her girl picks up right away.

"What's up?"

"Hey, what's up with you?"

"Just helping Auntie Trudy with the dishes. It was a great party, I wish you could've made it. How was your game?"

"Well, you know, one team's got to win, right? So why shouldn't that team be mine?"

Tara laughs. "Your girls dominated?"

"Total domination. They balled out, Tara. You don't even know. Every one of them is a baller on that team. Each and every one. I love it."

"They got a great coach."

"I don't know about that."

"Don't play with me, girl, I know you think you the shit."

"Well, if the shoe fits, right?"

For all her laughter, Naomi hasn't escaped the gloom from the ride home. "You ever feel kind of empty," she asks, "like after a game — or a track meet — and you say goodbye to everybody, and then everything's just so quiet? You know what I mean? Like there's all these people, and you're having so much fun, and everyone's appreciating you and you're appreciating them. And then, you get home and you're just alone. It's like you're more alone than you were before...before...I don't know what I'm trying to say."

"No, I feel you," Tara says. "I mean, I don't feel that way myself personally, but I understand what you're saying. If you want to be around people, you should come to the—Oh damn! I was about to invite you to the march tomorrow. My bad."

"Yeah, wouldn't that be something? I don't think Keenan would appreciate it too much. Or the people in the march, for that matter. I got to embrace my pariah status."

"Don't say that. You didn't pull that trigger. No one blames you for standing by your man."

Naomi appreciates Tara's words even if she doesn't believe them. She knows that the cloud of guilt and shame over Keenan hovers over her too.

She sometimes feels she has two communities to call her own, and sometimes that she has none. She is too much of everything, not enough of any one thing.

Her father is a mutt of European heritage. When Naomi was a kid, he would say to her and her brothers, "You know how many dutiful, gorgeous, petite women I could've married? But I wanted my kids to be heavyweights." Warrior Wilks, as he was known in his boxing days, maxed out as a super middleweight, something that obviously bothered him. "The moment I saw your mom,

I thought, there go my heavyweights." Naomi's mother is Dutch and Nigerian, and she stands an inch taller than Naomi's height of six-one. "So you should thank me for your height, kids. Except for you, Derek, you got too many of my genes, sorry about that. But Drew, Naomi: I did it for you. I had to put up with your wise-cracking mama for you to turn out the way you did. But heavyweights you are." It never seemed to occur to her father that she might not want to be a "heavyweight."

When he'd say this about her mother it was in jest, filled with grinning and chuckling, and Naomi didn't think too much of it as Vivian was, and still is, a striking, beautiful woman. Her father doted on her mother with unabashed affection. And then one day, right before she quit boxing to focus exclusively on basketball, Naomi caught him outside the gym getting into a car with an attractive petite woman. When she confronted him about it, he was repentant and promised never to do it again. The second time Naomi caught him — with a different woman — she told her mother. Her parents were divorced within a year.

"So how's Ty?" Naomi asks.

"Kinda different, kinda the same," Tara says. "He's quieter. Stiffer. He acts like he doesn't belong here anymore. Like he's a stranger."

Naomi gnaws on her lip. "Is he with you now?"

"No, he ran off with that fool Ricky to the Reef. They're going to try to hustle some tickets out of Antoine Deco for the fight tonight."

"Ty's going to see Antoine?"

"I'm just telling you what they told me."

Tyron and Antoine together again. She has difficulty imagining it. Envy cuts through her, like a scalpel grazing her heart, that they get to see each other and she doesn't.

"Has Ty been in touch with Antoine?"

"You know, girl, he did just get a new phone. I can give you his number."

"No, don't give it to me."

"I'll text it to you. That way you got it if you need it."

"Please don't. I c— I can't. I'll see him when I see him."

"All right. You do you. I'm with you."

"Thanks, Tara. Appreciate it."

"Appreciate you. But these dishes ain't washing themselves, so I better be out."

"Good talking. Hope you have a good night."

"You too. Bye."

"Bye," Naomi says, and waits for Tara to end the call before she lowers the phone.

3:39 p.m.

THE DESK CLERK holds her hand over the phone's mouthpiece, eyeing him skeptically. "What did you say your name was?"

Tyron stares at her. This is the third time he's had to tell her. "Tyron Shaw."

"I have Tyron Shaw here," she says into the phone. "He says he's an old friend of Mr. Deco."

"His foster brother," Ricky adds.

"His foster brother," repeats the clerk. "Apparently. Aha. Yes, I'll wait." She holds the receiver to her chest. "He's checking with Mr. Deco."

Ricky grins and slaps Tyron's arm.

"Who would ever turn you down, Ty?"

He humours Ricky with a smile. No doubt the desk clerk was on the verge of calling security a minute ago. Tyron hadn't wanted to play the veteran card, but Ricky played it for him. Perhaps it made some difference, and perhaps Ricky's insistence that Tyron was Antoine's foster brother did too.

"Oh, is that right?" she says into the phone, with a sudden bright smile. "Yes, I'll send him up." She puts down the phone. "Mr. Deco says you can see him." She gives them directions through the casino.

Walking away, Ricky gives Tyron a wry look. "So you been an officer in the United States Marine Corps for the last eleven years and your word is only good when some bullshit, borderline celebrity vouches for you? Good to be back, huh?"

"Yeah. Good to be back."

They pass through row after row of slot machines, flashing and chiming. Loud, bright, and disorienting. Tyron wonders why anyone would want to come here.

"Damn, the Reef is the shit, man," Ricky says. "They got places like this in Afghanistan?"

Tyron favours Ricky's smirk with a glance, but no more. He is tense. He shouldn't be here, accosting Antoine on the day of his fight, in this clamorous, artificial space, in this city he left behind long ago. He shouldn't be here.

They leave the casino and enter a cavernous hallway with designer stores on either side. About thirty yards in, the carpeted floor ends and a floor of transparent glass begins, beneath which is a giant aquarium filled with crystal blue water and fish, stingrays, sharks, even turtles and jellyfish. A glass mirror runs overhead, parallel with the tank below, giving the impression that you're both above and below water. This is what the Reef is known for, the attraction that pulls in tourists faster than any other resort on the Strip.

Tyron's eyes are on the crowd as much as they are on the sea creatures swimming among the purple and yellow coral beneath. "Over there, this many people in one place, you know what we'd think?"

"What's that?"

Tyron clenches his jaw. "We'd think a bomb was about to go off."

"Must've been some wild shit. I couldn't handle it, I know that. How'd you do it?"

He looks at Ricky, then points toward a set of elevators. "Let's move."

In the elevator Ricky says, "You excited to see your boy again?"

Tyron searches within himself. The only feeling he is sure of is trepidation. "I don't know."

Waiting for them on the twenty-first floor is a tall security guard with a black beard, sunglasses, and a Reef cap pulled low over his eyes. He starts the moment he sees Tyron, then turns his face as though to hide whatever surprise he felt and motions for them to follow.

Tyron complies, staring at the pistol holstered on the man's hip. The guard stops outside one of the doors and raises his fist to knock. He pauses, and looks over at Tyron.

"You want help with something?" Tyron asks.

The man takes off his sunglasses and looks at him with pale blue eyes. "It's a fake beard, Tyron."

Tyron checks the thin metal name tag on the man's chest: DAVIS.

"The name's fake too."

Tyron squints at the man, and then his jaw drops. "Keenan?"

The man gives a self-conscious smile. There is no doubt. Keenan. They hesitantly embrace.

"Damn. It's been long," Tyron says.

"Another lifetime," says Keenan.

Tyron steps back. He stares into Keenan's eyes. "You all right? I got back yesterday, you're all anyone is talking about."

"Not now." Emotions cross Keenan's face in waves. He starts to speak. Freezes. Then repeats, "Not now. It's good to see you though. I can't remem— It's good to see you."

"You remember my boy Ricky, right? We all played ball back in the day."

"I remember. What's up, man?"

Keenan holds out his hand, then drops it as Ricky keeps his at his side.

Tyron's face tightens. He is ready to shake some sense into Ricky, but Keenan stalls him with a look. "It's okay. It's a better reception than most people give me these days."

"How'd you end up here?"

Keenan shrugs. "I'm off the force. Needed a new job."

Tyron nods toward the door, beyond which their old friend waits. "You spoken to Antoine?"

"No," Keenan says.

"He doesn't know you're out here?"

"Not yet."

"You want me to tell him?"

Keenan thinks about it, then nods. "Sure. Tell him. Better he has some warning. We haven't spoken in . . . over ten years. Even Naomi hasn't spoken to him in years."

Naomi. Tyron feels like he's been sucker-punched. He tries to keep his voice level. "How is Naomi?"

"She's good. She's good. We're — we're good."

"Sounds good."

"She coaches now."

"I heard that. My cousin told me."

"Right, Tara. They're friends."

"Yeah," Tyron says, thinking that there are a thousand other things he wants to know about Naomi. Why did she retire? Does she like coaching? Have her features softened or sharpened with age? Does she still smile as easily, or laugh as effortlessly? Is her scent the same? Does she miss me? Does she think about me? Does she still love me? He takes a breath. "You guys got kids?"

Keenan shakes his head, staring at Tyron with his sad blue eyes.

Tyron is embarrassed at how much relief he feels. He thought he'd let her go. Realizes now that he'd just been distracted. It would take two wars to push a woman like Naomi to the back of your mind.

"So, Antoine's world-class now?" Tyron says, attempting to change the subject. "This for real?"

Keenan shrugs. "I never understood Antoine back when we were kids, and I sure as hell don't understand him now."

Tyron nods, remembering. He looks at the door to Antoine's suite. "I better go in."

Keenan backs down the hallway. "Good luck."

THE DOOR IS opened by a wiry Hispanic man, black tattoos snaking up and down his neck, creeping out from beneath the sleeves of his white shirt onto the backs of his hands. He says nothing to Tyron, merely looks him and Ricky over, then steps aside, opening the door wider. Tyron glances back as he steps inside, but Keenan is gone.

Not a room for a high roller, but the suite is spacious enough. A second Latino man, this one middle-aged and

weather-beaten but also wiry and strong, gets up off a
sofa and shuffles to another room, with the first man following behind. The third man in the room stands before
the floor-to-ceiling windows, looking out over the Vegas
skyline. The red, dusty mountains visible in the distance
are jagged against the deep blue of the Nevada sky.

The man turns to them, his eyes dark, calculating.

"I didn't think I'd ever see you again." Antoine's voice.
Weightier than Tyron remembered.

"Sorry to . . . sorry to show up out of nowhere."

Antoine says nothing, just stares at Tyron, who feels his
insides shifting in preparation for action. It's an instinct
he developed while in the Middle East, a sixth sense for
violence. Trouble didn't always follow this feeling, but
when it hit he was always forewarned.

"Who's this?" Antoine finally says.

Ricky strides forward. "Hey man, you remember your
homeboy Rick, right? We had some battles on the court
back in the —"

"I got to speak to Tyron alone," Antoine cuts in. "You
don't mind waiting outside, right?"

"Uh, yeah, I kind of . . ." Ricky looks over at Tyron, who
nods toward the door. Ricky sucks on his teeth, looking
from one to the other. "O-okay. Whatever."

Tyron watches as Ricky, deflated, retreats out the door.

"I see you haven't lost your charming disposition."

Antoine's face remains impassive. "What are you doing
here?"

"Honestly? Ricky wants tickets to the fight tonight. He hassled me to hit you up. I only got back to Vegas yesterday."

"From protecting our foreign interests?"

There is derision in the question. "That's right."

"You still with them?"

"The Marines?"

"Yes. The Marines."

"No, I'm not."

"How come? Got tired of killing Muslims?" With the question, Antoine's dispassionate face breaks into a spiteful smile.

Tyron feels himself stiffen. If he were to tell the truth, he would say yes. He was tired of killing the first time he had to do it. And he never stopped tiring of it. "I never planned on being in the Corps for the rest of my life. It was time for something new."

"Which will be what? Finding another way to kill people of colour? You can be like Keenan and join the police."

"If you want me to leave, just say so. I didn't come here for this."

"Of *course* you didn't come here for this," Antoine growls. "Of course you didn't. You came here, after years without a word, looking for a handout. That's what you came for."

Tyron exhales heavily. He isn't used to a civilian sniping at him like this. It makes his pulse thump.

"You're just like everyone else I used to know. You know what they say to me, all these ghosts from my past? Ever since I got out of prison and started winning—and especially when it became clear I wasn't going to stop winning—they all say the same thing. 'Don't forget me when you're famous. Don't forget me when you make it. Don't forget me, don't forget me, don't forget me.' And you know what I think each time I hear that? Don't remember me when I make it. Don't remember me. If you weren't *with me* when I was homeless... if you weren't *with me* when I was on the streets... if you weren't *with me* in prison... don't *fucking* remember me now. You couldn't visit me inside, you couldn't write me a letter, you couldn't send me a fucking email, and I shouldn't forget you? Don't worry, I don't. I don't forget who you are. Not ever."

Tyron returns the cold stare levelled at him. "I don't remember any letters from you when I was in Iraq. Or Afghanistan."

Antoine smiles. "Good point."

He takes a sudden step toward Tyron, whose muscles begin vibrating. "I always think of your parents when I see you," Antoine says. "You look like them."

Tyron gives a brief nod. He struggles to find something to say. Can't find the words to bridge the gap between them.

"You ever wonder who killed them?"

Tyron is so taken aback that he physically steps backward. Antoine is studying him closely now.

"I stopped thinking about that a long time ago. Why?"

Antoine hesitates on the verge of saying something. Then his face smooths and grows unreadable. "Just curious."

Tyron says, "Keenan's outside."

"What?"

"Keenan's working security at the hotel. He walked us in. He's waiting outside."

Antoine's eyes bulge with anger. Then he turns away and laughs. "It *is* fate!" He turns back to Tyron. "It is fate," he says softly, his eyes imploring. "All of us here together again on this day of all days. It's a sign. Something momentous is about to happen." His eyes flash and the hint of a smile appears on his lips.

Tyron watches Antoine. He wonders how quickly he can get out of the room if things take a turn. Antoine's speech is rushed, his mind clearly racing now. "I'll get you and Ricky into the fight. You can wait in the casino, I'll give you money." He turns and shouts to the bedrooms, "Carlos, *trae quinientos dólares y dos boletos para la pelea.*" Back to Tyron, he says, "Give your number to Carlos, he'll handle the details."

He jolts forward and puts his hand on Tyron's shoulder. Tyron almost flinches, half expecting a punch.

"You got my back, right?" Antoine says urgently. "If shit goes down, you got my back, right?"

"What do you mean? Like, in the ring?"

"I don't need help in the ring. If other shit goes down, you—"

"Like what?"

"Whatever! It doesn't matter what. If things happen, you look out for me, okay? Whether we were ever brothers or not, your parents loved me. You remember that. Your parents loved me and I loved them. You look out for me tonight. Yeah?"

"Yeah, all right man, I will."

Antoine stares into his eyes, searching, and finally gives a short nod, satisfied.

Carlos, the young man with the tattoos, waits silently behind them.

"I'll see you later," Antoine says. "Send Keenan in when you leave."

Antoine walks over to Carlos, whispers something to him, and walks back to the window.

Carlos approaches, a wad of cash and two tickets in his hands. Tyron exchanges numbers, takes the tickets, but refuses the cash. Across the hotel suite he says, "Hey Antoine."

Antoine turns, his gaunt face half silhouetted.

"Good luck tonight."

The boxer stares, for so long Tyron thinks there will be no other reaction, but at last it comes, a one-sided smile.

3:53 p.m.

KEENAN PUSHES AWAY from the wall with relief when Tyron comes back into the hallway—sharing an awkward silence with Ricky wasn't much fun. I should move, Keenan thinks. Life will never be the same for me here. He is afraid, however, that Naomi won't stay with him if he goes. He snorts. He is afraid she won't stay with him even if he stays.

Tyron's eyes look glassy.

"What's wrong?" Keenan asks.

"He's weird."

"He was always weird."

"He's weirder now. He wants to see you."

Well, that's ominous, Keenan thinks. "Let me get your number," he says, unsure if Tyron will give it to him with Ricky watching. But Tyron nods, and they punch each other's numbers into their phones. "We'll catch up later?" Keenan asks uncertainly.

"Definitely," Tyron says.

They slap hands and embrace. With a morose look over at Ricky, who glowers at him with fury and contempt, Keenan treks back down the hall.

Warily, he opens the door. Antoine is standing by the window.

"Come here," he says.

Keenan walks across the suite with long, slow strides, surprised at how Antoine's presence fills the room even though he is only five-ten and lean. As a kid, he could be right beside you and you'd forget he was there. Keenan was the one with presence back then. Before he became a pariah. Approaching the window, he sees how sinewy Antoine has become, how the veins branch across his forearms, how stripped he is of anything but muscle and bone.

They look out over Las Vegas Boulevard, immensely wide yet packed with cars.

"They come to our city for what, exactly?" Antoine asks. "They can't get drunk, high, and laid in their own cities? Can't waste their savings at home? They gotta come here to do that?"

"It's easier here, I guess." Keenan takes a breath. "How you been?"

Antoine slowly turns his head from the window and stares malevolently at Keenan. "How did you fuck up that bad?"

Keenan starts, unprepared for the hostility.

"Did they teach you to do that to Black people? Is that the thinking, take 'em out one at a time, eventually all America's problems will be solved?"

"Fuck you, man."

"Easy. We ain't kids no more. A lot's changed."

"No shit."

Keenan has a gun holstered at his hip and for a moment thinks he might need it, but Antoine's animosity recedes. No softness or warmth appear to fill the void, just a blank disposition, as he says, "How did it happen?"

Keenan can't put into words the thinking and instincts that develop over time as a cop—and, if he's being honest with himself, had been developing long before he joined the force. He was taught to shoot to kill anyone he deemed a threat to himself or others. But there is no gradation of threat. A terrorist armed to the teeth and a Black man who doesn't listen are both threats. Or maybe it's just that he told that kid to stop, to get on the ground—he, a police officer, who should be heard, who should be obeyed—and the kid didn't listen and he needed to be taught a lesson. Or maybe he was angry and he had never used his gun before in the line of duty, and he felt disrespected and he wasn't about to look weak, he wasn't going to be made to feel weak, he was a cop after all, and this seemed like the right time to finally step up. Or maybe it's that other cops were always watching, and you had to be hardcore or you wouldn't be trusted. Or maybe things just happened faster than he was expecting, and he didn't quite know what to do, and shooting the perp was the only action that came to mind. "I shouldn't talk about it," is what he says to Antoine.

"How's your father?"

Keenan's eyes narrow. "He's fine. He's retired now."

"He's keeping busy?"

"Not really. He mostly watches football at home or drinks at a local sports bar. How about you?"

"What about me?"

"How is your..." Keenan remembers too late Antoine's

family situation. He tries to think if there is someone else
he should ask about.

"Don't hurt yourself, Keenan. There's no one."

"You got a girl?"

Antoine shakes his head. "How's Naomi?"

"Great. She's really great. She's been following your success. She's proud of you."

It is the only time in their conversation that Antoine
looks taken off guard. His eyes soften and he seems about
to smile. Then a shadow crosses his face. "Any kids?" he
asks.

"Not yet. We might wait another few years."

"So, you my security detail for the rest of the night?"

"No. I'm behind the scenes wherever they need me. I
won't be in the arena."

Antoine's gaze slides back out the window. The
red sun is blazing even as it begins to wane. Watching
Antoine like that, his strange, simmering intensity,
Keenan realizes he has nothing to say. He realizes also,
in this moment, that he doesn't like him, that he never
really liked him. Perhaps he did as the third member of
their crew—fourth if you counted Naomi—but not one-
on-one. Antoine deserves to be alone.

"I might not see you again," Antoine says. "Good luck
with everything."

"Good luck with the fight."

They shake hands and then Keenan is back out in the
hallway, glad to be free of the man who for two years as

a teenager had spent almost every day in his company. Times change, Keenan thinks. For company, he would pick just about any stranger over Antoine now.

★ ★ ★ ★ ★ ★ ★ ★ ★ ★ ★ ★ ★ ★ ★ ★ ★ ★ ★

5

4:10 p.m.

TYRON AND KEENAN gone, and his fight still hours away, Antoine returns to his room, closes two sets of curtains, and stretches out on his bed. As his head hits the downy pillow, and he tugs the sheets around himself, he thinks of the nights he spent in alleys and empty lots, the nights in gang-run crack dens and austere prison cells, how he would rest his head on rough cement or filthy floorboards, how he might wake up shivering, wary for his life, or worse, with someone's hands on him and have to use his fists to get clear. Upon reflection, the comfort of this bed doesn't do much for him. Of course, given the choice between a cushiony king-sized mattress and the hard ground, he'd take the bed. But his ambitions have never lain in material things, which always seemed fleeting and inconsequential, an opinion Antoine developed as a boy when he and his father would break into wealthy people's homes.

As darkness drags him down, Antoine's last waking thought is that the dream will visit him again. To remember his father so close to sleep is to beckon it from the dark corners of his mind. The dream is so immersive and has maintained such a consistent narrative over the years that he can no longer tell exactly how, or if, it differs from the memory that gave birth to it.

He is twelve, creeping through the Las Vegas mansion of a billionaire. Everything is dark and blurry, including his father, who glides from shadow to shadow ahead of him, no longer Raul Deco as he is in the light of day, but a shadow himself. His utter silence, his absence of sound, gives Antoine confidence. They will not be caught. They are never caught.

The alarms have been disabled; the hidden cameras have been found; and the safe, behind a cabinet in a room at the back of the mansion, succumbs to his father's skills. It is their second heist of the night. The first, a law office off Industrial Road, had also been for documents.

The dream skips ahead in time the way dreams do. They are in his father's car beside a dumpster, underneath a long highway overpass. On Antoine's lap is a brown manila envelope containing the documents collected from the night's two heists. His father is nervous. Antoine can feel it. His father is never nervous. Not when he's getting chased down by the most vicious dogs, not in the company of the most beautiful women, not when he's questioned by the most persistent detectives; Raul Deco is never nervous. But he is nervous now. Antoine can feel it.

"Get out, *hijo*. Find someplace to hide. I'll be back soon."

For the first time in Antoine's life, he senses that his father needs him. Yes, perhaps he has been useful to his father as an extra pair of eyes, ears, and hands on their various jobs, but useful as a luxury instead of a need. Right now, his father needs him. Raul might not know it, but Antoine does. His father will make a mistake without him.

"What are these documents, *padre*?"

"It's a will. Copies of the same will. Now out. *¡Vete!*"

"Who's it for?"

His father looks at him, and Antoine—the thirty-two-year-old Antoine having the dream—understands this look. He is weighing whether or not to confide in his son, whether or not to show frailty before his boy, whether or not to look for support from the person he is guide and mentor to—none of which he has ever done before. In the end, he says only one word. "Cops."

"Cops?"

"They're waiting for me. Go."

Antoine is torn between obeying his father and adhering to his instincts. "Maybe you should leave one of the wills with me."

His father snatches the envelope from his lap. "Get out of the car, Antoine."

He slithers out of the vehicle, knowing that if he doesn't move, the edge he just heard in his father's voice will be followed by the back of his hand. The car pulls away, passing in and out of shadow in the half-lit dusty lot beneath the highway.

No matter how many times Antoine brings back the dream, no matter how hard he tries, he can never change its ending. He can never force himself to stay in the car. And the moment it drives off, he loathes himself for abandoning his father.

He hides behind the dumpster, watching his father's brake lights recede under the overpass. Like a soldier under fire, he scampers from one concrete pillar to the next.

The car is now far up ahead, its tail lights like the glowing red eyes of some small creature in the dark. He begins to run. The lights blink out.

His lungs burn, and yet his legs barely move. Like a mosquito caught in the sap of a tree, some viscous thing holds him back. But he has to catch up to his father. It's imperative. It's the most important thing he has ever had to do. He knows what will come otherwise. The chill in his blood can't be wrong.

Lost in the remnants and shadows, he runs from pillar to pillar. Until the glowing red eyes open once more. They are stationary. He can see his father now, standing outside the car, envelope in hand. Beyond him a black sedan is parked, and before it, no more than a silhouette in the shadows, a tall man stands waiting. He throws a black duffle bag into the slanting light from the highway above, and Raul warily approaches it.

It is then that Antoine sees the second man, using a pillar for cover, gun in hand, creeping up behind his father. Antoine is still so far away.

His father has checked inside the bag and slung it over his shoulder, and now he tosses the envelope into the shadows for the first man to take. Antoine opens his mouth to scream. The gunman comes out of cover and aims his weapon.

His father turns back toward his car, looking over his shoulder at the tall silhouette. He doesn't see the gunman. He doesn't see his death coming for him. Antoine's voice dies in his throat. They'll find me, he thinks. The gunman opens fire.

Eight times the pistol flashes: the gunshots echo in the cavernous space. His father writhes and jolts. Again Antoine wants to scream. Again his voice fails him.

The gunman collects the duffle bag from his father's still body and climbs into the black sedan. The engine revs in a guttural growl. Antoine scrambles around the nearest pillar so that he is hidden when the sedan screams past. He peeks around the concrete at the last moment and is given a snapshot of the two men in the car, a shaft of light on them in this one instant.

They are faceless. No hair. No eyes. No nose. No mouth. Each a blank white canvas of flesh. His dreaming mind unable to retrieve their features from this split second of memory.

The sedan is absorbed by the night, as if always a part of it. Antoine leaves the pillar. He walks out into the middle of the empty lot beneath the overpass to his father. The blood has already spread a distance from the body.

His tears stream, and still Antoine's survival instinct calmly says, if cops killed him, cops cannot find you with him. Go.

Antoine looks up from his father's face and sees in every shadow a pair of glowing yellow embers. They wink and blink and dance back and forth, and then the growls and howls come from all directions. One coyote emerges from the dark, the largest and boldest of them, its long, bared fangs glinting in the half-light. The pack begins to approach, lean bodies taking form around the fiery eyes. Fur bristling, tongues lolling, long jaws slavering for his father's pooling blood.

Antoine rises. He needs to run and run fast. But he can't. He can't leave his father again. He tries to lift him. The coyotes growl and slink closer. The cops will be coming. The ones in uniform. And somehow they will alert the faceless cops who murdered his father, and they will realize that Antoine was there, witness to their deed, accomplice to their thefts, a threat to their plans. A loose end they hadn't known needed to be tied.

He screams at the coyotes. They gnash their foaming jaws. The biggest launches at him. Fangs wide.

Antoine's eyes snap open. He is slick with perspiration beneath the fine triple sheets; his fists are balled up tight. There were no coyotes, no glowing eyes, when he abandoned his father for the final time. But days later, when he had to ID the body, he saw what the coyotes had done to it in his absence, and the chrysalis of their memory was planted in his mind. He presses himself up into a kneeling position. His fist is a blur. *Slap.* The pillow puffs up around his knuckles. He readies to fire another one.

Not yet, a voice inside him says—the same voice he has been obeying since he was twelve years old. Save it. Save it for tonight.

★ ★ ★ ★ ★ ★ ★ ★ ★ ★ ★ ★ ★ ★ ★ ★ ★ ★ ★

6

5:38 p.m.

"**B**ALLERS BALL, BABY, ballers ball," Ricky says, as he rakes in the blackjack pot with both hands.

"You're down overall."

Ricky sucks on his teeth. "For now."

Tyron laughs and shakes his head, then, scanning his surroundings, accidentally makes eye contact with one of the mermaids. She smiles playfully before cutting between two tables, a tray of martinis at shoulder height.

Tyron is embarrassed that only a smile from this woman, sent from a distance, is enough to cause a flutter in his chest. True, she is clad from the waist down in a fabric so thin it is half transparent, skin-tight grey-turquoise patterning made to look like fish scales. And true, all she has on her upper half is a near-imperceptible string bikini holding in place a pair of small seashells. And of course, it is true that she is one of the hottest women he has ever seen in person. But the real reason for his jittery excitement over a look from a half-naked woman is that he has spent so little time with women in recent memory. He is embarrassed at how long it has been since he last had sex. Forget sex, how long it has been since he last had a date.

"What do you think?" Ricky asks Tyron, as he motions to his new cards, a six of clubs and a jack of diamonds.

"I don't really play cards," Tyron says.

"Lighten up, Ty! Shit, we're in the hottest casino on the Strip and soon we'll be watching the fight of the decade. This is your homecoming, dude. You ain't a soldier no more, you a free man. Forget Auntie Trudy's cookout, *this* is your celebration! You with me?"

"I'm with you."

"Are you pumped?"

"Maybe a little."

Ricky punches Tyron in the shoulder. "Are you jacked?"

"Don't punch me."

Ricky punches him again. "Marine, are you jacked?"

"Yeah, I'm jacked." Tyron can't help but smile. Ricky could always make him smile.

"Then answer me this: Stay or hit?"

"Hit."

"Thank you! Hit me, man," Ricky shouts at the dealer.

The dealer flips a seven of spades.

Disdainfully, Ricky tosses his cards. "Twenty-three. Nice call, Tyron."

"So, you're a Marine?" says a bald man with glasses who looks to be in his sixties. Sitting to the right of Ricky, he leans forward to get a better look at Tyron.

"Yes," Tyron says. "Actually, not anymore. I suppose I'm a veteran now. I just got out."

"Name's Allen. I'm a retired principal." The gambler extends his hand.

Reaching for the handshake, Tyron sees that the cuff of Allen's sleeve is faded and grimy, overworn and under-washed. He looks in the man's eyes, and behind the lenses sees dark bags and burst capillaries. A gambling addict, Tyron suspects. Burning through his pension in this place. He won't be retired for long.

"And you?" Allen asks of Ricky.

"What about me?"

"Are you a veteran?"

Ricky mulls this question over like he could answer it several ways. "Not in the traditional sense, but I am a veteran of a lot o' things."

Allen looks for help to Tyron, who explains, "That means no."

The man shoves a handful of chips over to Ricky's pile and says, "I want to thank you for your service. What drink can I get you?"

Tyron nods but declines the drink.

"I insist," Allen says.

Tyron looks at Ricky, who is vibrating with anticipation. "You can buy him the —"

"You can buy *me* the drink," Ricky finishes for him.

"All right," Allen says, with a suspicious examination of Ricky. "What'll it be?"

Tyron's cell vibrates in his pocket. A text from Marlon. You thought any more about tomorrow? He asks Ricky what the deal is with the protest, explaining, "Marlon is hassling me to go."

Ricky sucks on his teeth. "I wasn't going to say nothing, but since you brought it up, you shouldn't have been talking to that guy like that."

Tyron's brow furrows. "I shouldn't have been talking to *who* like that?"

"To that fucking killer. The cop. Who the fuck do you think?"

Tyron's shoulders hunch up and his back stiffens. Ricky makes no apology, and the uncharacteristic behaviour in his friend hits home for Tyron just how devastating Keenan's actions and acquittal have been to the people of this city.

"People make mistakes," Tyron says.

"What?"

"You don't know what it's like when you got a gun in your hands and you're authorized to use it."

"You think it's okay to —"

"Did I say it was okay? Shit. All I said was people make mistakes."

Allen has motioned a server over and says, "A Jack and Coke for me, and whatever these two want. We got a veteran over here, we got to treat him right."

"A veteran, huh?" says a woman's silky voice.

Tyron turns to see the mermaid who smiled at him

earlier. She has green eyes, which look teasingly into his. Again he feels palpitations in his chest.

"You guys got a dark 'n' stormy?" Ricky asks.

She smiles at Ricky. "Yeah, we got that. And you?" she asks Tyron.

He shakes his head. "Nothing for me."

"Get something," the gambler says. "It's Vegas."

"And he ain't just a veteran, he's a war hero. Tell 'em about your medals, Ty."

"A war hero?" The mermaid bites her lower lip. "On behalf of the Reef, we'd like to accommodate you as best we can."

"You know what you should do," Ricky says. "You should give him a kiss. He just got home. How better to welcome him back to America than that? And you, I might add, are the very best America has to offer."

The mermaid considers it, raising each hand separately like she is weighing the decision on a scale. The moment Tyron realizes that it might actually happen, he begins shaking his head, but the mermaid is already leaning into him. "Welcome home, soldier."

Her lips are soft and full, and she holds them against his a good long time. Tyron opens his eyes. Stares at her. Once, in Iraq, he was half concussed when an IED went off nearby. He feels a bit like that now.

"So, one Jack and Coke and two dark 'n' stormys?" she says with a wink.

"Sure," he says. It is the answer he would probably give to any question she asked him in that moment.

After she is gone, he sees that the rest of the table looks just as stunned as he is. "That was hot," says a woman at the far end. Tyron returns their gazes with a sheepish grin.

Ricky slaps him on the back and says, "It's going to be a good night."

Tyron suddenly feels like he might be right. No Marines under his responsibility. No civilians under his jurisdiction. And a beautiful woman showing him attention. One night as a baller won't kill me, he thinks. I might even like it. And all thanks to Antoine. Hard to believe.

Out of all the people Tyron knew growing up, himself included, he never would've thought Antoine would be the one to rise so high. Still, the guy always had something unique about him. Some edge that the rest of them lacked. Tyron remembers it being there the first time they met.

Antoine had bounced around government programs and foster homes for two years before Tyron's parents brought him home one day. He barely spoke his first couple of weeks. They were both fourteen, and Tyron was tasked with taking him to school. Even then Antoine would say nothing walking or riding the bus, like he knew the whole thing was temporary. There had been other foster siblings for Tyron before Antoine, boys and girls who had been through hard times and had grown hard themselves, but none as silent as Antoine.

He only began to speak after the first incident with the police. He was caught one night breaking into a police station, which Tyron at the time thought was about the dumbest thing anyone could do. The cops held Antoine in a juvenile lockup for two days until Tyron's parents got him released. He hadn't taken anything or vandalized anything, so he was only charged with trespassing. The cops seemed to think detainment would break the small Hispanic kid, who looked a good few years younger than his age, but Antoine seemed not even to register that he had been punished. For him, it was all part of the natural order of things. When Tyron's parents asked him if he was okay, he gave them a look that said, Why wouldn't I be?

Back home, they sat him down and asked if someone had put him up to the break-in. "The police said you were going through their files and looking in their computers. What were you looking for?"

"Nothing," he said.

"Why did you do it?" He shrugged and stared back at them, waiting for his beating. "We're not mad, Antoine. We're not even disappointed. We just want to understand why you would do this thing."

Antoine had been sharp on the uptake since he came to live with them, but it took forever for it to dawn on him that Terrence and Viola Shaw were not going to beat him for getting arrested. Tyron would've laughed if he hadn't still been so creeped out by the kid. Though Antoine told the Shaws nothing that night, words slipped out of him in the days that followed.

And then one day he was just talking, like that's how he had always been. At least that's how he was at home with the Shaws. Outside the house was a different story.

5:52 p.m.

ON A BALCONY overlooking the aquarium, Keenan leans on the railing with his cell phone pressed to his ear. The alcohol has worn off and he feels irritable, as he often does after drinking. Not a good headspace to be in when calling the wife, he thinks. But he might not get a chance later, and he is trying. He is trying to be a better husband. Normally he wouldn't respond to her texts at work, but these aren't normal times. Listening to the dial tone, he wonders how far the drop to the water is. It would take a good jump to clear the tiled path around the tank. He's pretty sure he could make it; his hops aren't bad. After the plunge, what would the sharks make of him? Would his desperation draw them in? Whet their hunger?

"Keenan. What's up?"

He can hear the surprise in her voice. Not radio silence, not a cursory text, not even a long text. An actual phone call. It's a step in the right direction, he thinks. He hopes.

"I just wanted to tell you that it's going well so far."

"Yeah?"

"Yeah."

"That's good, Keenan. I'm happy for you."

"How . . . how are things at home?"

There is a pause, and again he can sense her surprise. "Home is fine," she says.

"Tyron's here."

She doesn't speak for so long that he wonders if she's still there.

"Babe?"

"You've seen him?" she asks.

"He got back into town yesterday. He's out of the Marines. He came to see Antoine."

"So you did see him."

"Yeah. Both of them."

"Really? You saw them both?"

"Crazy, isn't it? Like old times." He picks out the motions of a shark below. A fluid shadow in the fading light. "Actually, it wasn't like old times. It was different. But still, the whole crew back together again; first time in over a decade."

"Not the whole crew," she says.

He watches the shark catch up to a smaller fish and wonders if it will eat it. He would like to see that. The suffering. "Anyway, I just called to say hey. I'll be home late. Don't worry about waiting up for me."

"I'm coming down there."

The smaller fish darts to the side, but the shark takes no notice and slices on through the water with the same smooth rhythm. Dissatisfied, he asks, "What did you say, baby?"

"I'm coming down there. I want to see them."

"What?"

"I'm coming down there."

"No, babe, come on."

"I want to see them, Keenan. They're my friends too."

"So you'll see them. They're not going anywhere."

"Dammit, Keenan, I don't want to be left out while the three of you are back together partying."

"Jesus, Naomi, no one's partying. I'm working; Antoine has a fucking fight in a couple hours."

"And Tyron?"

Keenan sighs and hangs his head over the railing. "Okay, you're right, Tyron is partying. He's in the casino with his buddy Ricky."

"Ha! Ricky. He must've asked me out at least a hundred times."

"I remember."

"So I'll come down, I'll hang out with those two. Then after your shift we can all chill. And maybe we'll even get to celebrate with Antoine after he wins. Oh Keenan, I can't wait to see those guys."

Her excitement grates on him. The fact that other people can ignite such elation when the two of them have been so miserable lately pisses him off. Her voice is normally deep for a woman's and when she wants it can be sultry, but when she's excited, like she is now, it goes high. When he was a kid, hearing her voice high like that used to bubble up a fierce joy in him. And now? Now when her voice goes high, it's just a reminder of how much things have turned. How shut out he is to her heart, and she to his.

"Naomi, please. I'm working. I don't want my wife here at my job."

"Yeah, seems like you don't want your wife anywhere."

"Ah, I'm so sick of this shit."

"You're sick of it? How the fuck do you think *I* feel? Those boys are like family to me, Keenan. And I haven't seen them in years. I won't bother you while you're working; I won't even see you until you're done."

Keenan's cell beeps with call waiting. It's his father. He ignores it and says, "All right, whatever, come down."

"Why's everything got to be such a fucking fight with you?"

"I said come down. Fuck, what more do you want?"

He expects a tirade; instead he gets cold silence, which he knows is more worrisome. Eventually she says, "You got Tyron's number?"

"I'll text it to you."

"Cool. Hope work goes well."

And then she hangs up and he thinks, Nice job, Keenan. She really appreciated you taking the time to call. He wonders how it's possible for his instincts to be so wrong in just about every situation these days. As a kid, it was the opposite. Everything went his way.

He texts Tyron's number to Naomi, calls his father, and checks his watch. He really should be getting back to work.

"Keenan."

"Hey Dad. You called?"

"How's the job?"

"It's good, Dad."

"How's Monk?"

"Real good. He misses you."

His father snorts. "Bullshit. By the way, I'm going to put some money down on your friend."

"Oh yeah?"

"A lot. If I'd have known he'd turn out to be such a star, I would've let him live with us."

"Antoine's not a star."

"Oh, he will be. You seen any of his fights?"

Keenan takes a deep breath and looks up to the dusky blue-grey sky. First Naomi, now his father. He shakes his head. "No."

"He's no joke, that kid."

"I better get back to work, Dad."

"See ya, son."

A group of young women laugh as they walk around the enclosure of the aquarium, gulping margaritas from long plastic cups, each drink brightly coloured like a mad scientist's concoction. Another bachelorette party. The bride-to-be wears a white sash across her tight-fitting dress. On the far side of the tank are the resort's swimming pools — the ones for regular patrons. Beyond the aquarium are the gates to the high-roller mansions, each with its own pool. But these pools here have something the

high-roller ones don't: they are directly adjacent to the
aquatic tanks and share a glass divider so that patrons
can swim beside creatures of the deep. Not every pool,
though—swimming next to a blue shark isn't for everyone.

The bachelorettes sip their drinks, peering into the
aquarium. One of them looks up and sees Keenan watching them. She smiles. Not an overly flirtatious smile, just
a happy one, a content one. He begins to smile back but
stops himself and breaks eye contact.

In the seven years since he married Naomi, he has
never had anything regular on the side. Which he knows
is not saying much, but it's still better than some. There
are cops who have to lie to their mistresses when they go
out, let alone their wives. But no more of that. Nothing
on the side, no matter how brief. He is trying to be a good
husband. Even if he's doing a bad job of it, he's trying.

That bachelorette is cute, though.

★ ★ ★ ★ ★ ★ ★ ★ ★ ★ ★ ★ ★ ★ ★ ★ ★ ★ ★ ★

7

6:35 p.m.

TERRENCE SHAW HAD believed that boxing was a good skill for a young person to learn, which was ironic because he also believed in non violence and was opposed to boxing matches. "A person needs their head," he would say. "Fights will damage it eventually, no matter how good you are." But the skill itself—the training and discipline it required, the confidence it instilled, and the speed, fitness, and strength it developed—he thought was essential to a kid's upbringing. He liked chess too.

Antoine reminds himself that now is not the time to think of his foster father. Now that he is in the arena, in his own dressing room, with the undercard fights already begun. Soon he'll be out there, in front of thousands, with millions more watching around the world. Now is not the time to reminisce.

Except tonight is for Terrence Shaw too, says that guiding voice within him. Tonight is for all of them. Besides, what else is there to do before the warm-up begins, other than reminisce?

The waiting is the worst part of fight night. Antoine doesn't want to waste a thought, a breath, an ounce of strength before the battle begins, and yet he doesn't want to lose focus either. Too tense and he risks wearing away his stores of concentration; too relaxed and he feels unprepared for the gauntlet that lies ahead. So he must wait, balancing in between.

It was Terrence Shaw who first introduced him to boxing. The man started taking his own son, Tyron, to the Rising Star Boxing Club when the boy was eleven. Craig Quinn started taking Keenan when he was twelve. Antoine was fourteen when he joined the party, and fashionably late didn't apply here. Despite Terrence Shaw's reservations, the boys would fight each other on the days he did not attend their practices, and they would strike the head even though they'd been told not to go high when sparring, regardless of their protective headgear. Antoine got beat down. Again and again and again. Tyron and Keenan were a decent match for each other, with wins going back and forth, but how they adored their guaranteed victories over Antoine. Each sparring session he would summon everything he had. He would call up all the strength he possessed, from the marrow of his bones, from the pit of his stomach, from the furious thumping of his heart. And still he lost.

Tony "Warrior" Wilks was the owner and head trainer of Rising Star. He used to bring along his daughter, Naomi, as he had done with his sons, who had moved

on to professional fighting and running their own gym in
Atlanta. Naomi was at the gym almost every day, training,
boxing, or doing various jobs for the business. Though
the same age as the three boys, she was a good deal more
developed than they were. If it weren't for fear of Tony,
the young men in that gym would have circled her like
vultures. Even with Tony's presence, they still took bets
on who would be the one to pop her cherry, and they tried
to get away with as much leering flirtation as they could
without her father noticing. Once a young man was care-
less, grabbing her ass in view of Warrior Wilks, and then
the gym saw the former title contender in action.

Antoine never forgot that Tony let the young man
return to the gym — months later, after his jaw had healed.
The guy never looked at Naomi again and became one of
Tony's most committed fighters. Nevertheless, Antoine
couldn't understand that level of forgiveness.

Tyron and Keenan didn't like fighting Naomi. Not
because she was a girl, but because they didn't like losing, and she always won.

Back then Naomi was almost a head taller than Tyron
and Keenan, and she was head and shoulders above
Antoine. She was also more beautiful than any girl
Antoine had ever seen. He would challenge her to fights
just to be near her, even though she'd whoop him worse
than Tyron and Keenan. Looking up at her from the mat,
flattened, blood running from his nose, he couldn't help
but enjoy seeing her smile.

After practice, the boys and Naomi would go to the convenience store around the corner, and walk back slowly with the snacks they had bought, although Antoine and Tyron rarely bought anything, their pockets mostly empty. But sometimes Keenan would buy freezies or ice cream for the four of them, and then Antoine would feel that he wasn't so alone, that he had people to support and care for him.

All he wanted on those languid walks was to say something to Naomi that might make her laugh or smile. But his mind blanked whenever he opened his mouth, while Tyron and Keenan were suddenly wittier than ever. The only thing he ever managed to say to her was "You fought really well today" or "You were really good," which she appreciated at first, but she looked at him strangely when he kept saying it day after day. He meant it, though. Every time he said it, he meant it.

Eventually basketball took up too much of her time and she came less and less to the gym. The boys still saw her outside of boxing, but by then Antoine had even less to say to her. Back at the gym, he worked harder than ever.

But before Naomi moved on to focus on basketball exclusively, and Keenan decided that tennis was his main priority, and Tyron's track and field training took him away from the sweet science of bruising; before all that, while Antoine was still new to pugilism and not utterly immersed in it, he discovered the name of the man who had lived in the mansion he and his father had robbed.

The night his father was murdered. The man's name was Marty Bloom, and he was a casino owner. After his death, controlling interest of his company passed to his young wife, who sold it at a bargain rate to Norman Bashinsky. Bashinsky imploded the casino and built a new one over it. He called it the Reef.

6:37 p.m.

TYRON CAN'T REMEMBER the last time he saw so many people indoors. A terrorist's dream, he thinks. But there are a lot of security personnel here too. They seem competent enough. He grimaces. Competent enough, what the fuck are you thinking? Never underestimate the innovations of extremists.

Different desert, he warns himself. Different desert.

Part of him enjoys being buzzed for the first time in so long, the looseness and giddiness of it. Another part is repulsed at himself for dulling his wits—he *himself* choosing to do this, what an insane thing—and in such a crowd. So many people packed so close together as they slowly mill toward the arena. A terrorist's dream. Dulling his wits in a terrorist's dream.

"Oh shit, there's Jennifer Lawrence," says Ricky. "I told you there'd be some fine fucking women here."

You wouldn't even need a bomb, Tyron thinks. Not even a submachine gun. People this close together, just a semi-automatic pistol and you could take out a dozen before they got to you.

"I wonder if she plans on slumming tonight."

And I kept drinking and chose to dull my wits. I'm going to miss something. Fuck.

"Sure, she's had better. Better looking. Better in bed, probably. Famous, rich, successful. Just better men in general. But has she had funnier?"

As vigilant as Tyron tries to be, his mind shifts back to the mermaid, Layla, who kissed him again when they were leaving the blackjack tables. She gave him her number and told him to text her when he got out of the fight. And now he is once again happy that he has the alcohol in his bloodstream, happy that it is awakening something that had been dormant in him when the lives of his men, and all those civilians who were suffering before his eyes, were of such pressing concern. How good it would be to be with a woman again. Almost too good to imagine.

"Okay, she's definitely had funnier—there are way too many comedians in Hollywood. But like I said, maybe she's into slumming tonight. Maybe she's like, 'I want something different tonight, I want a guy who's inferior in every way to the guys I'm normally with.' It happens, you know, it actually does happen."

Tyron's cell vibrates and his heart checks against his ribcage. The mermaid. Layla. He pulls the phone out while he continues shuffling forward through the cavernous Reef hallway, packed from one side to the other with people. The escalators to the arena are just up ahead. His eyes widen when he reads the text.

"'Cause movie stars, they don't actually want to be with other stars. It's true. Stars always want to be the centre of attention. They always got to be the biggest deal in the room. Stars, if they're with each other, they're like... they're like, competing with each other, you know. They want to be treated like idols, not rivals. That's why so many crazy people are with shit boxes. You know what I mean? So what do you think? You think it's possible?"

Tyron looks at Ricky beside him for the first time in a long while. "I think you could be Jennifer Lawrence's shit box," he says.

"Man," Ricky says, shaking his head like he's holding back tears, "that's the nicest thing anyone has ever said to me."

Tyron motions for Ricky to follow him, then squeezes his way over to the wall, outside the flow of the crowd. When Ricky catches up to him he says, "You remember Naomi? That girl that me and —"

"Naomi, of course, who could forget Naomi? That killer cop stole her from you."

"No, it wasn't like that. Don't say that. Don't spread that shit either."

Ricky shrugs noncommittally. Tyron grabs Ricky by the shirt. "It wasn't like that. Don't tell people that. And stop calling Keenan a killer."

"Whatever. He is."

Tyron shakes Ricky. "I said don't call him that. Not in front of me."

Security has taken notice of them. He lets Ricky go. The security guard continues eyeing Tyron but makes no other move.

"With that kind of anger I'm pretty sure you could take out J-Law's bodyguards. They're big motherfuckers, but you got 'em, Ty. Then I can make my move."

Tyron forces a laugh, regretting his outburst. "I'm sorry, man."

"It's cool. So, what about Naomi?"

"She's coming here. Key told her about me and Antoine. The whole crew in one place for the first time since we were in college. Maybe even before then. She's stuck in traffic but she'll be here soon."

A look of concern crosses Ricky's face. "How you feel about seeing her?"

Tyron tilts his head to the side in a kind of shrug. "I don't know, man. This is one crazy day."

Ricky laughs. "It's about to get crazier, cuz. What you want me to do? I'll be your backup if that's what you need."

"No, you go into the fight. Jennifer Lawrence needs someone to creep on her, right?"

"Amen, brother. I'll see you in there."

They clap hands and embrace, then Ricky joins the current again and Tyron pushes his way back out through the waves of people.

6:44 p.m.

NAOMI IS WEARING lipstick. A dark red, almost purple, lipstick. She never wears lipstick, unless she's attending a wedding or something. She was surprised she even had something like this in her meagre makeup kit, then remembered it had been a gift a couple of years ago. Putting it on, this tiny act of vanity, concerns her. It concerns her because she would not be wearing it if she were not on her way to see Tyron. She could lie to herself, say that she put on lipstick because she's going to the biggest party on the Strip this year and wants to fit in, but she has never cared about fitting in. At her height, how could she, except on the court. She feels guilty already, but why? Because she is wearing something most women wear every day? And yet she knows that she is not most women.

Naomi looks out the cab window and wishes the traffic would move faster. Saturday night, fight night, she knows it's not going to, but she wishes it would. It has been so many years, what difference does another ten or twenty minutes make?

Her hands rest in her lap, her fingers between her thighs, and she can almost smell him. Yes, twenty minutes makes a difference. He's back. And out of the Marines. And Antoine's there too. A big success now, like he'd always wanted.

She was the only one of them to visit him in prison. In that bright, bland, white visitation hall that smelled of bleach, she asked him why he had never asked her out.

He stared at her, and then just shook his head. "I'm not in the habit of pursuing futile endeavours."

"You might have been surprised."

"No. You didn't think of me like that."

And he was right, she didn't. But she *did* care about him, and she was impressed by him. He never gave up. No matter how hard things got for him. That's how she knew he would make it out of prison.

The cab cruises forward then stops again, still a block and a half from the Reef. But of course, these are monstrous Las Vegas blocks. The casinos rise like mountains on either side of her, some flashy and sleek, others horrendously gaudy. She wonders if she should just get out and walk the rest of the way, but there is nowhere to get out on Las Vegas Boulevard except at the casino cabstands, and to walk these blocks in heels would just be ignorant.

Heels. A six-foot-one woman in heels. My God, you are trying hard.

But isn't that what women are supposed to wear when they want to attract a man: lipstick and high heels and a dark purple dress with slits down the legs, rising that long, long way up her thighs?

Not that she wants to take Tyron to bed. She just wants him to want her again, to remember what he gave up when he joined the fucking Marine Corps. "Antoine thinks you're making a big mistake," she'd said to him when they were twenty-one, just after the Olympic trials.

He laughed derisively. "Antoine's one to judge. Though I guess he does know a thing or two about making mistakes. Why are you still going down there to see him?"

"Someone has to! Shit, Ty, we're all he's got. Other than those psychos he rolls with who got him locked up in the first place. And since you and Key won't see him, it's up to me."

"So what did he say," Tyron asked, "about the Marines? Why is it a mistake?"

"He said the U.S. military is just a means to create the conditions in which American companies can exploit the Global South."

"The Global South?"

"The non-white countries of the world. And he said the Marines especially, because they're always forward deployed. He says that what you'll be doing is enforcing neocolonialism. You'll be the spear tip of neocolonialism. He said the only people you'll be serving are the corporate elite, and the only people you'll be fighting are the poor and the marginalized."

Tyron looked like he was going to punch the wall. "I am so fucking sick of this guy. The self-righteousness of this lowdown criminal, to judge me—this fuck!"

She had never seen Tyron so angry.

"The only good thing about my parents being gone," he said, "is that they never had to see what a degenerate Antoine has become."

"People run with gangs, Ty. Especially people who have no one. It's not like he's killed anyone."

"I wouldn't be surprised if he has. I've heard some things."

"Rumours."

"Even if they are rumours, I know he didn't get caught for half the shit he's done. If he had, he'd be in there a damn lot longer."

"Regardless, he has a point about the Marines."

"A point? You gone mad, woman?"

"It seems to me all he does in there is read and work out. Maybe there's something to what he's saying."

"He's doing more than that. That crew of his won't let him sit idle."

"Whatever! Forget him. I don't want you to go. So what, you didn't make it to the Olympics. In another four years, you will. I got drafted. I'll support you until you go pro."

He looked even angrier than before. "I'm not going to be supported by you," he said, his voice so low and cold that she knew it was over then.

A week before, at the trials, she had been so hopeful. He would need a serious personal best if he was to have a chance of qualifying in the decathlon, but she felt he could do it. He had such incredible motivation. The Olympics, endorsements, money, a little bit of fame, and yet all his competitors had those same motivations. But he had one extra. Her. She had already told him that she would not stay with him if he joined the Corps, and he had already told her that he was joining the Corps if he didn't qualify. Both were averse to breaking their word or changing course if they had set their minds on something. There could only be one happy outcome.

She had always loved watching Tyron compete. In his singlet, which left his broad shoulders and much of his heavy chest bare, and in his skin-tight Lycra shorts, which showed off his sinuously carved legs, he really was a sight to behold. He looked like he was born of the folklore her mother told her as a child.

The javelin throw was her favourite event. There was something about him running with that spear held aloft at shoulder height, picking up speed, faster and faster, a sprint now, and then stabbing his front leg into the rubberized ground, flinging his front hip backward and hurling his torso forward, the beauty of his release, his arm extending so fully, so fluidly, the javelin soaring in its tight spiral, like he was the champion on some ancient battlefield, and it was *his* projectile, flying further than the rest, that would draw first blood. Its whistling plunge deep into the field, pointing upright out of the grass, would give her chills.

Usually, after two days spent watching him compete, Naomi couldn't stop thinking about taking him to her room, to not even let him shower, just strip him naked, fling him onto the bed, and ride him. But after ten events, warm-ups and cool-downs included for each of them, he was a spent man. Tyron barely had enough strength to eat, his stores of energy depleted and then some, his meagre fat burned away, his muscles stripped for further fuel.

She would have to wait a day, even two, before she could have him. Even then he was tired and dazed, but he was hard and alive, and she could pull him on top of her and feel his strength flowing into her and hers flowing back into him, and she thought of him throwing that javelin as she came.

But on the sunny days of the Olympic trials, she felt no desire during the javelin event. She didn't feel that she could barely control herself when she watched him in his form-fitting track gear. And she knew that this was a bad sign. For him and their relationship.

He did end up recording a personal best, though. She could see that he was tense, but he gritted through it and pushed beyond his previous limits. The U.S. team had some real superstars that year—when don't they in the decathlon? Tyron didn't even make it as an alternate.

After he completed his final event, the 1,500 metres, she wanted to go down to the edge of the track to hug him, but she was weeping so hard that she rushed to the bathroom instead and locked herself in a stall. She never forgot that she wasn't there to give him condolences and congratulations after he had pushed himself so hard and still come up short. She was making it easier for him to go through with his decision, she knew, but she just couldn't leave that stall. She couldn't face anyone, crying the way she was, least of all him.

Naomi wipes away a couple of tears and gathers up her purse, as the cab pulls up to the entrance to the Reef.

★ ★ ★ ★ ★ ★ ★ ★ ★ ★ ★ ★ ★ ★ ★ ★ ★ ★ ★

8

7:17 p.m.

ANTOINE FOCUSES ON his breathing during his warm-up in the dressing room. The routine is ingrained. No need to consciously engage during the planks, the rope, the squats, the stretches, the shadow boxing combinations: he can execute them mindlessly. He wants to be mindless in the lead-up to the fight, because once the bell rings...

He is not looking forward to the state of extreme concentration he will have to enter. It is painful, more painful than the physical blows he will have to endure. So for now, he focuses on the breath, only the breath.

There is one thought, though, that he cannot escape. You have to win. You have to. Tonight, it is the only option. This gnawing thought worries him. Since his release from prison, his focus has always been on process, technique, tactics—not results, not outcome. But tonight he has to win.

He cannot shake the thought. And if his mind is on the outcome, then it cannot be on his technique, which is

what matters most. Execution. People make sports com-
plicated, but in the end it comes down to who executes
better. That's really all it is. Now, figuring out how to
execute better than the best in the world—that *is* com-
plicated. That is what Antoine spent his time in prison
struggling to decipher. That and the odd mission for the
Latin Knights.

It would seem from his successes in the ring since
his release that he has deciphered the secret, but he has
yet to square off against a fighter like Kolya "Clayface"
Konitsyn, the man with jaw and fists of clay. Konitsyn
has never lost a fight and knocked out his last nineteen
opponents. According to some, he is the future of the division. Antoine has never been knocked out. Even before
he went inside, he was never knocked out.

As his arms, legs, and core flow through combinations
with Alejandro, Antoine looks past the weathered old man
at the polished grey walls. I built this place, he thinks. I
built the Reef.

Marty Bloom's children swore their father had writ-
ten a new will right before his heart gave out, leaving his
company to them. Bloom's lawyer corroborated their story:
Bloom decided to change his will after a private investigator
hired by his children reported that Bloom's young trophy
wife was secretly a close associate of Norman Bashinsky,
who everyone knew was gunning to own a casino on the
Strip. This was long before Bashinsky's casino licences in
East Asia vaulted him onto the *Forbes* Top Five list.

When it came time to file a lawsuit, the Bloom children and their lawyer failed to produce the revised will. Corporate espionage! Theft! they cried, yet there was no evidence of a break-in at either Bloom's Las Vegas mansion or his lawyer's office. And the young wife, she had copy after copy of a will naming her the inheritor of Bloom's company, all conclusively signed in the hand of the late casino mogul.

The lawsuit dragged on, but in the end Bashinsky gave the Blooms a peace offering, a small buyout when he took over the company — all he really cared about was the land on the Strip, and all they wanted was a payout and an end to their legal fees. Everyone walked away satisfied.

Except for the man who handed Bashinsky an empire. His corpse was mangled by coyotes.

The breath. Focus on the breath.

7:18 p.m.

IF THIS PLACE was a terrorist's dream before, it's a paradise for them now. There are crowds everywhere, the bars, clubs, shops, restaurants, blackjack tables, slot machines, poker rooms, baccarat rooms, fish tanks, elevators, escalators, passages, walkways, lobbies, bathrooms, just about every available space is taken up by people. Most of them have their eyes on the televisions that are placed strategically throughout the Reef. The undercard fights are

in full swing, with a flyweight title bout ready to begin
and Antoine's match up next. Tyron wonders how he will
ever find Naomi in such a flood of stylishly dressed people.
Then he sees her, taller than every other woman there,
and remembers that it was never difficult to spot Naomi
in a crowd.

The older guys at the Rising Star Boxing Club used to
hound her about her looks: "Girl, what kind of mix could
make you turn out so good?" "Girl, that's a mix I could
get into."

Tyron catches her eye as he makes his way through the
currents of people toward her, and she pauses, and simply
stares and smiles. He smiles too, surprised at how easily
she can disarm him. Looking at her, for the first time in so
long, he relinquishes his thoughts of terrorists and crowds,
of bombs and blood, and he's not in the desert anymore.

She presses forward and they meet in the swell of
people. In her heels, she is taller than him, like she used
to be before he reached his full height of six foot two.

"You look great," she says.

He shakes his head. "Come on now."

"What?"

"It's you who looks..." Breathtaking is the word he
wants to use. While her black bangs fall to the side of her
face, her hair is cut short in the back, exposing the smooth
lines of her neck. "You look good," he says, reluctant to
use breathtaking on a woman who left him, a woman
who chose another man, a woman who is married.

She closes the gap between them and embraces him, and he closes his eyes as he encircles her waist with his arms and holds her tight. He catches the scent of her exposed neck, and an urge rears up inside him to bury his face against her and caress her skin with his lips.

"Good to see you," he says, after he has pulled away, in as plain a voice as he can manage.

She peers into his eyes. "You okay?"

"Why wouldn't I be?"

"You look worried."

He tries to think of a response but in the end ignores the question and juts his head toward the sports bar, where you can both watch a host of different sports and wager on them. "Want to get a drink?"

She nods and gives a half-smile, still staring at him like he is a mirage.

There is nowhere to sit and barely enough room to stand, but they get drinks—her a martini, him another dark 'n' stormy—and find a spot near one of the large TVs against the back wall. The flyweight fighters dart across the screen like characters in a video game, so fast and nimble they look unnatural, a film reel sped up.

"Antoine's up next," she says, speaking loudly over the Top 40 music and the crush of so many conversations.

"I'm nervous for him."

"Feels almost like it's us about to go out there, doesn't it?"

"It does." He watches the fighters, perspiring, gasping,

and he feels his own blood rise. A desire comes over him to be out there, in their shoes, in the thrill of combat once more. He thought at the Olympic trials that he would never again be so nervous, and then he found a new level of fear, anticipation, and excitement when he first went into battle. But the battles kept coming, and the fear drained away. And the person he saw in the mirror was no longer his parents' son but Captain Shaw. And that person doesn't have a place here, in this city, in this country, in any space that isn't a war zone. What am I going to do now? he wonders. What the fuck am I going to do now?

Tyron wills himself back to the present, and turns from the TV to Naomi. "Antoine's the only one still competing. Out of all of us, the only one left. You two made it the furthest. Only ones to go pro."

She muses on this, and a look of regret passes over her face. "You could've," she says, "had you stayed with it." She falters, realizing what she has alluded to. "Sorry. I shouldn't have brought that up."

He gives a light shake of his head. "It's fine, Naomi. It's long in the past." He looks up at the screen again and sips his drink. The fighters are in their corners, gulping water and catching their breath. "The truth is I never liked it as much as you and Antoine did. I didn't have the personality for it. That killer instinct, I didn't have it."

"No?"

"Not then."

"And now you do?"

Now I have it, he thinks, as the faces of the dead return to him. He clenches his jaw and pulls his gaze back into focus. Meets her look of apprehension.

"When it's necessary," he says. "But I don't like it. I don't like dominating other people. Ultimately that's what competing is about."

"But you're a Marine."

"I *was* a Marine."

"Right. Still. Isn't that—"

"Isn't that all about winning? Defeating the enemy?"

"Yeah."

"For some. For me it was about protecting my men. Defending civilians. My parents believed that sports were beneficial but that you shouldn't give up your life for them. There's too much important work to be done in the world. I didn't agree with them when they were around, but I do now."

"Do you miss them?" she asks.

It's different looking into a woman's eyes when they are above his own. They shine like the surfaces of deep, dark pools: easy to get lost in, hard to escape. Don't fall in, he thinks.

"Not as much as I used to," he says. "The Corps helped. It *is* a family."

He sees her mouth tighten, straining at its edges to pull down.

"Sorry," he says. "I shouldn't have brought that up."

"It's the truth. Why be sorry? They gave you what you

needed; I didn't, it's—" She looks at her glass, caresses the rim with a polished nail. Looks back to him. "And anyway, like you said, it's long in the past."

They sip their drinks in silence and stare up at the TV. One of the flyweight fighters leaves an opening in his defence and receives a well-timed blow to the face. His head snaps back but he keeps on fighting. The ambivalence Tyron feels watching the violence concerns him. He is both repulsed by the brutality, by its commodification, and calmed by it.

"What are you going to do now?" she asks.

"Antoine hooked me up with a ticket for the fight."

"I meant with your life."

"I know. I was making a . . . I don't know what I'm going to do with my life," he shouts over the music and the other conversations, and he thinks that it is an embarrassing thing to say so loudly, even if no one else is listening. "I really don't know."

"You've changed," she says, watching his face intently. "Something's changed."

"In what way?"

She pauses, as though ensuring she understands for herself what she means before she speaks. He remembers her being reflective like this when they were younger, but she has also changed. He is surprised by how much more of a woman she looks now. She was no girl the last time he saw her: at six foot one and a pro basketball player it was hard to think of her as anything but a full-grown woman,

but back then her face was rounder, softer, free of lines.
He could not imagine her as a mother in those days. He
can now. He thinks she is all the more beautiful for it.

"You're more sure of yourself," she says.

He laughs, which makes him think that his new drink
is getting to him, but he does not mind this time around,
now that he is with her. Terrorists aren't his responsibility anymore. Or at least, they are now secondary to the
wants and needs of his own life. "I'm thirty-two years old,
I have no idea what I'm going to do with my life, and you
think I'm *more* sure of myself?"

"You're more sure of being unsure. You never would've
admitted to something like that back in the day."

He smiles at her and sees that her drink is empty.
"Another one?"

She gives a hesitant smile and then nods. He leaves
her to wait in line at the bar. As he waits he checks his
phone and sees that he has missed a text. Another one
from Marlon. Young brother meet me at my place 6 am tmrw.
And there is a second one. Please. It's important.

I'll be there, Tyron writes back. He ponders whether
he would come to the same decision if he was sober, and
decides that he would. He likes and respects Marlon and
will help him any way he can, provided it doesn't conflict
with one of his principles—like turning his back on an
old friend.

Speaking of which, he thinks, don't forget that Naomi
is Keenan's wife.

In that purple dress, that slip of fabric hugging her the way he would hug her, how could any man not forget that she was off limits? He arrives at a clean solution. When he returns to her with the drinks, he'll bring up Keenan and keep bringing him up in their conversation.

It has the opposite effect of what he intended.

"I'm leaving him," she says.

"What?"

"I wasn't planning to tell you so soon, but it's not exactly like we're strangers. I'm going to leave him, Ty."

Leaning back, holding her drink off to one side, she looks like a movie star, all cool, casual confidence, so calm that he thinks either she is joking or she came to this decision a long time ago. "Are you serious?"

"I stayed with him through the trial because I didn't want to abandon him when he needed my help. But now that he's been acquitted, I can let him go." She turns to the side and stares off into the distance, the hint of a sad smile on her lips. "It's funny. Had he been convicted and sent to prison I would've stayed with him." She turns back to Tyron, and there are tears in her eyes. "We both escaped."

In that moment, Tyron realizes he had misread her behaviour: she wasn't joking, and she wasn't nearly as confident as she seemed; she was just better at hiding her pain. He wraps her in his arms, squeezes her against him, and cannot stop himself from kissing her on the cheek. When he lets go, she continues to hold on.

At last she pulls away and wipes the tears from her

eyes with a couple flicks of her thumb. It's the baller in her, reclaiming control. She looks up at the screen. "This fight's almost over."

Tyron follows her lead and sees that the flyweight bout is in its final round. One of the fighters has a horribly swollen eye and the other has a gash across his forehead. Nothing compared to the wounds Tyron has staunched himself.

"I just know Antoine's going to win," Naomi says. "It's incredible what he's become."

She watches the screen but Tyron watches her. He pulls his fight ticket from his pocket and hands it to her. "Here. You go. You'll have to hang with Ricky, which I'm sure he'll prefer, but you'll get to see Antoine live."

"No. It's yours."

"Take it. I want you to go."

"Really? You don't mind?"

"I only got the tickets for Ricky. And you were always a better boxer than me anyway. Take it."

She holds the ticket tight and grins at him. "What will you do?"

"I'll watch the fights here and meet up with you guys when it's over. Go. You don't want to miss Antoine's entrance."

"Thanks, Ty." She looks down at the ticket in her hand. "It really is great to see you again."

He nods. "You too."

7:27 p.m.

THROUGH FLUORESCENT-LIT SERVICE tunnels, Keenan hurries from the hotel to the arena. A fight broke out in the crowd and an old man fainted; in both cases security was called to step in, requiring more guards to fill their posts. He finds a stairwell at the end of the tunnel and springs up the stairs three at a time. He is to join the detail that takes boxers to and from the ring. The next match can't start without him.

Keenan emerges from the grey underworkings of the casino resort, returning to Norman Bashinsky's meticulous aquatic aesthetic. Some call the man a genius, a visionary ahead of his time. Others argue that he is a businessman so ruthless he puts the rest of the Fortune 500 CEOS to shame. Makes them look naive instead of Machiavellian. Keenan hasn't thought much on the subject, but he does remember when, some years ago, a high-profile, purportedly corrupt Chinese bureaucrat was murdered in a Reef hotel room. It wasn't the murder that stuck out to Keenan so much as what followed: soon after, Bashinsky received licences from the Chinese government to build several casinos in Macao. Wall Street fell in love with him after that, and as Reef Resorts stock rose, so too did Bashinsky's personal fortune.

Keenan passes through a security checkpoint into the interior of the stadium. A guard he met earlier in his shift is waiting for him outside the entrance to one of the dressing rooms. "We'll move out in a few minutes," he says to Keenan.

Keenan nods. "Who we taking?"

"Deco. He's just finishing his warm-up now. We'll get the call soon."

Antoine, Keenan thinks, you just can't get rid of me today.

Funny, though, that when they were kids it was the opposite. Keenan couldn't get rid of Antoine. Keenan had everything set up at the Rising Star Boxing Club: his best friend, a hot girl for them to compete over, a good coach in Tony. They *were* rising stars, all three of them; him, Ty, and Naomi all going places. They were the best athletes at their schools, the best young boxers at the gym, and the best of friends. Then this small, quiet, intense Latino showed up.

Keenan didn't mind that he had to compete with Tyron for Naomi's attention. He competed with Tyron in everything, why not the pursuit of her too? It was unfortunate, though, that he had never realized Tyron didn't feel the same way. Had he foreseen that, the distance between them might not have grown.

But while Keenan didn't mind Tyron as a rival for Naomi's attention, all it took was one look from Antoine and he wanted to smash the kid. They'd get in the ring to spar and he would pound the shit out of Antoine and feel that all had been set to rights. But Antoine would just crawl back to his feet, slink through the ropes, and be

the same as ever, only bruised and bloodied. Worse yet
was when Tony Wilks would commend Antoine on how
hard he worked or how much courage and toughness he
showed; the way Antoine's eyes would light up, like it was
the first compliment he'd ever been paid, made Keenan
want to pound him all over again.

It wasn't just at boxing that Keenan had to put up with
the kid. It seemed that wherever he went — basketball,
football, track — Antoine was always there. Thank God
Tyron didn't play tennis or Terrence Shaw would have
involved his foster child in that too.

Of course, Antoine grew on him over time. It helped
that Naomi never showed any interest in him, and it was
useful having a third member in their crew — fourth if
Naomi was with them. Besides, Antoine did get better
at just about everything, so that the three boys came to
dominate not only in the ring but on the football field,
the basketball court, and in the 4 × 400-metre relay. And
no one who wasn't packing heat would ever mess with
the three of them when they were together. There were
also things about Antoine that were amusing, like when
Keenan would buy the others ice cream or freezies. Antoine
would look so touched, as if Keenan had opened a vein for
him. Keenan would feel magnanimous in these moments,
proud that he was helping those less fortunate.

But when the time came to choose between being magnanimous or getting rid of Antoine, Keenan chose the latter.
A month before the killing of Terrence and Viola Shaw, a

strange thing happened at boxing practice. First, Keenan's father came into the gym instead of just dropping him off at the door—and even that was rare now that Keenan could drive himself. Then, he grabbed a hold of Terrence Shaw when he came in to drop off Tyron and Antoine, and took him to a corner of the gym. Tyron and Antoine were out for a warm-up run during the conversation, but since Keenan had arrived earlier, he was already inside putting on his hand wraps. The sound of his father's raised voice made him edge closer to where they were speaking. The men were on good terms, but their relationship went no further than parents whose sons were friends. To Keenan's knowledge, this was the first time they had ever spoken in private.

Semi-private. Craig Quinn noticed his son idling and barked, "Is this how you train? Move your ass, Keenan." The teenager hurried away; Craig Quinn was not a man to disobey when he was angry.

But Keenan had already heard much that surprised and intrigued him.

"Look, I think what you're doing is honourable. I really do. More than that, I actually agree with you: we can't have the most lucrative strip in America and the rest of the city poor as shit, I get it. But what I'm trying to tell you is that it doesn't matter if you're right. You're pissing off the wrong fucking people."

Terrence Shaw: "Who are these people I'm pissing off?"

"Christ, man, you're missing the point. I already told you

who they are, the wrong fucking people. I shouldn't even be telling you to back off; they'll have their eye on me next."

Terrence Shaw: "Did they send you to intimidate me?"

"Send me to intimidate you? You call this intimidation?"

Craig Quinn's face was a mottled red. A cop, six-three like Keenan is now, a big man with a furious temper, it was difficult to describe him as anything but intimidating. Yet Terrence Shaw did not look intimidated. Though not a small man, he was not as tall or as broad as his son Tyron would become — as Tyron was even then — and yet he did not seem afraid in the least.

"If you think this is intimidation, you really have no idea what kind of people you're up against. I wouldn't even give a shit but it's not just you, Terrence. You and your wife are behind this movement. Don't think they won't—" Here his father tried to lower his voice, but he was so jacked up that it came out louder than he expected. "—*take out a woman*. I wouldn't even give a shit, but I like your boy. He's a good kid. I don't want to see him turned into a fucking orphan."

Terrence looked for a moment into Craig's face, and then he said, softly and slowly, "Craig, changes have to happen. They have to. People have too little and they're suffering too much. And those fighting for them cannot always be afraid."

"For Chrissake, dammit, Terrence!" Here Craig looked around to see if anyone had noticed his outburst, which was when he caught Keenan eavesdropping.

A few moments later, on the other side of the gym, Craig Quinn grabbed his son by the scruff of his shirt and slammed him against a wall. Jabbing his finger almost into Keenan's eye, he said, "You never heard what you think you heard today. You never heard it. Which means you can't repeat it. Especially to your fucking friends. You say one word of this to them, I swear to God, boy, I will give you the beating of your fucking life."

Keenan was grateful that the gym was almost empty when all this happened. When Tyron and Antoine came back from their run, they asked him why his face was so red. He was afraid to cross his father, and even if he wasn't, he was too humiliated to explain what had happened. From what he could gather, Terrence Shaw never mentioned the conversation to his son, either.

Keenan had willed himself to forget the incident. In fact, he did such a good job of forgetting that the memory didn't surface even when he heard that Terrence and Viola Shaw had been killed in a gang shooting, the culprits never caught. It was only at the funeral, as he watched their coffins being lowered into the ground, that the conversation between his father and Terrence Shaw came back to him.

The details of the shooting were murky. It was assumed to be a drive-by that had gone wrong, the real target missed and the Shaws hit instead. All witnesses had seen was a car screeching away after the shots were fired. Everyone said—Craig Quinn, most of all—that the

Shaws had lived in a rough neighbourhood and that this sort of thing happened in places like that. To Keenan's reply that the Shaws were the most beloved people in their community, his father had shouted, "You think gangbangers give a fuck who they're killing? They're high out of their fucking minds. Wise up, boy."

Keenan didn't know who was responsible for the double murder, but he thought it best not to tell Tyron what he had heard that day in the gym. Tyron was distraught enough without a mystery to solve. As for Antoine, Keenan never thought it was his business, even if he was the Shaws' foster son. He wasn't their real son.

But Antoine wept like he was their real son. So did everyone. Keenan couldn't believe how many people were at the funeral and how many tears were shed. His own tears amazed him. He couldn't remember crying like that since he was a little kid. He hadn't realized how much the Shaws had meant to him until that moment.

At Keenan's request, the Quinns offered for Tyron to live with them. Tyron was grateful but declined, and he and Antoine moved in with Tyron's cousin Tara and her mother, Patricia. But the women didn't really have the means or the space to support two more, and Tyron soon realized that he was closer to the Quinns than he was to his own relatives. Also the Quinns had a far larger, more comfortable home that was closer to Tyron's high school. On top of that, Keenan had his own car and they could travel to and from school and various sports practices together, while living under the same roof. All in all, staying with the Quinns would allow Tyron to concentrate less on his basic needs and more on his priorities: schooling and sport.

But in truth, all of that was just window dressing to the fact that the Quinns adored Tyron, from Keenan's mother to his sisters to his older brother, and even to his curmudgeonly father. And right then, in the wake of his parents' funeral, Tyron needed them. He changed his mind, and everyone was on board with the move. The only question was, what was to be done with Antoine?

"It's up to you, boy, if you want us to take him or not," Keenan's father had said.

This felt like an overwhelmingly large decision for Keenan to make. "Do you want him to stay here?"

"Of course I don't want him to stay here. What do I look like, Immigration Services? You think I want to open my door to every Mexican that doesn't have a home? Christ, Keenan. I don't like that kid anyway, even if he wasn't a Mexican. He's too shifty. Like his father."

"You knew his father?"

Craig nodded. "A real piece of shit. A career criminal. The apple doesn't fall far from the tree."

"So he can't stay here then?"

"No, he can stay here. Just because I don't want him doesn't mean I won't take him. Your mother's got a soft spot for him for some reason. But it's your decision. He's your friend."

To be magnanimous or to get rid of Antoine? Keenan pretended to grapple with the decision longer than it actually took. The idea of living one room down from someone who so easily grated on his nerves was all it took to make up his mind.

Without her nephew included, Patricia wasn't going to put up Antoine. He seemed to think Tony Wilks would take him in, but the boxing coach explained that half the fighters in his gym had family troubles and it was impossible for him to offer safe haven to all of them, so to be fair he would offer it to none of them. Keenan suspected that this was true, but that Tony also didn't like the idea of bringing in a teenage boy, almost a young man, to live with his flowering daughter. Which was misguided. Other than Tony himself, there was probably not a better defender of her virtue than Antoine.

So while Tyron moved in with the large Irish-Italian family, Antoine once again became a ward of the state. For about six hours. He continued training at the Rising Star Boxing Club, which was how Keenan, Tyron, and Naomi still got to see him, but everywhere else he fell off the map. He disappeared from school, from the social housing for minors where he was meant to live, even from official records—there were rumours that all files on him in the possession of state enterprises vanished. If a cop or a social worker showed up at the boxing gym looking for Antoine while he was there, they would be waylaid by the other fighters and word would be sent to him to escape out a back door.

Tony stopped charging him for training, probably out of guilt that he didn't let a twice-orphaned boy share his roof, but it served him also to have Antoine there. At sixteen, almost seventeen, Antoine was the hardest worker in the gym—perhaps, as Tony had once said, the hardest worker he had ever seen. And the fact that he still wasn't the best, or even close to it, set a precedent for everyone else. "This guy's never going to be a contender and look how hard he trains. You want to be a world champ, you call yourself committed, you better step up your game."

Of course, they were wrong. Antoine was the only one from Rising Star to claw his way up to contention; the others all petered out as amateurs or low-level professionals.

Tony would give Antoine food too. Whether this was more guilt or generosity, Keenan couldn't tell, but it was a good thing he did. Always a lean kid, Antoine began to look very thin in those days. Very thin. If anyone asked him where he was staying, he had a set response. "How is that your business?" If pressed further, he'd add: "The time to worry about me has passed. Leave me alone now." And if you were to press him after that, you had a fight on your hands. While Antoine wasn't the best boxer in the gym, he was a hell of a lot better than he used to be, and his fists never stopped coming.

Antoine didn't have to say where he was staying for them to know the truth—his grubby and dishevelled appearance told them in plain words: some nights he was sleeping on the streets. Keenan told him that it was his parents' decision that he couldn't stay with his family, and Antoine gave him that discomfiting, unblinking stare of his. Antoine never said a word, and Keenan wondered if he knew the truth.

7:45 p.m.

THE NUMBER OF celebrities in the crowd is humbling, even for a minor celebrity like her. *Former* minor celebrity, she reminds herself.

Naomi climbs the steep flight of stairs to the top of the arena. Even the nosebleeds seem filled with the rich and famous—so many fake breasts and oven-baked tans, bespoke sports coats and designer dresses. The Gibbons-Suarez main event is just one fight away and the alcohol is flowing; the anticipation is a bubble that keeps sucking in more air.

"Naomi! Naomi!" Ricky shouts as he squeezes past two middle-aged men wearing blazers and ripped jeans. He steps forward to embrace her and she stretches out one arm for a handshake. To his credit, Ricky closes both hands around her single one, as if that was what he'd been going for all along: a big windup with the arms for a hearty handshake.

"It's been such a long time, Naomi. Way too long. Way too long. How you been?" Before she can answer he adds,

"Ty messaged me that you were taking his ticket and I saw you coming up the stairs. You look great. I mean, even better than you used to, which is . . . well . . . What's better than great? Really great, I guess."

Taken aback by his energy and activity, Naomi tries to think of a response, but he has taken her hand in his and is pulling her along with him, up a few rows and then down one of them to their seats. People generally get out of her way, especially when she is in heels, but this crowd stares up at her, sullen and superior, reluctantly shifting their knees, and she is reminded why she avoids this side of Vegas. Ricky plops down right in the middle of the row, a spot with a fine view: the entire arena beneath them, filled with people from top to bottom.

From this high up, the ring looks small. It's strange being in the crowd. More nerve-wracking on this side of things, she thinks, as she wants Antoine to win so badly. He deserves it: to have success on a scale like this, to be vaulted into stardom. Deserves it, both for how hard he has worked and for how much he has endured.

Naomi can scarcely believe just how nervous she is. She wishes she could reach inside herself and crush those fluttering butterflies. It's an uncomfortable sensation, one she is unused to because she never got nervous for herself. Not when she was competing. Not really. Not even for the WNBA Finals. Nothing like Tyron used to get at least. Or Keenan. With Antoine, who could tell? He wasn't exactly the type to share his feelings, and as far as facial expressions and body language went, he was almost always intense, brow furrowed, dark eyes searching, like he was constantly competing. If he was nervous, then he was always nervous; and if he was calm in life, then he was calm in the ring. At this point, she supposes, it makes no difference: if you're always one thing, then you're adapted to it no matter what. And yet she did see something else in him once—something she had never seen in him before nor has since.

It was more than a year after Tyron's parents had been killed, almost at the end of high school. Tyron was living with the Quinns and Antoine was staying God knows where. Naomi, Tyron, and Keenan were at the gym only occasionally, other sports taking precedence. But Antoine was always there, quietly training on his own.

It was a Saturday. Naomi was at the gym because her dad was driving her to a game after he finished up some classes. She found Antoine at the coffee table by the front desk reading a boxing magazine. He greeted her with his typical reserved nod and a quiet "Hey Naomi"—though there was that extra bit beyond his eyes, like he wanted to say more. It was there every time they spoke, and she had given up on waiting for him to divulge it.

After a few pleasantries he went back to reading *The Ring*, and she sat next to him to do the same. She felt the change in him before she saw it, a prickling of her skin that she couldn't explain until she noticed he was transfixed by the pages in his hands. Slowly his knees straightened so that he was standing now, and she stood too, wondering what he could be reading for it to hypnotize him in this way. At last he looked up from the magazine and seemed to remember where he was. He looked at her beside him and smiled slightly. Without warning, Antoine took her face in his hands and kissed her on the mouth. Then he stared at her, saying everything she had always guessed at in one look: I love you, I know you don't love me, either way I've moved on to more important things. Then, with brisk purpose, he walked out of the gym with the magazine clutched in his hands, and she was left behind, stunned by how good the kiss had felt.

When she had gained control of herself, Naomi snatched up another copy of *The Ring* from the table and flipped through its pages until she found the article he'd been reading: a puff-piece about the newly opened Reef Resort and Casino on the Strip, and the first boxing event held in its state-of-the-art arena. She read the article three times over and still had no clue why it had produced such a reaction in Antoine.

The article outlined the usual details: who won, who lost, upcoming bouts for the fighters, reactions of the crowd, some snippets about the casino owner, and a description of the arena and the aquarium-themed Reef Resort. What jumped out at her most was the image of sharks and stingrays swimming beneath the feet of gamblers, shoppers, and hotel guests. Bright fish everywhere,

you didn't need to go all the way to Australia to see the
Great Barrier Reef when you had it right here in Las Vegas.
The whole thing was the vision of the new casino mag-
nate, Norman Bashinsky, who, the article reported, had
an armed escort with him at all times. However, at the
recent fight, Bashinsky threw caution to the wind and left
his escort behind to visit with each of the winning fighters and congratulate them in person. "I like winners," the
article quoted him as saying. "Those are the people I want
to spend time with. If someone is good enough to win in
my place, he deserves to get a handshake." The tradition
had just begun, but Bashinsky planned on continuing it as
long as the Reef was in his possession. "And the only way
I'm ever giving up the finest resort on the Strip is if they
pry it from my cold, dead hands. Even then I won't let go!"

Naomi thought Bashinsky sounded like a bit of a nut,
but then again all these casino moguls did. The Reef
sounded awesome, though. But what — *what* — had
brought about that change in Antoine?

She put the magazine down and sat back into the sofa.
Thought about that kiss again. He must've wanted to
do that for a long time. What a different person he had
seemed.

Naomi wondered if Antoine was a virgin. She had wondered it for a while. Of course, he might not be. Even
before the Shaws were killed, he would disappear for
long stretches, sometimes a day or two. And now he was
completely on his own; who knew what other lives he

had? Perhaps there was another girl out there, someone he could tell all the secrets that glinted behind his eyes. But she doubted it. Her guess was that this was it, his one moment of release. She had seen it. She had felt it, flowing from his lips into hers.

RICKY IS SAYING something to her, which she only half hears through her musings. "I'm sorry?"

"I said, what are you up to these days?"

"Coaching." She doesn't want to explain it further, yet she sees that he's expecting more. "I'm an assistant with the men's and women's teams at UNLV, coach a girls' AAU team, a girls' high school team, some camps and clinics for younger kids, and I do some personal training on the side."

"Whoa," he says. "So you like coaching, then. You must if you do so much of it."

Her eyes are on the empty ring and the tunnel leading to it, and she is annoyed having to keep glancing away to answer him. From what she can tell, Ricky hasn't changed much since high school.

"For sure. My dad's a coach. My brothers are coaches. It's in my blood."

"You're not still playing ball, then?"

There seems to be some activity around the ring, various officials mobilizing. She feels the butterflies inside her mounting. It's been seven years since she last saw

Antoine. Seven years since she told him she was engaged to Keenan. Seven years since he told her to stop visiting him in prison.

"No. Retired a few seasons back," she says.

"That's right, I think I heard that. Tara must've told me. So how come you retired?"

She turns to him, frustrated, wanting to come up with a clever lie or half-truth to deflect the question but instinctively being forthright, which frustrates her even more. "I was a bench player my whole career. I was never going to be a starter. The money's not great in women's sports, for most of us at least, even if the work is hard as hell, and I was thinking I might try to have a baby... What are you up to these days, Ricky?"

"Shit, Naomi, you know I got like ten different hustles, don't you? So you and Tara are tight these days, right?"

"Yeah, we're close," she says.

He nods knowingly. "What do you think about her?"

"What do I think about Tara?" What is wrong with this guy?

"Yeah. You think she's—" He shimmies his shoulders. "—looking for a new guy, maybe?"

Naomi stares at him. "Are you serious?"

"Why wouldn't I be?"

"You?"

"Well, you don't got to be mean about it."

"I'm sorry." She can't curb her giggles. "Did you meet her last guy?"

"Couple times. Why?"

She looks at him sideways. "He's like the complete opposite of you in every way."

"Okay. Okay. Well...well...it didn't work. It didn't work with him, Naomi, how you like that? You trying to bring me down, you actually just making me more confident. You're making me more confident."

"Oh, is that what I'm doing? I'm glad. I'm glad that's what I'm doing."

"'Cause he's the opposite o' me—you just said it—he's the opposite o' me, and she don't like him. So maybe— *maybe*—I'm the guy she's been waiting for."

She had control of herself but this sends her into new bouts of laughter. "No one's been waiting for you, Ricky."

He sucks his teeth and shakes his head. "You are just straight-up cold."

"I'm sorry. I really am. I'm sorry. I know you're a good guy. I know you are. And you know what...you've convinced me. I think Tara would really like to go out wi—I'm sorry, I can't get through it with a straight face. You're just not her type, Ricky! You *are* a good guy, but you're not her type. I don't know what you want me to say."

He shrinks into silence and she focuses on the ring again. The announcer climbs between the ropes, a microphone in hand.

"Could you put in a good word for me?"

She turns to Ricky, flabbergasted.

"Please," he adds.

"Don't give me no puppy dog eyes, okay? Do you even like Tara, or is she just the next prospect on your list?"

"Are those two things mutually exclusive?"

"That's what I thought."

"No, I'm playing, I like her. I genuinely like her. You want me to bare my soul? You want me to get all vulnerable? I want to be with her. I want—"

The lights cut out. A spotlight opens on the tunnel entrance. This is it, she thinks. Despite her quickening nerves, she grins.

"I want a rela—"

"Not now, Ricky. Antoine's coming."

7:56 p.m.

"IT'S TIME," **SAYS** the event handler as she sticks her head inside the dressing room. She has on a headset and carries a tablet. Antoine looks up at her. *It's time.*

He turns from the door and spreads his arms like he's being crucified. Alejandro slips on his shimmering black robe. On the back, the head of a coyote, mouth open, fangs bared. The robe's hood hangs low over Antoine's face, leaving only his jawline visible beyond its shadow.

Gloves on, he pounds the fists of Alejandro, of Carlos, and of his cutman, Simón. They nod to him, their faces grim, expressions sombre, but their eyes are filled with devotion and belief. He looks out the door and sees Keenan waiting in his ridiculous fake beard. Keenan nods to him with an uncertain smile of encouragement, but Antoine isn't greeting anyone right now—especially not Keenan.

Out in the tunnel, surrounded by his security detail and handlers, Antoine walks with swagger and purpose down the halls of the Reef arena. Even here, behind the scenes, the walls are sea blue and lagoon turquoise, stormy grey and seaweed green, the colours flowing and blending in waves. Hanging on these watery walls are paintings of the fighters who have won in this stadium, great champions immortalized with stylized brushstrokes. Hopkins, Ward, Mayweather, Suarez, Gibbons. Antoine doesn't pause to look at the paintings. He doesn't care who or what came before him. For Antoine Deco, the history of boxing begins and ends with this fight.

The tunnel bends and up ahead he sees the opening to the arena. It is black, dotted with camera flashes, winking stars in the vast expanse of space. For all Antoine's recent success, this is his biggest stage yet.

He steps from the tunnel into the cavernous space of the arena. There is a roar from the crowd. Undercard, underdog, underestimated, he is still the hometown fighter, the object of their support. With the spotlight on him and the rest of the lights off, he can see the crowd only as silhouettes. But he can feel them. Their energy, the energy of thousands, and he feels like he could burst into flame. There is music playing, a reggaeton track his team supplied. He can hardly hear it over the din of the crowd.

Inside the ring now. He doesn't recall climbing through the ropes, which worries him. Stay here, Antoine, a voice inside him says. All the world could be watching, but it doesn't change what you have to do. Stay here.

You didn't come here for this, he thinks. This is just another step forward. Stay focused. Do what you have to do. Execute.

He leans back into his corner, spreads his arms wide over the ropes, and sneers with disdainful confidence.

★ ★ ★ ★ ★ ★ ★ ★ ★ ★ ★ ★ ★ ★ ★ ★ ★ ★ ★ ★

9

8:05 p.m.

TYRON THINKS THAT Antoine's entrance is good but Konitsyn's is better. Yes, Antoine looks like an athletic grim reaper in his sleeveless robe, carved bronze arms and black tattoos on full display, but Kolya "Clayface" Konitsyn looks like a champion.

His entourage is almost twenty people. It includes a world-famous rapper and a world-famous actor, not to mention two world-famous trainers and one of the biggest promoters in the sport. The Slavic-looking men on either side of him are giants, bearded monsters who glare at the crowd and the TV cameras, daring anyone to make a move on their champion. The entire entourage wear grey T-shirts with CLAYFACE emblazoned in big auburn letters above an image of the Batman villain who inspired the name: a hideous creature with hands morphed into sledgehammers, soulless white eyes, and a wide, pugnacious grin.

Konitsyn is so polished he almost shines. His body has been shaved clean, as has his famously indestructible chin.

His straight hair has a plain, traditional cut, not too long, not too short, brushed to one side. His wide eyes exudes both benevolence and smugness. His skin is stretched taut over sinuous muscles and rope-like tendons. His abs, without a sliver of fat, are nevertheless wide and thick, the engine in the twisting of his torso. He is known for knockouts—nineteen in a row and looking for his twentieth. The man has fists and a face of clay. He has never lost. He smiles at the camera like a campaigning politician, and it is hard to imagine anyone that confident ever losing.

Antoine looks menacing, but Clayface looks formidable.

Tyron learns of Konitsyn's history from the television commentators. With the match involving a local fighter, and with the Gibbons-Suarez showdown impending, the bar has turned off its music and turned up the volume on the TVs.

"It is clear that nobody wants to fight him," one of the commentators says of Clayface. "We now know that two fighters ranked ahead of Dex Deco were given the opportunity to be part of the biggest event in our sport, and they turned it down. It's a big payday but it's just not worth it to suffer the kind of trauma Konitsyn inflicts on his opponents. Credit to Deco for putting himself in harm's way, and giving himself a shot at a potential title fight, if he can pull off the upset... But what an upset it would be."

"Most definitely," says a younger man, with a gruff, staccato cadence. "I like Antoine Deco. I like him a lot. He's

a great fighter. He's got great speed, great hands, great
defence. He's worked hard to reinvent himself after incar-
ceration. But no one, so far, has been able to withstand
the power of Clayface, and as good as Dex is, I don't see
that changing tonight."

Tyron balls his own knuckles into a fist. He is amazed
that Antoine has done it, made it to the pinnacle, beneath
the bright lights and the flashing cameras, what they all
dreamed of as kids. He still can't quite believe it, how far
Antoine has come.

But then, look at Naomi and all she's accomplished.
Look at Keenan, and how far he's fallen. It's been a long
road for all of us, he thinks. A long road. But where is the
road taking us?

Tyron doesn't think Antoine will win. How could
someone he used to whoop beat a title contender? Doesn't
seem possible. He even wonders if Antoine will make it
out alive, judging by each new detail he learns of Konitsyn.
It seems that every middleweight is ducking the man,
including the belt holders in the division, which is why
he has yet to climb to the very top. Antoine is the only one
to jump at the opportunity to fight this knockout machine.

Tyron doesn't want to watch his former foster brother
be beaten to a pulp. Lord knows, he's seen too many dis-
figured bodies. Nevertheless it surprises him, this resid-
ual fraternal concern. For years he thought that the next
time he heard Antoine's name would be to learn that he
was dead, and Tyron had accepted that, long ago. Instead,

here Antoine is, against all odds, a success. Tyron wonders what Terrence and Viola would make of it.

They would be proud of their son, he thinks. But worried for him, like Tyron worries now.

The commentators quiet down as the sonorous voice of the announcer booms across the chic sports bar. "Next is a ten-round middleweight clash between two of the fastest-rising stars in their division. Our first combatant, fighting out of the red corner, wearing black and gold, officially weighing in at 159 pounds, his professional record: twenty-five victories, fifteen by way of knockout, and only three defeats. From Las Vegas, Nevada, on a fourteen-match win streak, Antoine 'Dex' Deco!"

The crowd in both the bar and the arena erupts. Antoine doesn't raise a glove. He doesn't nod his head. He simply stands in his corner, staring at Konitsyn.

Despite how certain Antoine looks, his opponent was born for this moment. Came from a family of boxers. A star from the beginning. Scouted, trained, and groomed to be the best.

"And his opponent, fighting out of the blue corner, wearing white, and officially weighing in at 159 pounds, his professional record: twenty-seven victories, twenty-four by knockout, with zero defeats. From Tashkent, Uzbekistan, nineteen knockouts in a row, Nikolai 'Kolya' 'Clayface' Konitsyn!"

Tyron is unsure if Antoine does have the support of the hometown crowd. Their cheering and applause for

Clayface is at least equal to what it had been for Antoine; they know who is on the path to mega-stardom, best to get on the bandwagon now.

The referee calls the fighters to the centre of the ring. As he recaps the rules, they stare each other down. Clayface's smugness is gone. Eyes deadened, he looks like an assassin. They are both five-ten, both weighed in at 159 pounds although both are heavier now, and the difference in reach is negligible. Apart from the difference in skin tone, and the addition of Antoine's gang and prison tattoos, their bodies look similar, though Antoine's legs are slightly thicker and Clayface is heavier on top. Antoine also has more veins branching across the surface of his flesh. As for their faces, Antoine's, shaded in stubble, is longer, more gaunt, and his brow is low, slanting up to his buzzed black hair. Clayface, clean shaven, has a high, flat forehead and a thin, bow-shaped mouth. Both have thick noses, flattened more than a few times, but neither is misshapen. There seems a beam between their eyes, a meeting of lethal intent. Each looks like he has killed a man before, and the longer Tyron watches them, the more likely that seems. He cannot imagine any co-operation between them, but when the referee tells them to touch gloves, they do — a quick pound, the gaze between them unfaltering.

Then they are back in their corners, and Tyron finds that his mouth is dry. The bell dings.

8:20 p.m.

NAOMI LEANS FORWARD, fingers digging deep into her thighs, and wishes she were closer. Not that much has happened yet. Two rounds of Konitsyn stalking Antoine around the ring in patient, calculated steps, feet never crossing—front foot up, back foot up, front foot up, back foot up—while Antoine is the opposite, springing backward, darting forward, fists flashing then defending. But for all Antoine's activity he has not connected cleanly on anything—too wary to get in close, which Naomi can understand. Even from this distance, she can see how explosively Konitsyn can strike. Not on his jab feelers. Or on his feints to set up the real combination. But when he truly attacks, so sudden and powerful, it is preternatural. Each time he does it, her breath catches. But Antoine's escapes are also animalistic and disconcertingly fast. Until an exchange when he is not fast enough.

It happens in the third round. Konitsyn catches Antoine with a right hook to the jaw. A glancing blow, but enough to make Antoine stumble as he retreats, enough to make the crowd gasp and rise halfway to their feet, enough to make Naomi wince as if it is she who has been struck. Konitsyn rushes in for the kill. He side-steps quickly to keep Antoine boxed in near the corner, and then he launches a barrage of punches. His fists are remarkably accurate. Each one seems to find the only hole in Antoine's defence. Body. Face. Body. Clean shots getting through. And then Antoine slips a punch and connects on an uppercut to Konitsyn's jaw. The man's neck arches all the way back; his chin shoots skyward.

The crowd pops all the way to their feet and cheers. There are none louder than Naomi. "Yes! Yesss!" she screams. "Wooo, Antoine!"

He advances now as Konitsyn retreats. The favourite is not as agile as Antoine, and yet his defence with his gloves is near impregnable. Antoine throws combinations with vicious speed, his entire body rotating into them, but few punches get through. Then Konitsyn comes back with another attack of his own and the blows rain down, both fighters on the offensive. The crowd grows more raucous. There is a loud clap, and ten seconds of furious fighting later, the bell rings.

8:23 p.m.

THE BELL RINGS. Antoine bounces backward and turns halfway toward his corner, eyes lingering on his opponent. The man gives him a tiny nod of approval, commending him for that final exchange.

Save your praise, Antoine thinks. You don't know me.

Sitting in his corner, Antoine tries not to gasp. His opponent is fast. He'd figured he would be but had hoped he was wrong. And Konitsyn can hit. It was all anyone could talk about before the fight, the cinder blocks in his gloves, and they were right: that hook did its damage. And a few of those jabs in the corner too. Not good to be hazy this early, Antoine thinks.

He blinks his eyes, hoping that will clear them. Simón pours water over his head while Alejandro rubs petroleum jelly over his face. The actions revive him a little. He can also feel oxygen returning to his lungs and spreading into his shoulders. But it is too soon, the haze in the eyes, the burning in the chest, the lactic acid in the limbs. The pace is so much quicker than every other fight he has had. Attacking, defending, everything. Antoine needs something else. Something to separate himself. Otherwise his opponent is too strong. His technique too solid. Body blows don't do much against layer after layer of wrought-iron flesh. And that's when the shots get through. Is there enough time to tenderize it? he wonders. Got to try, regardless of outcome. An investment that has to be made.

Got to take the fucker's head too, he thinks. Use the head to set up the body. He felt that uppercut. Didn't know I could pop like that.

This is Antoine's boxing obsession. Increasing his power. Between every fight he has raised his level. Tried to squeeze out every joule of strength he possesses. He can hit harder than ever, a true power-puncher now, to complement his defensive prowess. But even with his power additions it is not enough, he knows. His enemy is too good.

Got to take his legs out. Keep him moving. Never let

him rest. The body, the head, the legs, break him down. Forget the score, just break the *pendejo* down.

He frowns, foreseeing the rest of the fight. Still not enough. Got to do it early, he thinks. The secret juice. Got to drink it now. Can't wait till the sixth round.

Antoine's routine is to wait till the midpoint of a fight before he calls up the memory of his father's murder. Or more specifically, the memory of his failure to protect his father from murder. The memory of his cowardice. It's like being burned alive.

When his opponents hit the wall, he is a demon. When they start to slow, he is faster than ever. When their will falters, he lusts for blood.

True, he hates himself for days afterward when he opens this pit of self-loathing. And the fire it ignites burns away every last bit of fuel in him, so that it's often weeks before he fully recovers. But it is separation — the holy grail when it comes to sports. This memory, the well of rage, is separation from his competition.

I won't sustain it, though, he thinks, as the referee calls time and Antoine pops back up to his feet.

His enemy advances, gloves up, cold determination in his pale, ghost-like eyes.

If you fade, you fade. Now is the time. No point waiting till you're knocked out.

Antoine slips a punch, darts forward, fires a jab and a straight right. Springs back and skips to the side.

Coward, Antoine thinks. You let your father die.

8:26 p.m.

EVEN WITH HIS elbows held tight against his ribcage, Tyron keeps getting jostled by the people around him. Antoine's fight continues to draw more to the already overcrowded bar, with all eyes on the screens.

The pace of the fight has picked up and the audience can feel it. The commentators have scored the first three rounds to Clayface, but the momentum has shifted. Antoine is the aggressor now and Clayface is on his heels. Damn, he moves fast, Tyron thinks. But what grips him tighter than the speed and ferocity of Antoine's attacks is the fury in his eyes. There it is at last, Tyron thinks, what was lurking in his foster brother all along. *There it is.*

I should've visited him in prison. The thought comes to him unbidden. He mulls it over. No, it was already too late.

As Antoine swarms Clayface, catching him in the eye and on the temple, Tyron wonders when he could've saved Antoine from what he has become. There must've been a way.

At the end of the fifth round, Clayface hobbles back to his corner, shell-shocked. His moniker remains apt, though its meaning has changed. No longer something that has been hardened by fire, rigid and rock-like, but something that is soft, malleable, shaped by the forces around it. A blood vessel has burst in the fighter's left eye, pooling red visibly invading the white, while around the eye socket the tissue is swollen.

At that moment, Tyron realizes what he could have done differently in the past. He could have turned the Quinns down. He could have stayed brothers with Antoine. He is surprised that he has contemplated this so rarely. Even then, when it was happening, he didn't consider the implications his decision would have on his foster brother. But I was a boy, Tyron thinks. I wasn't ready to be there for someone else yet.

When the fight starts again, the dip in Antoine's energy level is immediately apparent. There is not the same aggression, the same intensity to his focus, nor the same speed to his movements. Clayface picks up on it before the commentators do, though they come around when they see body shots snapping through Antoine's defence.

"It seems that momentum has swung again. The first three rounds were for Clayface. Rounds four and five unquestionably for Deco, and now round six going the way of Clayface," says the older of the two commentators. "Unlikely that Deco can find a way to steal the round, but the way this fight is going I wouldn't be surprised."

"Deco showed us all how much game he's got. But Clayface is still the stronger *fighter*. He withstood Antoine's surge and now he's giving it *back*," says the younger commentator, the staccato cadence of his speech emphasizing his points. "Ahh, that's a good jab to the kidneys. You see, Deco's trying to protect his head from a *knockout*, so Clayface goes to the body. He's not only a knockout *machine*, he's a smart *boxer*."

"Deco is trying to stay out of range of Clayface's power, but the favourite knows how to cut off the ring and he is doing it to perfection here. Deco just doesn't seem to have the same burst he had in the last two rounds."

"No doubt. He used up a lot of energy to take control of the fight, but now fatigue is setting in. I been there before and it ain't pretty. Especially when you're up against the finishing power of Clayface."

Tyron shuts out their voices. Come on, Antoine. Come on.

The four of them may be fractured. They may have scattered with the wind since they were kids. They may have no right to claim any connection to one another anymore. But for years they trained together, and this is it. The biggest stage for any of them. They can't fail now.

"Come on," Tyron growls out loud. "You got this, man. Don't give in, you got this."

8:34 p.m.

A GLOVED FIST catches Antoine beneath the ribs and the air pops from his lungs. He's surprised his insides don't come out too. His opponent swoops in to finish him off. Antoine sees the counter to be made, but his body betrays him: all it can do is clinch his enemy and hold on for dear life. Antoine's face is tight, closed against the pain in his abdomen.

It will pass, he tells himself, what he always tells himself when confronted with physical pain. But he has thought this too many times over the last five and a half rounds, and the pain continues to accumulate. His ribs are in agony now.

Konitsyn tries to break free. Antoine clings tighter, knowing it will mean the end if he lets go. He does this as a drowning man, as he cannot get air back into his lungs. The ref breaks them apart, and Konitsyn lunges forward, swinging a haymaker at his chin. Antoine covers up and the blow ricochets off his gloves. The bell rings.

There is no nod from the man this time. He glares at Antoine, disgusted that the bell has saved him from certain defeat. With his swollen eyes and his blood-filled eyeball, Antoine's opponent looks hideous. Fearsome.

Antoine stares back at him, but inwardly he is shocked that he wants to look away. He has never been afraid in a fight before. Afraid of losing, perhaps, but never truly afraid. Not afraid for himself. Not afraid of pain. It sickens and worries him, this fear he feels now.

He walks to his corner, while Konitsyn remains in the middle of the ring staring him down. The ref eventually nudges the enemy to his own corner, and the man reluctantly saunters away.

Slumped on his stool with Simón doing his best to revive him, Antoine wonders what he will do now. The juice didn't work. It wounded the beast instead of killing it, while it left Antoine physically and mentally spent. What now? There must be a way. There is always a way. But he is out of ideas. Or perhaps there are ideas in there, but his brain is too muddled to go looking.

Antoine blinks. Alejandro is crouched before him, snapping his fingers in front of his eyes. Unlike most trainers, Alejandro talks sparingly to Antoine during a fight. They agree that Antoine should know what he is supposed to do, and must be left to execute it without distraction. Only when Antoine strays from the plan, forgetting some detail or weakening in his resolve, does the old man step in to take command. The scarcity of his words makes them ring all the louder in Antoine's ears.

"*Sobrino*," he says, for he calls Antoine nephew. "It is one more round that you need. No more. He is tired, I see it. He is too angry to notice yet, but I see it. You have done well to hurt him and anger him. He will come after you all round. And you, *sobrino*, you keep him chasing. Take the counter when it is there, but keep him chasing. Rest as much as you can. Round eight is when you strike."

Antoine's eyes lock on to the old man's. It is something to have someone believe in you. To see it in their eyes.

Antoine nods. The old man smiles. He gives a gentle slap to Antoine's cheek.

"Five percent better," Alejandro says. "*No más.*"

Antoine closes his teeth around the mouth guard Simón offers.

The bell rings.

8:37 p.m.

"YOU CAN DO it, Antoine!" Naomi screams. She is aware of
the neighbouring richies eyeing her with distaste. Even
Ricky seems for once to be giving her some distance. Let
them judge. If there is any way to help her boy win this
battle, she will take it. "Antoine, you can do it!" And then,
half to piss off those glaring at her and half because the
words are broiling within her and need to get out, she
cries loudest of all, "Beat this fucker!"

Others ahead of her—inspired by her ferocity perhaps—call out Antoine's name, shout words of encouragement. She wills their cries to inspire those lower down,
so that her message may descend that long way to the ring
where Antoine is fighting for his life.

The arena is immense. No sky above, it feels to her like
a cavernous hall, burrowed into the roots of some great
mountain. No night, no day, only the teeming masses in
their sealed-off tomb, clamouring for violence. A scent of
blood in the air. No wind here to scatter it away; it satur-
ates her breath.

We are a mob, she thinks. A mob closed off from the
rest of the world. A mob drunk on brutality. For this is
indeed a brutal fight. Even in escape, Antoine keeps going
after Konitsyn's head, keeps knocking his brain onto a
collision course with the inside of his skull. There is
an inflamed lump near Konitsyn's right temple, almost
the size of a golf ball and growing, the product of an

inadvertent head butt. Naomi can see it in gory detail on the gigantic screen above the ring. Antoine is bleed-ing from a cut above his left eye and another from his lower lip.

And then there is the sweat sliding off each of them. Sweat cascading when a fist hits its mark. All of it susten-ance to the mob. Drunk on liquor, a fervour is waiting to take hold of them.

This, Naomi can sense as the seventh round passes into the eighth and Antoine attempts a resurgence. But she has been keeping score in her head, and the rounds are unquestionably five to two, with no knockdowns and no penalties. Even if Antoine wins the remaining three rounds, the best he can do is a draw. And the eighth is the first that is inconclusive, with exchanges going both ways and long stretches of inactivity, each fighter seeming to lick his wounds. Antoine needs a knockout, she thinks. It is the only way he can win. He must know it too. But there are only two rounds left, and his opponent looks indomitable.

The ninth round. Antoine attacks and so too does Konitsyn. It is as if they want to heap every brain-addled disease on one another: Parkinson's, dementia, CTE. This is beyond winning. This is about who can put the other in the grave first. The crowd loves it. They cheer feverishly. The bell rings and the battered fighters wobble to their cor-ners, neither one looking as if he will ever come out. And Naomi realizes how she can help him.

"An-*toine*. An-*toine*. An-*toine*," she begins to chant as she stands up. She looks over at Ricky. Grabs his arms and starts pumping them up and down, nodding at him to follow her lead. "An-*toine*. An-*toine*."

One flirty smile is all it takes to get that horndog jumping up and down, bursting his lungs to spread the chant as far as possible. She looks at the richies around her as she continues to chant, and motions for them to follow. Carrot or stick, flirtatious smile or intimidating glare, sexy woman or towering baller, she knows just what to use and who to be with each person, until she has tapped into that wildness that is in all of them.

"An-*toine*! An-*toine*! An-*toine*!"

Their section is howling it now. But it is not enough. She yells at those beneath her, still in their seats. "Get your ass up! This is our hometown boy! He needs us!" She flings her long arms up into the air. "An-*toine*! An-*toine*! An-*toine*!"

Those below look up at her in fear and wonder, then jubilation, as they too are swept up in the roar of the pack.

"An-*toine*! An-*toine*! An-*toine*!"

The cameras take note of her. She is up on the giant screen punching her fist into the air with each syllable. The chant doubles, triples in strength.

This is the unique skill of the bench player, their gift to the starters, to ignite the crowd, to light a fire on the court, to take a torch to the stadium. Naomi was never an all-star, but in this she excelled.

"An-*toine*! An-*toine*! An-*toine*!"

8:47 p.m.

HE RETURNS TO the world. Where he has been he does not know. Where he is now is also a mystery. A loud, blurry place. Where the sound carries.

There is a ringing in his ears. No, the ringing is outside him. Yes, the ringing is in his ears but there is also a bell ringing outside him. A man with a bludgeoned face and bloodshot eyes stares at him in bewilderment. Antoine remembers where he is. He remembers who he is.

The ref is yelling at him to go to his corner, and his people there are yelling for him to do the same. They vociferously motion with their hands for him to come over. It seems a very long way and an inordinately difficult task to cross that canvas floor. He takes a step and feels like he will topple over. He concentrates, takes another step. When he makes it to the corner, he asks Alejandro if he was knocked out. "No, *sobrino*. You were strong. You were very strong."

"What round is it?" Antoine asks.

The old man's eyes widen.

To staunch bleeding, Simón sticks a cotton swab soaked in adrenaline hydrochloride up Antoine's nostrils, so he inhales through his mouth. Pain shoots across his ribs.

He looks at Alejandro while Simón goes to work on his various cuts.

"It's round ten," says the old man. "The final round. You have to knock him out. They won't give you the decision."

Antoine knows it is imperative that he wins. But he cannot remember why. Everything before this fight has faded into a distant and irretrievable past.

He shakes his head. "I can't—" he starts to say, but Alejandro cuts him off.

"Listen, *sobrino.*"

Listen to what? The crowd chanting at a fight? Mere background noise to what's happening in the ring. What goes on beyond those ropes is no concern of his. But Alejandro insists, so he listens.

Antoine's face slackens. He brushes Simón's hands aside and rises. Looks out at the crowd.

"An-*toine*! An-*toine*! An-*toine*!"

The entire arena is chanting. Their voices as one. Deafening. He spins around, looking up at the rafters, his own name echoing from those heights above. Lowers his gaze to the seats closest to him, row after row of animated faces screaming his name, pumping their fists, stomping their feet. How is this possible?

He looks to Alejandro and Carlos. They shrug and shake their heads, their faces open in disbelief in a way he has never seen on either of the stoic men.

"An-*toine*! An-*toine*! An-*toine*!"

He feels a prickling across his flesh that becomes a burning. It is like the secret juice of rounds four and five, but so much more. He is awake now. In a way he had not thought possible moments ago.

"An-*toine*! An-*toine*! An-*toine*!"

He turns to his opponent and sees him staring out at the sea of people surrounding them. His face is also slack with awe. But he is not buoyed up by it; he is not emboldened by it. He cringes from it.

The bell dings and Antoine springs into battle.

8:48 p.m.

TYRON FINDS HIMSELF throwing his own mini-punches in time with Antoine's hurtling blows. A smile lingers at the corners of his mouth, waiting for that man on the screen to topple. But Clayface is still standing, and as the commentators keep reminding listeners, he will win the fight if he can survive this round.

The time remaining is at the bottom of each screen— 2:27 — and the entire bar, jammed together, watches breathless as the clock ticks down. Clayface is a different boxer to the one who started the fight. He defends instead of attacks, panting like a stray dog that has been run ragged. Antoine has ground him down.

And yet, while Clayface has given up on knocking out Antoine, he has not given up on winning the fight. He retreats, he covers up, he wraps Antoine when he is near. The clock ticks down. Less than two minutes to go.

Antoine has the crowd behind him. They are still with Antoine, no longer chanting his name but bellowing and shrieking each time he lands a punch. The commentators sway with the wind, suddenly calling the favourite "Konitsyn" when they have called him "Clayface" all fight, and referring to Antoine as "Dex" when they have mostly called him "Deco."

You got this, man, thinks Tyron. Hit the body. Take what he gives you.

Antoine seems to hear Tyron. He fires a slashing left hook into Konitsyn's ribs, throwing his weight into it so fully that his feet almost leave the ground. Konitsyn winces and angles down to cover his side, his hands dropping. And in that instant Antoine rifles a right jab to the skull. Sweat sprays. Konitsyn's head whips back. He stumbles drunkenly. Tyron roars, "Come on!"

No one hears him, though. They are all yelling.

8:50 p.m.

ANTOINE LOWERS HIS arms, baiting the dopey bitch. The buffalo has one charge left before he can be put down.

It almost looks like the man has red cataracts, so glazed and bloodshot are his eyes. The blue swelling around the left eye has nearly swallowed the eye itself. And that lump on his right temple just keeps getting bigger. The man throws a tired jab. Antoine ducks it and pops two shots to the body. Jukes the opponent's counter, gets in a quick hook to the side of the head, and springs outside of range.

He hears Alejandro shouting at him that there is less

than a minute left, but he is beyond panicking. Something happened when the crowd revived him. That formless nothing where his mind had gone was a kind of death. And he's come back from it.

Konitsyn is swaying. He steps backward, struggling to keep his gloves up. He has knocked out nineteen opponents in a row: it's been years since he fought a tenth round.

Antoine darts forward, feints a left jab, and comes around with a right hook. Then it is combinations, unceasing combinations, like he is up against the bag while still slipping the errant swings that are the last gasp of a dying man.

Antoine's opponent teeters, eyes vacant. Knees buckling, he begins to drop. Antoine can let him fall or get one more shot in. He cannot risk the man getting up again. The bell would save him then.

Before the ref can stop him, Antoine winds up and uncoils. His glove drives into the opponent's falling skull. Flung outward, the boxer collides against the canvas with a rattling thud. His eyes are shut. He is as still as a corpse.

The referee begins his count over the body, but it's more likely that Konitsyn is dead than getting back up within ten seconds.

Konitsyn's team shout curses at Antoine, but he ignores them. Turns to his own corner and sees shining faces, those characteristically impassive men now jubilant and proud.

He stands there, on the edge of the ring, fists by his

sides, muscles taut, triumph building inside him, waiting
for the ref to finish his count.

Who would've thought, he thinks to himself. Who
would've thought... that you could actually pull this off.

The ref finishes his count, rises to his full height, and
waves to the scorekeepers that the fight is over. Antoine
hinges at the hips, clenching his fists to his face, a strangled
cry of victory escaping him. The crowd erupts. Antoine
straightens, relaxes at last, springs onto the ropes, and
basks in their cheers. His team swarms him and he falls
back into their arms.

No one could've imagined this for you, Antoine. You
proved them all wrong. It is the happiest thought he has
ever had. *You proved them all wrong.*

8:51 p.m.

IN HER EXCITEMENT, Naomi lifts Ricky off the ground.
She can't stop laughing. Ricky self-consciously straightens his button-up shirt after she puts him down, and
she high-fives the richies around them, the coach in her
coming out.

Far below, Antoine is being mobbed by his team, officials, casino representatives, interviewers, and camera-
men. They are all packed into the ring, along with some
of Konitsyn's entourage, as well as security guards and
paramedics. As for Clayface, he still hasn't moved, though

fight doctors are attempting to revive him, holding his eyelids open and shining their little flashlights.

Naomi has a smile that won't go down. He'll get a title fight. Perhaps become a world champion. Be a millionaire. That little boy she used to beat up. She clasps her hands together and holds them to her chest. There are tears in her eyes.

"I'll be back," she says to Ricky, and "Excuse me" to the richies as she passes by. She descends the steep stairs down the bowl of the arena, high-fiving people along the way.

8:54 p.m.

WHILE ALL THOSE around him are cheering over what they've just witnessed — or rushing to the bathroom now that the action is over — Tyron merely shakes his head in disbelief, a bemused smile on his lips. The commentators are also incredulous. "When Konitsyn shook the canvas, so too was the entire division shaken. What a thrilling performance by Antoine 'Dex' Deco. Surely that was a fight for the ages. And that's right, our main event, Gibbons-Suarez, is still to come. What a card this is shaping up to be."

"I can tell you this, Joe, each of these fighters will have his own main event soon enough. And fighting each *other*? After what we've just seen, a rematch would be the biggest draw in the sport."

Onscreen, a third commentator crowds Antoine in the
ring and aims him toward the closest camera. He starts to
speak into his microphone, but even this man, for whom
words are his living, is at a loss for them. After a shrug and
a laugh, he says, "Antoine . . . how did you do it?"

Antoine looks at his interviewer and then into the camera. His face is battered and bleeding, his breathing ragged. He wipes sweat and blood from his left eye with the
back of his hand, now cut free of its glove. From the defi-
ant expression on his face, it seems to Tyron that he will
launch into the kind of diatribe he gave him this afternoon. But then Antoine's puffy eyes soften. "I don't know,"
he says, his voice strained. "I don't know why the crowd
helped me like that. It made a difference."

Hearing this answer, the crowd cheers louder, an echo
of the thunder they produced that final round.

"Do you think you're ready for a title fight?" asks the
commentator.

Antoine levels a stare at him. "I'm ready for *any* fight."

Tyron laughs under his breath. There it is, he thinks.
There's that good ol' Antoine antagonism. Glad you didn't
change too much, brother.

★ ★

10

9:00 p.m.

ANTOINE TAPS KONITSYN'S fist after the man has come to. He nods at Antoine for the second time, and this time Antoine nods back.

Once outside the ring, on his way back to the stadium tunnel, Antoine's elation gives way to turmoil. What if? The question keeps repeating in his mind. What if he were to actually *be* Antoine Deco, professional boxer? Nothing is set in motion yet. He could call it all off. Tomorrow he'll have million-dollar deals on the table. He could do anything. Get a wife. Have children. None of this ever seemed like an option before.

People in the crowd lean over the railings on either side of the walkway and stretch their arms out in the hope that he will high-five them. He doesn't. But he cannot fully suppress the gratification and pride their validation gives him. It is distressing, this change within him. Life has prepared him for many things, but success is not one of them.

Antoine sights a very tall and very beautiful woman in a

dark purple dress leaning over the railing further than the rest. She keeps shouting his name, trying to get his attention. At first he doesn't believe it. Thinks the punchiness is making him see things. But there is no mistake. Naomi.

He breaks from his team and security detail. Walks right up to her. She embraces him, despite his heavy sheen of sweat, and squeezes him tight. Others pat his shoulders and back. He ignores them and takes note of how her body feels against his.

"Antoine, you were incredible. I've never seen anything like it," she says into his ear. "I'm so proud of you."

He steps back and looks at her. "What are you doing here?"

"Ty gave me his ticket. I can't believe that you *won*." She smiles that vivacious smile of hers. "I knew you would win and I can't believe it at the same time."

Carlos taps him on the shoulder. The casino handler is motioning for them to keep moving.

He hugs her again and says into her ear, "I'm glad you saw it. And I'm glad I saw you. Thank you."

He lets her go and he doesn't look back.

INSIDE THE HALLS of the stadium Keenan is waiting on guard outside his dressing room. You again, Antoine thinks.

To his team he gives one nod, and they continue down the wide tunnel, knowing where they are supposed to go and what they are supposed to do. The casino aides and the security detail leave to ferry the next pair of fighters, Gibbons and Suarez—the true attractions of the night—leaving only him and Keenan in the hall.

"Well done," Keenan says.

Antoine nods at the man and goes inside.

He forgoes a shower, instead towelling himself dry, and puts on a fresh set of clothes: grey running shoes, spongy sport socks, loose-fitting black mesh cargo pants, a black cotton T-shirt, and a thin grey nylon warm-up jacket. He leaves his boxing gear on the floor but packs the rest of his belongings into a small backpack. Then he sits on the trainer's table and waits.

The adrenaline wears off and his head begins to throb. It hurts to breathe. His limbs are leaden and his hunger ravenous. He wolfs down energy bars and gels, and pumps water into his mouth as fast as it will come out of the bottle.

He checks his watch. 9:16 p.m.

The main event must have started already. But he can hear nothing, as the room is soundproofed. Pop stars use these dressing rooms too; they must need quiet before they perform.

He flexes his fingers. This, too, hurts. Their stiffness feels arthritic. His knuckles are bruised and scraped raw.

Why'd Naomi have to be here? Why'd she have to look so fine and act so fine? Why'd everyone have to behave like they cared just because he won a single fight?

Why now—*now*, as he waits—do doubts have to start creeping in?

There is a knock at the door. It opens before he can respond. The first person to walk in is a burly man about the same height as Antoine. He has a grey buzz cut and a combative face. He nods at Antoine upon entering, then steps aside to allow another man to come forward. Outwardly Antoine remains impassive. Inwardly his head-ache dissipates, his gaze sharpens, and his muscles slough off their stiffness.

Antoine knows the man to be in his eighties, yet the extensive cosmetic surgery gives his face an indetermin-ate quality. His eyes are brown and alert, and his thin wavy hair has been dyed a dirty blond, the colour it was when he was a young man. He is very short, even shorter now than he once was, and he cuts a trim figure in his charcoal grey suit. Antoine has looked at photos of this man for many years and on two occasions he has seen him from afar, but this is the first time he's been close to him. Antoine struggles to keep his knee from bouncing and he resists the urge to swallow, though his mouth feels thick with saliva.

"Antoine," the man says, in a nasal voice gone gravelly with age. He extends his hand. "I'm Norman Bashinsky. It's a pleasure to meet you."

Antoine's lips tighten, pulled between a grimace and a smile. His hand is trembling, so he squeezes it into a fist until it is in line with Bashinsky's small hand, then opens the fist and closes it around the man's papery skin. During the handshake Antoine trembles and the old man gives him a patronizing smile. "Don't be nervous," he says. "Think of me as just another one of your fans."

Antoine gives a couple of quick nods and removes his hand from Bashinsky's grasp.

"This is my director of security, Raymond Monk." Bashinsky motions to the other man. "He'd also like to shake your hand. That was one hell of a show you put on for us, son."

Monk's handshake is too tight, like he's trying to prove something. "I haven't seen a fight like that in years," he says to Antoine. "You're a great boxer."

Again, Antoine nods and gives that tight smile, afraid of what his voice might sound like if he tries to speak.

Bashinsky looks around the dressing room, at the empty chairs. "Your people made a quick getaway."

"I . . ." Antoine's voice catches in his throat. He swallows, but his voice still comes out thick and unwieldy. "I'll celebrate with them after."

Bashinsky chuckles. "I know exactly what you mean. When I have a big day I like to—"

Antoine launches off the trainer's table with a right jab at Monk's throat. He feels the man's Adam's apple crumple beneath his knuckles. Within the same combination he springs into a left hook at Bashinsky's temple, his feet leaving the ground as he propels his fist into contact. He leaves a dent in the old man's skull. Before Bashinsky's body hits the ground, Antoine has pounced on Monk, hands around his crushed throat.

Monk scrabbles feebly at his neck, but Antoine pins his arms down with his knees and digs his strong thumbs into the man's windpipe. Grip strength is something Antoine has worked on for many years. In truth, it does not take that much strength to choke the life out of a man. What is difficult is keeping your grip when the jugular starts to pulse. It thrums repulsively. The unnatural twang of a grotesque harp string. Each throb makes you want to snatch your hands back in revulsion. It takes practice, holding on to those large veins and arteries jerking for air. For life. All creatures fight when death is forced upon them.

Antoine started with cats. He could've snapped their necks, but he strangled them because he wanted to feel that throbbing. He wanted to watch their eyes bug out — the way Monk's eyes are bugging out of their sockets right now — without letting go or throwing up. How they used to buck and twist and tear at his forearms with their hind legs. Seeing his own dripping blood made him feel better, some atonement for this unholy preparation. The blood reminded him that he was not a psychopath. A psychopath cannot tell the difference between right and wrong, whereas he knew that what he was doing was absolutely wrong. His own body did its best to betray his commands. No, Antoine was no psychopath. He was someone who had the ability to push himself beyond any limit. Any instinct that kicked in, no matter how strong, any challenge that lay before him, no matter how insurmountable, fell beneath his ceaseless determination.

Monk's eyes are so huge now, little red capillaries bursting in the whites of them, that Antoine wonders if they might actually pop from their sockets. That or simply explode. Instead, the man's contortions abruptly end, his arched back lowers to the ground, and his blue tongue hangs from the side of his mouth.

Antoine is sure he killed Bashinsky with that punch, but he straddles the little old man anyway, wraps his thick fingers around that frail neck, and digs his thumbs in. There is no pulsing in this throat. Not like when he used to strangle pit bulls and German shepherds. In their final throes, they could do a lot more damage to him than cats, and he would have to lie behind them on the ground, keeping his face turned away from their clipping jaws, constricting them in headlocks and leglocks. His initiation kill for the Latin Knights was by strangulation. It served two purposes: it was his first human, and it was a grislier execution than the gang was expecting. Rookies to the crew normally used a pistol with a shaking hand. That got Antoine respect right from the start, which he cemented in prison by volunteering for any hits the Knights wanted done. They called him Windpipe after his first inside, and his rep was strong throughout the prison because he didn't need a shiv. And because he could out-box any inmate.

Antoine stands and takes a moment to survey the two bodies. So quickly done, he thinks. He hoists his backpack and settles it snugly onto his shoulders. Then he exits the room.

9:23 p.m.

THE DOOR OPENS behind Keenan. He turns to see Antoine quickly shut it behind him. "They're having a conversation," Antoine says. "They want their privacy."

"Cool," Keenan says. "You dressed quick."

"Got to get to the after-party. I'll see you."

Antoine walks briskly away. Keenan thinks there is something odd about how he hurries, especially for a man who has just suffered through ten rounds in the ring and come out with the greatest accomplishment of his career. Keenan would expect release, relaxation, contentment, but there is none of that in Antoine's rushed gait. He supposes that's Antoine's secret, that intensity even now the reason he could beat a world-class fighter like Konitsyn.

The boxer passes out of sight, lost down a bend in the hallway, while Keenan wonders whether he should have gone with him. He was told to guard the dressing room as long as Antoine was in there, and that others would come to lead the boxer away. But Antoine left so suddenly that Keenan didn't think to ask questions.

Whatever, it's not like Antoine can't handle himself. And Monk and Bashinsky are inside; Keenan doesn't want to leave them unguarded. Weird that they'd have a private conversation in Antoine's dressing room, but if something comes up, you got to discuss it wherever, Keenan guesses.

He waits, thinking what a boring job private security is. He misses the force. Lately he has been trying not to wish that he could take back that moment. It serves no purpose to constantly regret, but — *Christ* — if only he could take back that moment! His life is now divided between before and after it happened. Because of that one moment, I'll never be happy again, he thinks. He admonishes himself. Quit your grumbling, you whiner. Thanks to you, that kid doesn't even have a life to be miserable in.

This is a long conversation these guys are having. Normally Keenan wouldn't disturb such important people, but an anxiety that he can't explain is gnawing at him. He knocks on the door. Waits. There is no answer. He knocks again. No answer. He depresses the handle and opens the door just enough to stick his head inside.

Keenan throws the door wide and removes his pistol from its holster. He moves swiftly between the two bodies and shoves in the door to the bathroom. Clear. He looks at the bodies. Doesn't bother checking for a pulse; he's seen dead men before. He runs.

His Reef cap flies off as he sprints down the stadium hallway. There is no sign of Antoine. Keenan does not stop running. The passages are eerily quiet. Everyone is out in the arena monitoring the megastars, Gibbons and Suarez.

Monk was my father's friend, Keenan thinks as his legs pump. I've known him since I was a child. What the fuck, Antoine? Keenan has to catch him.

There are two arena staff up ahead. They leap against the wall before Keenan barrels them down. "Antoine Deco! Have you seen him? Antoine Deco. The boxer. He just won a fight. Did he come this way?"

The man and woman stare at him bewildered, and it isn't until he grabs the man by the arm that the woman points further down the hall and says, "He went into the parking lot."

Keenan hasn't sprinted like this in years. He chases signs that point to parking.

What the fuck? What the fuck? Monk and Bashinsky *dead*? What the *fuck* is wrong with Antoine? He just won the biggest fight of his life.

Keenan kicks open the heavy door that exits onto an elevated walkway between the stadium and a multi-level parking garage. The night is crisp. A breezy chill has swept away any remnants of the heat. Pistol in both hands, arms extended, he advances across the walkway. He checks over the side but there is no activity on the tarmac below. He enters the parking garage.

Gun and gaze swivelling, he scans the cars surrounding him. There is no one in sight. He listens. Thinks he hears footsteps on a lower level. He lopes down the curving road to P2, and there up ahead of him between the cars, still walking briskly: Antoine.

Keenan takes flight and by the time Antoine has turned he has closed most of the distance between them. Keenan sets his feet and aims his weapon. "Antoine! Hands where I can see 'em! Don't move!"

Antoine's swollen face doesn't react. He stops where he is and raises his palms to shoulder height.

Gun trained on the man's solar plexus, Keenan walks forward until they are less than ten feet apart. Now that he is stopped, Keenan notices how much his lungs and throat are burning. His voice hoarse, he says, "What the fuck, Antoine? You killed those guys?"

Antoine stares at him, his eyes impenetrable, his body perfectly still.

"Tell me what the fuck is going on."

Antoine keeps staring. He lowers his arms to his sides, blinks, and says, "They killed my father."

Keenan's face scrunches in confusion. "Who?"

"Monk and Bashinsky. And one other. They killed the Shaws too."

Keenan begins to lower his gun. "What?"

"Bashinsky had a team of corrupt cops working for him for over twenty years. They did all kinds of shit for him, including hits. My father and the Shaws were killed by these men on the order of Bashinsky."

Keenan's world is spinning. He swallows, trying to

return saliva into his mouth. Antoine hasn't budged. "How could you know all this?"

Antoine gives a half-smile. "This is my life," he says, his voice no longer flat. "Ever since you knew me, this is what my life has been about. Everything else was a front." He smiles in earnest now, but to himself, not to Keenan. "My real life."

Such fulfillment on the face of a man who just committed a double homicide makes Keenan's stomach churn. He raises his gun. "Get on the ground, Antoine."

Antoine looks at him, the smile gone. "You can't stop me with your hands," he says. "Which means you'll have to shoot another unarmed man. Are you ready to do that?"

A bead of sweat drips from Keenan's eyebrow into his left eye. He shuts the eye against the sting. He is perspiring everywhere. His hands are slick with it. "Get on the ground."

Antoine juts his chin in the direction behind Keenan. "I think my friend has a problem with that."

Keenan doesn't take the bait. He motions with his head for Antoine to get down.

There is a low whistle from close behind him. "*Gringo.*"

Keenan glances back and sees a young, wiry Hispanic man, with black tattoos creeping out from beneath his shirtsleeves onto his hands — which hold a large grey handgun a foot from the back of his head.

Keenan lets his breath out. Deflates with the escaping

air. There's no hope against the two of them. But I've fucked up too many times to fuck up again.

He feels nauseous. A thought strikes him. Dying like this wouldn't be too bad. Everyone wins.

He whips the gun around as the wiry man swipes at him with the butt of his pist—

★ ★ ★ ★ ★ ★ ★ ★ ★ ★ ★ ★ ★ ★ ★ ★ ★ ★ ★ ★

11

10:38 p.m.

OUTSIDE ONE OF the Reef's nightclubs is a large aquarium inset in the wall where small sharks move quietly through the water, their hollow eyes and slightly parted jaws looking mechanical in their fixed positions. Naomi finds Tyron standing before the glass—or plastic polymer that looks like glass but is stronger and better-suited for viewing, as she learned from a Reef guide on a previous trip to the resort. Tyron starts awkwardly when she calls his name.

"What's up?" she says, after hugging him to celebrate Antoine's victory.

"Nothing," he says. He checks the time on his phone. "How was the fight? The big one?"

"You didn't see it?"

"Bar was too crowded. And I didn't need to see any more after what Antoine did."

"Right? Wasn't he incredible?"

Tyron nods. "Incredible. I never would've thought it."

"I did. I knew he could do it. But it was good you missed

Gibbons-Suarez. Gibbons won in a decision but nothing happened. Antoine's was the fight of the night."

"Where's Ricky?"

She laughs. "He met some people and went off with them. Said he had to 'network.'"

"Network?"

"Whatever that means," she says, shaking her head. "I don't want to get ahead of myself, but I just feel... I just feel like Antoine winning that fight... and you being back here and Keenan not going to prison... it's like... it's like we're all going to be back together again. I'm just so happy. I missed you guys so much."

Tyron's features are immobile, but she can see the concern and doubt in his gaze. "I hope so," he says, finally. Suddenly, perhaps affected by her words, embarrassment flushes his face and he says to her, "There's a woman coming to meet me. She'll be here any minute."

"A woman?"

"Like, a girl."

She laughs again. "Is that why you're being so weird? I'm married, Ty. You're allowed to do what you want."

He gives a shrug. "I thought you were getting a divorce."

"As of tonight, I'm still married. You have fun, Ty. I want you to." She smiles, but more to herself than to him. Mission accomplished, she thinks. He wouldn't be embarrassed about this chick if I hadn't sparked something in him. "So, who is she?"

"A waitress from the casino."

"Look at you. Picked up some game in the Marines, did you?"

He shakes his head and smiles self-consciously, and she grins to see that smile again. It always amazed her how humble this man could be when there was so much he could be arrogant about.

She catches herself being too happy. Too, too happy. Too much as always. And what always happens after happiness like this? A dip. A fall. A plummet. Always. She tries to be cool, to stay level, but she can't help it; she is on a high from the fight that she hasn't felt since she retired from pro ball. It doesn't feel like she will ever come down. Everything around her is wonderful and bright and amusing and to be appreciated: the sharks lazily gliding before them, the long line of scantily dressed people waiting to get into the club, the gamblers, boxing enthusiasts, and tourists walking past them in a never-ending stream.

"What are you going to do?" she asks.

"What do you mean?"

"What are you going to do now with your girlfriend?"

"Come on," he says, failing to repress a smile. "I don't know what we'll do, but you should... you're welcome to—"

"Really? Your fiancée won't mind if I tag along?"

"I forgot how sassy you can be."

"My only hope is that your wife is more demure, as a wife should be."

"Hey!" A woman's voice. High-pitched.

Naomi turns to see a young woman with green eyes and soft brown hair streaked with blond. She wears heels and a short forest-green dress, so thin and tight it looks like it should be peeled off like cellophane. Naomi's satisfaction over tugging on Tyron's heartstrings curls up like a salted slug.

"Hey Layla," Tyron says.

He leans in to hug her and the girl kisses him on the cheek, half catching him on the lips.

"Layla, this is Naomi, one of my closest friends from back in..." He glances at Naomi and says, "She's one of my closest friends."

The girl nods to Naomi and says, "What are we all doing?"

"You guys do your thing," Naomi says. "I don't want to intrude."

"Please, you're coming with us, babe." The girl motions with her hand at the club beside them. "Let's go in there. This is my spot, I can show you guys a good time."

Naomi and Tyron share a look between them. Tyron shrugs and Naomi grins. She wanted a night out and it looks like she's going to get one. She checks her phone for messages but there are none. Keenan must still be working. She nods, and Layla leads them forward.

"Affectionate girl," Naomi says quietly to Tyron, as Layla kisses the cheeks of the bouncers.

"You see why I like her."

Naomi smirks, and Tyron returns the smile.

One of the bouncers, a hulking man who dwarfs Naomi and Tyron, pulls aside a red rope for the three of them to pass into the club. At the threshold, Naomi looks back guiltily at everyone waiting in line.

★ ★

12

11:12 p.m.

NEON LIGHTS CUT through the darkness like blades, fused to the rhythm of the pumping music. At long last, Tyron begins to understand the appeal of nightclubs. He has never experienced this scale before in a bar, and he wonders where and how it connects with the rest of the casino. Whisked down endless halls and indoor pavilions, he finds it so easy to lose his bearings in this place, even when navigation is what he prided himself on in the Corps. And especially easy with the alcohol swirling in his skull.

He has decided to give up worrying about terrorists for the night. For all nights, in fact. Let that be the duty of others from now on. Otherwise, why come home if he is just going to live as he did over there? While everyone else grumbled about the invasive pat-down and search to get inside, he was impressed by the bouncers' thoroughness. Can't take any chances in a terrorist's dream.

He shakes the thought away. Fuck, it's time to live, man. You're not an athlete no more, you're not a soldier, you're . . . He almost has the thought *you're no one*, but catches himself in time. You're thirty-two years old, it's time to live. Whatever you are these days.

The club is huge, and initially overwhelming. There are booths, tables, bars, a large dance floor, an upstairs, a downstairs—and that is just the inside. The back of the club opens onto a large outdoor space with pools, fountains, cabanas, more bars, and another dance floor, joined to the indoor one by a wide black stage that sits on the precipice of the two worlds. A bleached-blond DJ is at work at his mixing tables, while several sets of people chill on the edges of the stage.

Layla yells into his ear, "Some really big names are playing tonight because of the fight. It's only going to get crazier. Come on, let's get some shots."

Outside, at a bar on the far side of the glittering fountains and pools, far enough from the music to speak without having to talk directly into each other's ears, Layla's bartender friend lines up three shots of tequila, each with an accompanying lime wedge on top. Tyron looks at the short, round shot glass and the clear tequila inside. He looks at Naomi and Layla beside him.

He reaches for his glass as they reach for theirs, yet his hand halts midway. A voice inside tells him: Your responsibilities don't end just because you're discharged. And you got that meeting with Marlon at 6 a.m.

Lime in the left hand, shot glass in the right, Naomi and Layla are waiting.

He counters the voice: If not now, then when?

He picks up the shot, which draws smiles from the women. "To Antoine," Naomi says. He gives a nod to her, good call, and the three of them tap glasses.

As the tequila drains down his throat, the answer to his internal question comes to him. Never. Your responsibilities are never done. There is too much to do. There is always too much to do.

Naomi shimmies her head, recoiling from the heat of the distilled liquid, and Tyron is reminded of their life together in college. That same shimmy has been with her since the first time she tasted liquor. It was rare for them to get drunk, usually only at the end of their sports seasons, but those nights, and their lovemaking after the drinking, left an indelible mark on him. She had that shimmy then, the same as now. He never realized before how much he liked it.

His own throat and chest burn from the alcohol. Responsibility turned you into a eunuch, he thinks. You're allowed a few mistakes.

Layla has her friend line up three more shots. "One more round, then we hit the dance floor," she says, her eyes sparkling.

He looks at Naomi and they hold each other's gaze longer than they should. This time her toast is to the crew being back together again, adding as she puts her arm around Layla's shoulders, "And to our newest member."

Layla laughs, they tap glasses, and drink. Tyron looks up at the Reef Resort rising all around them and at the soft black sky above, much too well-lit for any stars to shine. In Vegas, the stars are down here, he thinks, and we all get to pretend to live like them.

Growing up, the Strip was for tourists. No one he knew had the money to experience its sights and sounds. He used to wonder why people would spend so much to come to his city, because all he knew of Vegas was its poor and their underserved communities. That was the world his parents brought him up in — endless fundraisers and food drives. But he understands the attraction for tourists now. On the dance floor, the lithe bodies of two beautiful women flowing with his to the pulse of the music, the night air cool as their temperatures rise, he understands that the Strip is meant to be transportation to a world away. A world of shimmering sexiness and possibility. A world so opposite to the one he knew in Vegas.

Though he can see through the facade, he is caught up in it nevertheless. He smiles at these young women, and they smile back at him as they brush their bodies against his.

A.M.

★ ★ ★ ★ ★ ★

★ ★ ★ ★ ★ ★ ★ ★ ★ ★ ★ ★ ★ ★ ★ ★ ★ ★ ★

1

12:24 a.m.

"**Q**UINN, I DON'T know if you intentionally fuck up like this, or if you are actually this incompetent. I can't figure it out. You got an answer for me? Maybe you are the unluckiest son of a bitch on earth, always at the wrong place at the wrong time, but fuck it, Quinn, I would think *you* of all people would pull the trigger when you needed to. You couldn't even be consistent in your incompetence."

"I'm sorry, sir."

"Don't say sorry again. Don't fucking say it, Quinn. Jesus Christ. I'm going to explain something to you, and I'm going to do it real slow for that pea-sized rock you call a brain. When it's an unarmed Black kid running away, you *don't* shoot him. When it's a perp who just committed a double homicide, you *do* shoot him. Understood?"

"Sir, I knew him growing up. We were friends. I had him contained, I didn't know his accomplice would sneak up be—"

"No shit, you didn't know. What a news flash. Thompkins, go tell the reporters that Quinn was ignorant of something. Fucking hell, Quinn. Fucking hell. Do you understand that that man in there was the fifth-richest man in the world? The entire world, Quinn. He was worth forty billion dollars or some crap like that. He bankrolled politicians. He financed construction projects across the globe. He brokered meetings in his resorts between government and business elites. Hell, he even influenced foreign policy. He was a big fucking deal. A *big* fucking deal. There will be major fallout from this. And what were you doing out here while he was getting strangled to death? Twiddling your *fucking* thumbs?!"

"Sir, forensics believes the blow to the skull killed Bashinsky before the strangulation."

"Shut the fuck up, Thompkins!"

"Yes sir."

Undersheriff Jake Fischer opens his mouth to continue his tirade, but Thompkins's interjection has him apoplectic. The tall, red-faced man huffs like a cartoon character, which Keenan would find funny if he weren't the one being chewed out.

The lump at the back of Keenan's head has grown. It continues to throb. His nausea also remains, but at least his dizziness has subsided. The paramedics' initial assessment is that Keenan has a concussion, though he will have to see a doctor when he is allowed to leave the crime scene, which doesn't look like anytime soon.

"The undersheriff is right," Detective Clyde Miles says, taking the opportunity to provide his input while Fischer catches his breath. "Bashinsky's death is a big deal. The feds will be on it in no time."

"Which is why we need this mess cleaned up before they arrive," Fischer says, halfway calm.

Miles stares at Keenan. "Monk's death is a big deal too. He was one of us, even if he was off the force."

"Fuck Monk," Fischer says. "A more corrupt cop you couldn't find."

Miles's eyes flick to Fischer, then flick away as if there had been no reaction at all.

Anti-corruption is the platform on which Fischer has built his tenure as undersheriff, which everyone in Metro has found hypocritical, as there are stories about Fischer when he was younger. Of course, no one would ever say anything about it to Fischer directly—a man in his position is not someone to cross. It was Fischer who came down hardest on Keenan after the killing of Reggie Harrison. He proclaimed, after Keenan retired, that such egregious misconduct and lawlessness would no longer stand in the Las Vegas Metropolitan Police Department. Miles, on the other hand, had stood up for Keenan, and fought for him to keep his job.

The undersheriff smooths down what is left of his thinning hair. "What were you doing, Quinn, while your boyhood sweetheart murdered a former cop and the fifth-richest man in the world?"

"Sir, my assignment was to guard the door against any-one trying to get in to harass Deco. I didn't think—"

"You didn't think? I'm glad you finally said it. No, you didn't think. Just like you never think. Just like your father never had a fucking thought in his head either."

Keenan stares at Fischer. Miles does too. Fischer stares back at Keenan, smug and confrontational, daring him to try something.

"With all due respect, sir, the room is soundproofed. I didn't hear anything. How could I have imagined that right after Antoine became a star he would throw it all away by killing two people? Is that something you would've expected?"

Fischer opens his mouth to rifle more shots, but Keenan cuts him off.

"And Monk was with Bashinsky, and armed. Deco was unarmed. I would assume Monk would be able to handle himself and protect his boss when up against an unarmed man, but clearly he didn't imagine Deco would turn on them either."

"What happened exactly?" Miles asks. "How did you first become aware of what he'd done?"

Keenan looks around him. They are outside the dress-ing room, standing right where he was when Antoine committed the murders. The police have cordoned off this entire section of the arena. No one, outside of them, the crime scene investigators, a handful of Reef employ-ees, and the upper crust of Reef Resorts executives, knows what has occurred. And Antoine, of course, wherever he is now.

While there are investigators inside the dressing room, outside in this stretch of hallway are only Keenan, Fischer, Miles, and Fischer's underling, Thompkins, the only one of them clean-shaven, despite the late hour. A slight, thirty-something man with wire-rimmed glasses, he is also the only one under six feet. The other two are within an inch of Keenan's height of six-three. Clyde Miles has a wizened, sunbaked face and curly salt-and-pepper hair, looking like he just rode in from the Wild West. The creases around his eyes and mouth, and in the hollows of his cheeks, look like they were carved with a knife. His mouth is small and his lips thin, as though his genetics knew he would not open them often. Jake Fischer's genetics seemed to have had a read on him too; his lips are fleshy and red and always flapping.

"I was standing right here, and Antoine opened the door behind me," Keenan says. "By the time I turned around, he had already closed it. He said Bashinsky and Monk were staying inside to talk about something, that they wanted privacy, and then he walked off. It seemed strange at the time, and I felt something was off, but like I said before, I had no reason to think that Antoine would've done anything like this. I didn't know if I should go with him or stay where I was, but I had been told to guard the door, not him, so I remained at my post. I figured that Monk would tell me if I needed to do something different when he came out."

"Why didn't you check on them immediately?" Fischer asks.

"Like you said, it's the fifth-richest man in the world having a private conversation. I didn't want to interrupt."

"So why did you then?" asks Miles.

"I don't know. I just knew something was wrong. Antoine walked away so quickly. It took me a minute to realize how fast he had gotten out of here, but once I did, and the two of them not coming out yet, I just felt like I had to check."

Miles again: "How long between Antoine walking away and you going in?"

"I would say three minutes at the most."

"And inside?"

"I saw the bodies. Pulled my gun. Cleared the bathroom. Then I ran after Antoine. Eventually I caught up to him in the parking lot."

"Which is when you spoke to him?"

"That's right."

The conversation comes back to Keenan. He is grateful that the pistol-whip didn't knock it from his brain, because there were things in there of grave importance. He has been so bombarded by this blowhard that he hasn't been able to break down all Antoine said, but he knows that there are deep secrets to be teased out. Secrets that are essential to his own past. And Tyron's. And, obviously, to Antoine's. Their entire crew seems to be caught up in Antoine's revenge plot.

Keenan has considered the fact that Antoine might've lied to him—lying would hardly go against the morals of someone who just committed first-degree murder—but he has discarded the possibility. Antoine had no reason to lie just then; he had never been a liar, even if he clearly knew how to keep a secret, and the release and fulfillment in Antoine's voice and face could not be staged. And there was one other factor that persuaded Keenan of the veracity of his words: everything Antoine said rang true. As he heard the words, an inner voice said to Keenan, Yes yes, what you have always suspected, finally laid bare. Antoine has connected the dots for you.

"What did he say to you?" Miles asks.

Keenan looks between Fischer and Miles, debating how much to tell them. Already Antoine's words have made him suspicious of anyone in Metro.

"Come on, Quinn," Fischer says. "Out with it."

Keenan watches for their reactions. "He said that Bashinsky had a team of corrupt cops doing hits and other assignments for him for over twenty years. He said that Bashinsky and Monk and one other killed his father." Keenan draws in a breath for the final reveal, that Bashinsky and his corrupt cops were behind the killing of the Shaws, but this he holds back. Bringing the Shaws into this right now seems irrelevant. Besides, what he saw that day in the gym when his father warned Terrence Shaw against political activity right before his death might make him look suspicious. His father.

Keenan doesn't even want to think what his connection could be to all this.

There is no reaction on either man's face. Just rapt stares with pinched brows.

"Where'd Deco come up with this idea?" Miles asks.

"That's what I asked him," Keenan says. "I said, 'How could you know all this?'"

Keenan pauses, remembering the look of deranged satisfaction on Antoine's face when he gave his answer.

"He said, 'This is my life. My real life.' It was creepy." Keenan draws his tongue along his upper teeth, thinking about it. "Makes sense, though. There was always something going on with him, you know. He wasn't like a regular kid. There was some hidden thing consuming him. You could tell. This was it, investigating his father's murder. He also disappeared all the time, sometimes for days. And he'd get into trouble with the cops." Keenan's eyes widen and he looks significantly at Miles and Fischer. "He got caught breaking into a police station. This was right after I first met him. My buddy Tyron told me about it. He didn't take anything, he was just charged with breaking and entering because all he did was look at their files." Keenan almost gasps remembering this detail, while Miles and Fischer share a concerned look between them. "He's been planning this a very long time," Keenan says, to himself as much as to anyone else.

"No doubt of that," Miles says, arms folded, leaning his long body against the wall. "He must've known that

Bashinsky visited all the winners personally. Hell of a motivation to win a fight."

Keenan turns sharply to face Miles, realizing that he is right. This is why Antoine never gave up on his boxing. This is how he could will himself to the upper echelon of the sport. This is what fuelled him against Konitsyn. He wonders how long ago it was that Antoine learned of Bashinsky's custom. Antoine trained like a fiend from the beginning and he couldn't have always known. Still, Keenan wonders how good the boxer would've been without this knowledge.

Thompkins says, from three paces behind and to the left of Fischer, "Sirs, I believe what Detective Miles has suggested is extremely accurate. I have read that internal motivation is a major factor in developing high-level performance. It would seem that Deco's dream of having his moment alone with Bashinsky gave him the internal resources to rise so high."

Fischer hangs his head and pinches the bridge of his nose. "Thompkins, just shut up."

"Yes sir."

Thompkins stares straight ahead, arms at attention like he is guarding the White House, and Keenan almost smiles looking at him. A Stanford grad, the rumours are that Thompkins only joined Metro to preface a career in politics. Still, as much as he looks like a nerdy suck-up, he did spend some time in SWAT. No small feat, thinks Keenan.

"I don't give a damn why or how this psycho did what

he did," Fischer says. "We have to find him and find him fast." His mouth twists into a grimace, and he takes a stride toward Keenan, jabbing his finger into his chest. "Do you realize how bad this looks? You of all people being asleep on the job while the highest-profile murder of the decade goes down behind your back? Fuck! Half the Black people in Vegas are going to be outside this building in the morning to protest you, you fuck. Why are you even here? You hadn't brought enough bad press on our department? You thought, Let's see if I can take the entire organization down single-handedly?"

"Easy," Miles says. He puts a reassuring hand on Fischer's shoulder; Fischer glances back and seems to appreciate the gesture.

"We need to find this other man Deco is after," Fischer continues. "That's one lead at least."

"If there *is* another man," Miles says. "Maybe Deco said that to make us think he's still in the city. Not already on his way to the Mexican border."

"For what it's worth, I think he was telling the truth," Keenan says.

Fischer levels a contemptuous glare at him. "You do, do you? You know your father was partners with Monk back in the day."

Keenan's face drops. The word "no" rises to his lips, but he cannot bring himself to say it. His father *was* partners with Monk. What else did they team up on? Keenan feels like he has to sit down.

"You were partners with Monk too, weren't you?"

Miles asks the question of Fischer, who spins on him, growling, "What are you insinuating?"

Miles holds up his hands, palms out, and gives a slight shake of the head. "Nothing."

Fischer stares him down, then turns back to Keenan. "There was nothing else Deco said to you?"

"No sir."

"All right. Now, you don't tell a fucking soul about your involvement in this mess. Understood? Anyone finds out about it and there'll be pandemonium in this city. You burn that fucking beard that you were wearing, and that mysterious security guard who ran down Deco will remain anonymous. Got it?"

"Yes sir."

To the others, Fischer says, "Thompkins, get an official statement from him; Miles, check on the investigators." Then he walks away, eyes on his phone.

Keenan stops him with, "Sir, let me call my dad first." Fischer looks back at him. Piercing through the graveness and stress in his small brown eyes is a glimmer of sympathy. He nods and marches off, putting the phone to his ear.

Keenan has missed two calls and several texts from his wife. Most of the texts express her excitement over Antoine's victory and how they'll have to celebrate with him later. A subsequent text asks where he is and lets him know that she is with Tyron at a nightclub in the casino and he should join them. He calls his parents before responding to her.

Voicemail on both their cells and the house phone. He leaves urgent messages on all three asking them to call him as soon as possible. Then he writes to Naomi, Something BIG has happened you'll hear about it soon but I'll tell you everything at home. I have to see my parents now.

Keenan puts his phone away and says to Thompkins, "Let's do this quick."

★ ★ ★ ★ ★ ★ ★ ★ ★ ★ ★ ★ ★ ★ ★ ★ ★ ★ ★ ★

2

1:12 a.m.

A **BEAD OF SWEAT** trickles down the back of Naomi's
neck. A touch of cool amid the heat of her dance.
And his dance. And the girl's dance. It seems they have been
dancing forever—and *will* be dancing forever. Dancing
and drinking in their own world. A world of darkness and
flashing lights and famous DJs mixing to the pulse of the
crowd. And shots, drinks, and more dancing, their young
strong bodies pressed tight, and the world spinning, and
Ty so close, so close once again, in her arms like he was
always meant to be, back in her arms after all these years.

But she won't kiss him. Even drunk, she won't go that
far. And he doesn't kiss her, though she can see how it
burns inside of him, that desire to press his lips to hers.
He doesn't kiss the girl either, which she thinks is kind
of him. She can see how he wants to. What straight man
wouldn't, a girl like that? Layla rubs her hands, her hips,
her ass against him; she kisses his neck, his earlobe, his
cheeks; but when she goes for his lips, Tyron glances at
Naomi, then turns his face away.

Naomi is caught between wanting Ty to get with the girl, to remove the temptation of being with him, and simply wanting Ty. Once she had thought he would be the father of her children. How can you be close to a person like that again without some of those old feelings returning? If she stays on this dance floor, things will go too far. "I need a break," she shouts, and she thinks she will leave them there but they both follow her.

On the far side of the fountains and pools, near the bar where they have been getting their drinks, there is space and relative quiet for Naomi to collect herself. She takes out her phone, more to give her a reason to distance herself from Tyron and Layla than to actually check it, but as she grips the glossy black device she remembers Keenan. Like everything else that isn't a part of this club, this self-contained magical place, Keenan has been forgotten. She wishes she had forgotten him for good when she reads his text. Something big has happened, he'll explain later, he's going to see his parents now? Typical Keenan. Half including her with half-truths that tell half the story.

She looks at Tyron in conversation with Layla, and thinks that she should sleep with him. It's what she wants, it's what he wants, and who gives a fuck about what Keenan wants? He deserves it after all he's put her through.

She takes a deep breath and reads the text again. Keenan isn't one to visit his parents normally, and he's going to see them now in the middle of the night? Perhaps something happened to them. Concern vanquishes her anger. I'm here if you need me, she writes back. If not I'll see you at home.

She walks back to the others and says, "I have to go. Something's going on with Keenan."

"Does he need help?" Tyron asks.

Naomi smiles at how reliable he is, then shakes her head.

She hugs the girl and kisses her on the cheek. "Great to meet you, Layla."

"We've got to do this again," Layla says, holding her hand above them and gesturing to them all with an encircling motion.

"For sure," Naomi says.

She takes Tyron in her arms and kisses him on the mouth. She can feel through his lips his past love for her flowing from some hidden space deep within him to that hidden space deep within her, reserved for him alone. She wants to say, "I love you. I'll always love you." Instead, when she separates her lips from his, she whispers into his ear, "Don't worry about me. Be with Layla if you want."

He looks closely into her eyes, and she cannot tell what he is thinking.

She lets him go, retreats a step. "It's great to have you back, Ty." She smiles and lets out a huff of amazement. "What a wonderful night."

1:29 a.m.

TYRON AND LAYLA watch Naomi walk away through the crowd. She looks statuesque, so tall in her purple dress, her gait so long and athletic, even in heels. She passes out of view, and Tyron keeps staring after her, like a man on the ocean and she his horizon.

"Are you in love with her?" Layla asks.

It takes him a long time to answer. "I used to be," he says, his gaze still far away.

"And now? Are you still in love with her?"

"Probably."

"I see it. She's got presence."

He returns Layla's probing look, then glances up at the bleached night sky and thinks, Didn't imagine all this when I was in Aunt Trudy's backyard today.

"What do you want to do now?" Layla moves closer as she asks the question and weaves her fingers between his.

"My boy is coming to meet me here."

"The one from the blackjack table?"

"Yeah. Ricky."

"And after that?" she asks, stepping even closer.

He stares into her green, cat-like eyes, feels her body grazing against his. "Not tonight, Layla."

She nods. "I'm going to go, then. I'm working tomorrow."

"Okay."

She reaches her arms around his neck, and he thinks

as he kisses her goodbye how long it had been since he last kissed a woman. Now he has kissed two in a matter of minutes. "Sure I can't change your mind?" she asks, lips brushing his ear.

He cannot sum up the range of thoughts and emotions that rip through him like a desert wind to explain why he won't go home with her tonight. So he awkwardly murmurs, "Another night," and wonders if he is blowing a future chance with her.

But Layla seems unfazed. She softly kisses the side of his mouth and says, "Text me later," and then she is gone. And Tyron is left alone, feeling like he needs to catch his breath even though he is rooted to the spot.

RICKY FINDS HIM ten minutes later, sitting on the stone barrier around one of the fountains, and plops down beside him. "Man, I just been striking out tonight. How you been doing?"

Tyron looks at his friend. "Nothing on my end either."

Ricky sucks on his teeth and shakes his head. "Women, huh."

"You enjoy the fight? The big one?"

"Ah, it was a bust. Defensive the whole way through. Everyone was saying that Antoine's fight was the real deal. He's really going to be big-time from now on. We got us a big-time hookup, baby." He slaps hands with Tyron. "Big-time!"

Tyron grows pensive. "I'm not sure. With Antoine you never know."

"Nah, man. Celebrity parties. VIP treatment. We got it made, dog. He needs an entourage, and we're just the men for the job."

"I think he's already got an entourage."

"You can never have too big of an entourage. You should know that. I'm sure he needs an ex-military body-guard, anyway."

"Even if he does, what about you?"

"The ex-military bodyguard needs a sidekick, don't he? Shit."

They laugh and check out a group of women in a bach-elorette party getting drinks at the bar.

Tyron says, "Marlon wants me to meet him at 6 a.m. tomorrow. This *morning*, I should say." He checks the time on his phone. "That's four hours from now. I got to get some rest, man. I'm still jetlagged."

"You know what you should do? Just stay up the whole night. You've come this far, might as well keep pushing it."

"That's great advice. You should be a health guru."

Ricky laughs. "I thought you were serious for a second. You got me, man . . . Wait. Why's Marlon want to see you at 6 a.m.?"

"I don't know. But I told him I would, so let's bounce."

Ricky throws up his hands, aghast. "Oh Ty, we're *here*! We're here, man. We're here, the women are out, we're *here*. People across the world are spending fortunes just to be where we are right now, and you want to go? Come on, man. You look good. I look…better than average. Let's do this thing, let's make it happen. Hook me up."

"All right, man," Tyron says, rubbing at his aching eyes. He heaves himself up. "Let's do this. Another half hour, then I'm out."

Ricky springs to his feet and stares up at Tyron. "You know you're a great friend, don't you?"

Tyron is about to brush aside the compliment as he does most sent his way. But he pauses, and looks at Ricky, some of his guilt over kissing Keenan's wife assuaged. "Thanks," he says. "You're a great friend too."

1:31 a.m.

KEENAN LURCHES TO a halt in front of his parents' mid-sized bungalow. He leaps out of his car, bounds up the tiled path to the front door, and unlocks it with his key. It's pitch-black inside; he shuts and locks the door behind him. He debates turning on the front hall lights and decides to—

A dazzling beam of light strikes him in the eyes. He holds his hands up as he turns his face away.

"Jesus, Keenan, I almost shot you! What the fuck are you doing?"

Sparks flash behind his closed lids. "Can you turn the light off, Dad?"

"I almost shot you, boy. Christ almighty in heaven,

what the fuck are you doing creeping in here like a criminal in the middle of the night?"

"Dad, turn off the flashlight."

Keenan fumbles for the light switch and flips it on. His father at last lowers the flashlight; Keenan, however, still sees stars bursting across his vision, the bright beam and concussion not mixing well.

"Dammit, Keenan, answer me."

Rubbing at his eyes with his thumb and index finger, Keenan says, "I tried calling the house."

"We turn the ringer off at night, you know that."

Keenan cannot remember if he did know that or not. He does know that never before had he needed to get a hold of his parents at this hour.

"Is it Keenan?" his mother calls from deeper in the house.

"Yup. Just our boy trying to give us a heart attack. Fine lad we've raised. Why didn't you ring the bell for Chrissake?"

Keenan's vision is coming back to him, fuzzy shapes emerging out of the stars. "I didn't want to wake Mom. It's you I need to talk to."

"Ha! Didn't want to wake your mother. Nice going, you just gave her a heart attack instead. She thought someone had broken into the house to *murder* us."

If Antoine is after my father, at least they seem prepared, Keenan thinks. Finally, outlines to the shapes come into focus, and he can see that his father is pointing a pistol at him.

"Dad, fuck, lower your weapon!"

"Oops...sorry, boy. Got caught up in the moment."

Rosie Quinn emerges from down the hall, a thin, dark-haired woman with black eyebrows and a sweet smile. She squeezes by her much larger husband, looking wild with his faded pajamas, grizzled stubble, dishevelled hair, and long arms hanging limply, holding a pistol and a flashlight. She embraces Keenan and kisses each of his cheeks.

"How're you doing?" she asks.

"I'm okay."

"Really?"

"What difference does it make, Ma?" Before she can fret, Keenan says, "Dad, I have to tell you something. It's important."

Craig rolls his eyes: What of importance could *you* possibly have to tell me? Keenan has seen that look on his father's face a thousand times. But he doesn't back down. Not this time. He holds his father's stare.

"Well, come on, then," his father says, motioning with the gun for him to follow.

He turns on the light in the living room, and the three of them crowd inside. Craig puts the pistol and flashlight down on the glass coffee table, then grins at Keenan like a kid who just got his way. "I won twenty grand on your friend. I told you he was a sure thing. Though I had my doubts during the match. My God, what a battle. That little Mexican's got some fight in him, that's for fucking sure. Twenty grand, boy! Your mother and I are thinking of taking a cruise."

"It's all he's been talking about, he could hardly fall asleep," Rosie says. "He was so happy when that Russian man didn't get up. Just ecstatic."

"Want to come with us on the cruise? Not like you're actually working right now. Twenty grand, we got money to spare. You can bring Naomi. God, I love that woman. How she ever married your sorry ass is beyond me."

"Craig!"

"He knows I'm joking. But it's true, to think of the decent, hard-working, impressive men she could've ended up with. I give you credit, boy. You always knew how to charm a pretty woman."

"Dad, it's Antoine I came here to talk to you about."

"What about him?"

"Prepare yourself, okay?"

"Prepare myself? We about to have a duel? What do you mean, prepare myself?"

Keenan's stomach twists now that he has to deliver the news. "It's bad, Dad. It's really, really bad."

Craig looks at him suspiciously, then says to his wife, "Rosie, why don't you go into the kitchen. Get Keenan some food."

"I want to hear this," Rosie says.

"You hungry, boy?"

Keenan looks between his parents. Now that he thinks

about it, he is famished. But he is reticent to be the excuse for his father to kick his mother out.

"You hungry?" his father asks again, louder now.

"Yeah. Yeah, I'm hungry."

"Get in the kitchen. Get Keenan some food."

"What's the news, Key?" Rosie asks.

"Get in the kitchen!"

"All right!"

She storms out of the room. The sight is so familiar, his parents fighting, his mother storming out, that Keenan hardly registers it.

"Spit it out, Keenan," his father snaps.

"After Antoine won his fight, he went back to his dressing room and..."

"And what?"

"He murdered Raymond Monk and Norman Bashinsky."

His father bursts out laughing, as if Keenan has made the funniest joke, though there is a twang of hysteria in the throaty chuckles, some part of him seeming to recognize the truth.

"I'm not joking, Dad."

"Fuck you, you *are* joking."

"I'm serious. He strangled them."

Craig nearly trips lurching at Keenan, grabbing him by the scruff of his shirt. "Tell me you're lying."

"I'm not lying."

His father's ashen face contorts. Both hands now on Keenan's shirt, shaking him. "Tell me you're lying!"

"I'm not lying!"

Keenan slaps his father's hands down and shoves him in the chest. Craig stumbles back. He stares at Keenan in disbelief. Keenan stares back. Not this time, old man. His father's eyes are wild. Hateful. He charges at Keenan.

Like a pair of buffalo, snorting and grunting as they battle for supremacy of the herd, the two tall men grapple between sofas and chairs. Rosie comes running to the edge of the room.

"Stop it!" she cries.

Craig twists and yanks with his arms. Keenan's heels lift off the ground. He strains. Keeps his toes down. He is not thrown. Unbalanced, though, his father bull-rushes him into the wall. Keenan's shoulders collide with a picture frame. Glass breaks. Pain shoots up his back into his neck.

"Enough! Both of you, enough!"

Not this time, you old bastard. Keenan tightens his grip. Heaves his father backward. He digs deep, pivots, then wrenches with his arms.

The old man is thrown. He lands on the glass coffee table.

A shriek of glass. A shriek from his mother. "Keenan!"

His father squirms in the shattered glass. Rosie hurries to his aid, but Craig is already on his knees, hands scrabbling in the broken glass. "I'm fine," he barks at her.

"Oh God, Craig, your back is bleeding."

"I'm fucking *fine*, I said!"

His hand finds the pistol, and he shakily rises to his feet. Keenan doesn't retreat. Do it, he thinks.

Craig spits at him, "I'm not going to shoot you, you fucking idiot."

He hobbles past Keenan out of the room, without another look at his wife or son.

"How could you do that to your father?" Rosie asks, her face drained of its normal olive hue. "He's your father."

She follows after Craig, stops, and turns around. "You should be ashamed of yourself."

A door slams at the back of the house. His mother rushes away.

KEENAN'S FACE IS red. His breaths come in short, shallow gasps, rage and humiliation constricting his chest. He looks at the shattered glass scattered across the living room rug. At the broken picture frame on the wall with a photo of the Quinns taken when he was still in high school, the whole family dressed up and smiling as one. The American dream.

Keenan rotates his shoulder. Feels the lump at the back of his head. He goes to the door and swings it open. Looking out at the poorly lit street, he wonders if Antoine or one of his crew is already lurking in the shadows. He studies the parked cars and alleys between the houses. A man could hide almost anywhere, with the streetlamps so intermittent and the houselights almost all turned off.

Keenan cannot leave and he cannot shut the door. All he wants in this moment is to get away from his parents, and yet he cannot abandon them to Antoine. And that's if Antoine even thinks his father is the third man. If not, there's nothing to worry about. No ghosts in those shadows. It all depends on whether or not Keenan's father was involved in the murder of Raul Deco. And if he wasn't, then who was?

He looks back down the darkened hall, the shadows haunted by his parents' muffled arguing. He had wanted to take them to a hotel or the airport to ensure their safety. But he cannot face them again. He'd almost rather face Antoine than them. He looks out at his car on the street and realizes he can get out of the house and still keep watch.

Three steps down the path a thought strikes him: Why would Antoine tell you about this third man if he was after your father? Antoine had kept his plans secretive for so long, why would he reveal the final phase now unless he thought it held no effect on the outcome? Maybe he's not after Craig, after all. But if not him, then who?

In his car, Keenan reverses a few houses down the block and turns off the engine. Nothing stirs. Not so much as a breeze.

His head aches and he still hasn't eaten.

His mind begins to wander, and he finds himself thinking about the protest scheduled for the morning, now only hours away. He had forgotten all about it.

I'm a curse on this city, he thinks.

He leans his head back. His eyelids droop.

He punches his thigh, shakes his head, pops open his eyes. Scans the street and the yard outside his parents' home.

I can't do this alone.

He takes out his phone and calls the number Fischer gave him. Holds it to his ear, listening to the ring.

"Thompkins here, who may I ask is calling?"

"Thompkins? It's Quinn, where's Fischer? He gave me this number."

"That's correct, it is his number. However, all Fischer's calls go through me. If I deem the call pertinent enough, I forward it to the undersheriff."

Keenan winces. "Fischer must have his own phone, Thompkins. Just give me his actual number."

"That would be a negative, Quinn. If he wanted you to have his personal number, he would've given it to you. Now, how can I help you?"

Fuck, Keenan thinks. "I want you to send a car to my dad's house. Marked or unmarked, it's up to you. But he needs protection."

"From Deco?"

"Yeah, from Deco. Don't you want to catch him? I got the bait right here. If he's after my dad, this is where he'll be. He'll fall right into your lap, so get some men out here for both our sakes."

"Duly noted, Quinn. I'll alert the undersheriff to your

concerns. Is there anything else I can help you with?"

Keenan snorts in exasperation. The man sounds like a customer service rep. "Just make sure you get someone over here, all right?"

"It's a busy night, Quinn. I can't promise anything. But I will alert the undersheriff to your concerns, and I'll send a patrol car to scout the area."

Keenan grits his teeth and shakes the steering wheel with his free hand. The car rocks. "Just do as much as you can. Please."

"Understood. We'll be in touch."

The call beeps off.

Fucking Thompkins. I can't trust any of them.

I need a friend, Keenan thinks, which is when he realizes he hasn't told Tyron yet what Antoine said about the death of his parents.

★ ★ ★ ★ ★ ★ ★ ★ ★ ★ ★ ★ ★ ★ ★ ★ ★ ★ ★ ★

3

2:49 a.m.

CAPTAIN TYRON SHAW lurches awake to a dry desert night. A thunderclap and the walls of Combat Outpost Mic Check quiver. Dust falls onto his chest and light shines through new cracks in the walls.

"There's a lot of them this time, Captain Shaw," says a breathless sergeant appearing out of the gloom.

Tyron can hear it all now: small-arms fire, mortars, rockets. Fully clothed in body armour and desert cammies, his earplugs already in, his gloves already on, his elbow and knee pads already strapped, he rises from his cot, pulls on his Kevlar helmet, lowers his night-vision goggles, and takes hold of his M4 assault rifle.

He moves swiftly through what was once a packaging factory on the outskirts of Baghdad. Passes Marines hunkering down, trying to keep themselves small, so that the shells that manage to break through the walls and ceiling don't find them with their shrapnel.

Observing his men, Tyron finds, once again, that he is not afraid. The worst fear comes during downtime, the anticipatory moments of danger and death. But when actual danger and death come hunting for him, when the gates of hell seem to drop open beneath him and he balances on the precipice, he does not fear. There is only the battle. There is only the fight. No life behind it, no life before it, nothing to lose until the storm settles once more.

He marches to a corner of the building into what was once the factory's office, demarcated by flimsy plywood walls, but is now COP Mic Check's surveillance centre, the remnants of the walls torn down after rocket attacks blew them to pieces.

"What do we got?" he asks his surveillance team.

They show him green-tinged camera feeds on various monitors, all obscured by smoke and swirling dust. "Looks like they're hitting us with everything they have," says Staff Sergeant Higgins. "The blast walls are soaking up a lot of the shit, but plenty is getting through."

To echo his point, a mortar explodes outside and the walls shake.

Goggles raised, Tyron examines the images. North of them, insurgents are firing from rooftops with rockets, RPGs, and small arms. East of them, in a dirt field, men hiding in a ditch are setting up what look to be EFPS. The snipers have already taken out two of them, but the remaining insurgents are more careful with their cover. And the feeds from the west show nothing but burning tires, black smoke, and explosions.

"Get air support," Tyron says.

Higgins gets on it.

Tyron continues to watch the footage. The only side they're not getting hit from is the south. This is an aggressive attack. The most aggressive by far since they relieved an Army unit at this position six weeks ago.

"No air support, captain. Too much dust in the air. And the whole AO is a shit show. Battalion's getting hit everywhere."

Tyron stares unblinking at his company sergeant. No help on the way means this place will be rubble by morning.

"Did Intelligence report anything about an attack like this coming?"

"Not that I heard, captain. But gut feeling, I'd say they mean business. Come full strength and cancel Christmas for the lot of us."

"I get the same feeling." Tyron looks at the monitors, then at his men. "I like Christmas. How 'bout the rest of you?"

One voice: "Hell yeah, captain!"

"So let's light these fuckers up."

TYRON LURCHES AWAKE to a dry desert night. His head is spinning. Where is he? On a couch. In someone's living room, not his own. His mouth is dry and his bladder full. He stands shakily and it comes back to him: this is Tara's apartment.

He presses a hand to his forehead. He'd been dreaming of that night in Baghdad again. The one that earned him those medals. It had been so real, so visceral, like he was reliving it again.

He'd thought—and hoped—the dreams would stop once he was back stateside.

He stumbles his way to the bathroom, guided by the glowing lights of kitchen appliances. After he has relieved himself, he splashes water on his face and looks in the mirror. It surprises him how little his face has changed over the years. There are thin scars here and there, narrow misses from the endless roadside bombs, but it's only in the eyes that he sees a real difference from his younger self: their steeliness, the heavier shading beneath them. He half wishes that it were a different face, so that people would realize it is a different person inside.

Tyron switches off the bathroom light and returns to the couch. The clock on the stove tells him it's almost 3 a.m. He has barely closed his eyes. What does it matter? No operations to prepare for. No responsibilities. If he has to sleep more after he sees Marlon, he will sleep more.

He lies back down on the couch, and wonders if he will again be transported back to Baghdad. The thought pushes him away from sleep. So too does the anger inside that he cannot explain. If he looks at his life practically, his position couldn't be better: he has made it home from two wars healthy and intact; he has money saved from his years in the Corps; he has no dependants, a degree, and a stellar military record; he can live anywhere, do anything; he has been welcomed home and showered with affection by his community; he has had a great night with an old friend; and he has kissed two women. He should be content, happy even. And yet he feels angry.

It is deep inside him, this anger, like a bruised bone. What therapy could reach it, clean out inflammation buried beneath so much flesh? He often forgets its existence, and then come moments of stillness, when there is nothing to mask it, when there is nothing to quench that simmering burn.

Tyron closes his eyes. Tries to sleep.

★ ★

4

3:26 a.m.

KEENAN PULLS INTO his driveway in a new development on the northern outskirts of the city. His head and shoulder blades throb, and he has to blink his eyes regularly or they start to burn with exhaustion. Inside he plods up the stairs. Naomi is stretched out on their bed in her short white nightie, half covered by the sheets. He looks at her forlornly, remembering when he would have leapt onto the bed with her at such a sight.

He hadn't been able to get a hold of Tyron by phone, and decided against leaving a voicemail or sending a text. Telling someone their parents were assassinated isn't something to leave a record of. He'd waited indecisively in his car outside his parents' home, and woke up over an hour later, not remembering when he had fallen asleep. Feeling impotent to protect his father and unsure if he even needed protection, Keenan decided to go home, to rest a short while and think things through.

Naomi stirs as he gets undressed in the dark. "You're home," she says, half asleep.

He turns on the lamp. "I'm home."

She blinks her eyes open, then sits up straight. "What happened to you?"

"Why?"

"You look so pale."

"You won't believe it."

He kneels on the bed in a T-shirt and boxers. "After the fight, Antoine killed two people. It'll be all over the news in a few hours."

Her eyes widen in alarm, and he tells her everything from start to finish. The clock ticks past 4 a.m. before he is done.

★ ★ ★ ★ ★ ★ ★ ★ ★ ★ ★ ★ ★ ★ ★ ★ ★ ★ ★ ★

5

4:09 a.m.

AFTER KEENAN HAS completed his story, Naomi takes him in her arms and holds him. He clings to her, the way a shipwrecked man clings to an outcrop of rock. She doesn't feel much like a rock, more of a crumbling sandbank, still half drunk from all those shots at the club, but she tries her best to be what he needs from her. In truth, she thinks the alcohol might be helping with the shock of it all. It is difficult to believe.

"Are you going to tell Ty about his parents?" she asks.

"I tried calling him but he didn't pick up."

She looks away from Keenan, wondering if it is because of their kiss that Tyron didn't answer. She won't tell Keenan about it because there's nothing to tell. Just two drunk ex-lovers kissing goodbye. Still, she feels a slight stab of guilt. They are still married, for now at least. But she won't tell him, especially not now with the world collapsing around him.

"What will you do?" she asks.

He lies back on the bed. "I don't know. I feel I have to

get to the truth. Whatever it is." He rubs his eyes with his palms and looks at her. "What do you think I should do?"

Keenan wants her advice? Things really have got to him. "I think," she says slowly, "that if this third man isn't your father, Antoine would know it. Maybe your dad wasn't involved. Maybe you just do nothing and we'll all be okay."

"My dad was involved with Bashinsky. Somehow they were linked. He might not have been one of his trigger men, but I know he was involved in other things. There are too many connections, too many scraps of things I overheard as a kid." He slaps the mattress. "If he wasn't such an asshole, I could just ask him. But he'll never talk to me about any of this. Especially now." He adds with an unhappy laugh, "He'll probably never talk to me again, period."

She studies him, just a foot away on the bed, as he looks down, his mind playing out possible scenarios. Even now, pale and distraught, he is handsome. Lush red hair, an oval face with dark eyebrows like his mother's, a smattering of freckles across his nose and cheekbones, a soft mouth, and a long, lean, broad-shouldered body. He looks like an underwear model, just as he did when they were younger.

But for all his looks, he never turned her on the way Tyron did. The great appeal of Keenan's features was the status they brought her among other women. She'd only realized that in the last year. He was wanted by so many women, and the woman he wanted was her. That must make her special. That must make her more desirable than all these pretty, regular-sized women.

And then he became a pariah, and she didn't feel that pretty or special on his arm anymore. Nor was he the confident, charming ladies' man who had been there for her when she was getting over Ty, and won her over with his persistence. Instead he was sullen, bitter, and guilt-ridden. She would find him in the middle of the night, in the glow of his computer, staring fixedly at photos of Reggie Harrison.

Naomi wanted to tell him that it was going to be okay. He had done a terrible thing, but nothing could be done about it now. She wanted to tell him that she forgave him.

But she never did any of those things. She couldn't bring herself to lie.

She stayed with him through his acquittal because he needed her, and she had made a vow to be there for him through thick and thin. But the whole "till death do us part" thing, that didn't work for her. She was an athlete: she knew mistakes were part of the game, and correcting mistakes was how you moved forward. He was acquitted. That was it, he was not going to prison. She had done her duty by him.

And now he's in another fucking crisis. But not again. She will be there for him, as she always will be, but not as his wife. Not again.

"I have to figure this out for myself as much as for my father," Keenan says. His tone has a firmer edge to it. "For

Tyron too. And for the police. If there is corruption in the department, I should root it out. It won't make amends, but at least it'll..." He chokes on his words. He swallows and looks at her. "I'll know I tried."

She reaches out to touch his face, her heart aching for him. But her mind is made up. Even as he closes his eyes and nuzzles his cheek against her hand, she doesn't change it.

"The only people who still support you are the police," she says, another sad thought coming to her. "If you go looking into corruption in their ranks..."

"Then absolutely everyone will hate me," he says, finishing the thought for her. He takes her hand from his face and kisses the back of it. "The good thing about being unpopular is you lose your fear of it."

"Do you still have people in the department who can help you?"

"Some...a few...one, maybe. Fitz. He'll make inquiries for me, I think."

"Does he owe you a favour?"

"I think I owe *him* a favour, but I'll be persistent."

"You sure you want to do this? Why don't we just go get your parents and get out of town? We can fly down to L.A. for a few days. I can get your dad out of the house. He listens to me more than he does you."

"Jesus, does he. Even tonight he had to remind me that you're too good for me. It's embarrassing, this crush he's got on you."

"Well, now it works to our advantage. Maybe I can get the truth out of him."

"I doubt it," he says. "But I don't want you going near him. It's bad enough my mother is with him."

"Why? You think Antoine will hurt me?"

"He might. If you're in the way . . . for sure he might."

"Antoine wouldn't hurt me. I'm probably the best person to protect your father."

"Antoine's not the guy you remember. He really has lost his mind. He could do anything. We can't take that chance."

"I saw him. After he won his fight, I saw him." Seeing his perplexed look, she explains how she had been in the crowd and hugged Antoine on the edge of the walkway. "He said he was glad I saw his fight and he was glad he got to see me. It makes sense now, the finality in his words. But the point is, he still cares about me."

"I'm sure he does still care about you, but I don't think it'll matter. The guy's a psycho."

"He left you alive, Key. Keep that in mind."

Keenan has no response to this.

"I think what you said before is right: he wouldn't tell you he has another target if that target was your father. Either way, let me look after your parents. I'll get them to a hotel. Maybe to the airport. And I'll get as much as I can out of your dad. That'll leave you free to find the real third man."

"I can't ask you to do that."

"You're not. I want to do it. I want to help. This is the

best way I can. Antoine won't move on your dad if I'm
with him. I'm sure of it."

"I don't know. If something happens to you, babe ... It
might not be Antoine coming either. He has dangerous
people working for him. They won't have nostalgia holding them back."

"Key, we're a team," she says. "We're family. Your parents are my family. We're all in this together. I can handle
myself."

He squeezes her arm. "You're sure?"

She nods. "You're sure you want to go after this cop?"

"No. I'm not sure about anything these days. But I'm
not afraid for myself anymore. The only thing that scares
me is something happening to you or my parents. But
for me ... there's a strange power that comes from being
hated. I never knew that until tonight."

It seems as if he will tell her something deeply personal,
but he simply looks at her with sadness and gratitude.

"So this is for sure, then," he says. "This is how you
want to do it?"

"Yes."

"Thank you," he says. He leans forward and kisses her.
"Thanks, babe." He straightens his back and widens his
shoulders as though the weight he was carrying just slid
off. He nods to himself and stares ahead, strategizing. "I
want you to take my spare gun. Just in case."

"All right." She can shoot; she's been to the gun range
with him enough times.

"You'll go to my parents' place, move them, and find out what you can from my dad. I'll get in touch with Fitz and see what he can do."

"Can you trust him?"

"I don't know. I don't think there's anyone I can trust right now other than you. But it's worth the risk. And there's one more thing."

"Yeah?" she prompts when he doesn't continue.

He stands and begins to pace the room. He stops and looks at her, his eyes fierce. "Are you leaving me?"

"What?"

"Are you going to leave me?"

"You want to do this now?"

"That's an encouraging response. Yeah, I want to do this now."

"Keenan, there's so much going on. Don't you want to wait till all this is over? When we have time to —"

"No, I don't—"

"Time to think about it, talk about it, get to a—"

"No. No, I don't want—"

"Now is not the time to make a big decision like —"

"Now *is* the fucking time, Naomi! Dammit, I'm done waiting. It's been almost a year that I've had this hanging over me. Whatever's coming over the next day or two, I want this settled. I don't want this uncertainty at the back of my mind. And if something does happen to me, I'd rather have this resolved before I . . . I just want to know, babe. I just want to know."

Naomi gets off the bed and walks to him. She takes his hands in hers.

"I'll always love you, Key, but..."

He laughs sardonically and hangs his head. "This is a good start."

"But as a couple, I don't feel the same way I used to. I'm sorry. I've tried. I've tried to get those feelings back. But I just don't have them anymore."

"What changed?"

She opens her mouth to speak.

"Wait," he says. "I know." He drops her hands. "If I could take that day back I would."

She feels tears coming to her eyes. "So would I."

He walks back to the bed and slumps down on it, leaving her standing, watching him. She squeezes back her tears and wipes away the one that slips through.

"I never asked you this, Key...in all this time I never asked you because I knew everyone was asking you this question, and I didn't want you to have to defend yourself to me. But how did you do it? How did it happen?"

He spends a long time staring at the floor, thinking, and the only sound in this early hour of the morning is their breathing, steady and deep, but heavy with emotion and fatigue.

"They tell you that the Strip is the lifeblood of the city," he says. "The tourists, the businessmen are the lifeblood of the city. And our prime objective is to ensure that that blood keeps pumping. Unobstructed. The people who don't belong there should stay where they can't disrupt the flow of money. We are told, implicitly, and sometimes explicitly, to make sure they know where they belong."

"Who's they?"

"Do I have to say it? You know who I mean."

"Yes. Say it. Who's they?"

"They. Them. Black people, brown people, poor people. Make sure they know who's boss. Make sure they know who's in charge. Make sure they're afraid of challenging the order of things. And definitely make sure they know where they don't belong. So no matter how rough things are in those communities, tourists can come here from anywhere in the world and stay on the Strip, or off the Strip, and feel completely secure. We don't make the city safe. We compartmentalize it."

"And if someone doesn't comply you shoot them?"

"It's not like that. No one says 'Shoot them.' But you are taught that if someone is a threat to you or someone else, then yes, you do shoot them. And you have this mandate to intimidate. It becomes normal after a while. There are always eyes on you. Other cops, I mean. You've always got to look hard. You can't let any of these people step on you. You put all those things together: someone doesn't listen, they piss you off, they don't comply—they're already a threat to the lifeblood of the city, now maybe they're a threat to you or your partner. And that's it. You take someone's life."

He gets off the bed and walks to the window. He slides the curtain open and lets in the predawn light. "I don't blame you for wanting out," he says, with his back turned to her. "I don't feel the same about myself either."

She closes her eyes and her tears seep through. She cries for him, for her, for their broken marriage, for Antoine and what he's become, and for her evaporated dream that the four of them could be together again. It has all gone so wrong. She opens her eyes and Keenan is beside her, holding her, kissing her, wiping away her tears. She melds into his embrace, savouring the familiarity of his touch and his scent, knowing it might be the last time she experiences either.

★ ★ ★ ★ ★ ★ ★ ★ ★ ★ ★ ★ ★ ★ ★ ★ ★ ★ ★ ★

6

5:06 a.m.

CAPTAIN SHAW TAKES 1st Platoon with him outside the wire from its southern perimeter, while 2nd and 3rd Platoons hold position and lay suppressing fire on the enemy. Tyron and his men weave their way through the dust and smoke.

Tyron likes the smell of it. He has never smoked, not once in his life. Not one cigarette, not one joint. But the scent of smoke, of burning... Maybe he was born for Iraq, for this is indeed a torched nation, a country ablaze. Fires lick their garbage. Bombs scorch their markets. The burning, acrid scent that is everywhere in this place, that most American soldiers loathe, choked by it, wishing for leave just so they can take a clean breath, has become Captain Shaw's guilty pleasure. He inhales it. Feels the sooty blackness drift into his lungs. Because it smells good to him. And because it is condensed destruction and death. It is what Iraq has become. It is what he has become.

He studies his men as they creep toward the dirt field where the enemy is planting explosively formed penetrators. He watches the platoon commander, Lieutenant Lake, who keeps looking up whenever an explosion flashes overhead. This fight could last till morning. It could last through tomorrow. Tyron sneers. For the Iraqis, this fight could last another generation or more. But tonight it is only his men he has to worry about. The fight will be long and he does not want them worn out by fear.

He knows they are brave and they will not hesitate when the moment comes, but he can still see the tension in them. Their shock at the scope of this battle. It is dawning on them that this is not an ambush on a convoy; the enemy is here to kill every last one of them.

"Hold," he says, and his order goes down the line.

Crouching on the edge of the field, taking cover behind what's left of a blown-out building, Tyron traces his planned line of attack with his finger in the sand. "I want smoke rounds that entire way," he says to Lake. "One squad there, cover fire. One squad here, smoke. One squad with me, closing with the enemy."

"You're on point, sir?"

He hopes Lake can see his big-toothed grin. "Aye aye, lieutenant."

CRAWLING THROUGH A murky, rank ditch, smoke billowing all around him, Tyron hears the ripping report of AKs up ahead, answered by the precision firing of his Marines.

Adrenaline spikes through him as he reaches for a grenade. Fortune favours the brave, motherfucker, he recites in his head. He snakes closer. The wind blows, the smoke swirls, and he sees the firing gunmen lined up along the ditch ahead of him. They see him too, turn their fire on him. He presses himself down, hears their bullets crack and whistle above him. Feels the spray of dirt from those that hit before him. The wind dies and the smoke thickens once more. He pops the pin, holds a beat, rises to his knees, and smoothly chucks the egg-shaped explosive. Face back down into the dirt. Cries of alarm up ahead mixed with gunshots. And then a boom.

The sky rips apart. Shock waves funnel down the ditch. A blast of smoke, sewage, and shrapnel scattering before it. The wave rakes over him. And a split second after, there is a ferocious crash from the west.

He springs up, wipes his face, and scans his surroundings. His grenade triggered the EFPS, which exploded all at once. The discs of metal they sent hurtling crashed into the upper wall of the combat outpost, leaving gaping holes and rubble behind. None of his men would've been hit; he told Lake to radio in that the east side of the COP must be cleared. As for the insurgent gunmen, there are only pulpy pieces of them left, nearly indistinguishable from the rest of the gunk that fills the ditch.

His ears ringing, his brain stunned, his throat constricted from gagging, Tyron turns and looks back at his men. "Clear," he says.

TYRON'S PHONE CHIMES to life. His eyelids open and he pushes his torso up from the couch. He squints at the phone and remembers the alarm he set last night, a distant memory now. He swings his legs off the couch, turns off the alarm. He still feels drunk. For now at least, it's imbuing him with a kind of giddy energy, though he knows a crash is coming.

Looking at the phone, he sees two missed calls from Keenan. Why would Keenan be calling him at such a late hour? He cannot remember if he ignored the calls when they came in or never noticed them.

Still jacked up from his dream, he heads to the bathroom, strips off his clothes, and gets in the shower. He leaves the water cold and lets the icy blast hit him full in the face. Already, last night feels like a long time ago. Those dreams: he was reliving that battle. His survival instincts kicked into high gear over a dream? He dips his head and lets the cold water splash the back of his neck. He was calmer when he was actually in the fight than he is now.

I need to get away, he thinks. Somewhere wet, cold, green. Where people don't know me. Where I can start fresh. From scratch.

Those calls from Keenan aren't helping him slow his heartbeat either. Naomi must have told him about their kiss.

What a mistake. Dishonourable. Disloyal. Not the man Tyron has tried to be. And yet, despite the guilt, he can't help thinking about the kiss. God, he is happy around Naomi.

He tries to remember what possessed him to leave her to join the Corps. Those days return to him: the loss, uncertainty, and isolation in the wake of his parents' deaths. Even five years later he was adrift, and the thought of not being in university anymore, not being on the track team, to lose that structure and support terrified him. He couldn't put all his needs on her, but he couldn't deny how great his needs were, and so he gravitated to a world that was entirely structure, support, and community, built on endless goals and objectives to keep his mind occupied.

He needed the Corps. And it needed men like him. It still does, more than ever, so long as America's wars are endless and forever multiplying. He needed the Corps, but he was only willing to join because deep down he always thought he'd win her back one day. Had he realized that he would be losing her forever, he wonders if he would've made the same choice.

It wasn't exactly like Keenan had moved in on his best friend's girl — Keenan had dated Naomi first, after all — but Tyron had assumed Keenan would leave her be with him gone, knowing how much she meant to him.

Tyron kills the water. He dresses fast, makes a sandwich, and eats it quick. He brushes his teeth and leaves the apartment, hoping he hasn't disturbed Tara. He takes the stairs four flights down and exits into the light of dawn.

He can't blame Keenan. It would've been stupid for

him to pass on a woman like her once Tyron was out of
the picture. And Key never made a move while Tyron and
Naomi were together. But *you* have now, Tyron thinks.
You've made a move on her while they're still married.
You've lost honour because of it.

He dreads the next call from Keenan.

TYRON PASSES AN empty lot where he has a view of the
sun climbing over the shoulder of a mountain to the east.
The entire edge of the sandy brown peak is black, with
burnished gold behind it. He recalls early morning patrols
in the Corps. If there's one thing the desert has — here and
in the Middle East — it's breathtaking sunrises.

He keeps walking. The sunrise is blocked by low-rise
apartment complexes and small, single-storey houses
cut off from the street by chain-link fences. The streets
are quiet. No one else is about at this time on a Sunday
morning.

He cuts across a main road, void of cars, and sees a
coyote in the distance. It glances at him as it pads along
the asphalt. It seems almost to nod at him, fellow hunter
of the dawn. Then it slips behind a church, and Tyron
wonders if he imagined it.

He checks his phone and sees that he is early, so he
slows his pace.

Ten minutes later, at precisely six, he is outside Marlon's
door.

★ ★ ★ ★ ★ ★ ★ ★ ★ ★ ★ ★ ★ ★ ★ ★ ★ ★ ★

7

6:00 a.m.

"**T**YRON, GET IN." Marlon looks left and right down the street, then hurriedly shuts the door once Tyron is inside. "You see anyone suspicious on your way over?"

Tyron is surprised by the question. "I didn't see a single person. Suspicious or otherwise."

Marlon flips the door lock and fastens the chain. "This way," he says.

The small house is heavily shadowed, with no lights on and the curtains drawn. Marlon leads Tyron down a narrow hallway to the back of the house, where a wooden staircase goes down to the basement. The stairs creak as the two men descend. Marlon flicks on a couple of lights, which buzz like a pair of bumblebees and illuminate the cement-floored workshop. There are shelves and cabinets across the walls, and a wide selection of tools hung neatly on pegs. The centre of the space is taken up with work-tables and benches, but in one corner there is an old boxy TV with a faded grey couch and a couple of folding chairs sitting before it.

Marlon turns on a power saw, which echoes gratingly off the walls, then he motions for Tyron to sit on the couch while he pulls up a chair. Tyron finds all of this exceedingly strange; he hopes it isn't visible in his face.

"Sorry for all this, young brother." Marlon waves vaguely at the saw and the basement in general. He speaks just loud enough for Tyron seated beside him, but any further and his words are lost to the mechanical whirring of the saw. "I'll explain in a moment. But first, have you heard what happened last night with your friend Antoine Deco?"

"Yeah, I heard," Tyron says, trying to match the same volume as Marlon. "I watched the fight."

Marlon's deep-set eyes tighten, and he peers further into Tyron's. "You haven't heard," he says. "After his fight, Deco killed two people. At least that's what the police are saying."

Tyron involuntarily laughs. "You're not serious?"

Marlon nods. "No one can believe it. It'll dominate the national news for a while. Sports news too."

Tyron stares into Marlon's eyes. He doesn't distrust him for a moment, yet still he can't believe it. Marlon turns on the TV as evidence. Tyron doesn't need the saw turned off to hear the newsfeed: Antoine's face is plastered across the screen, with the words "Murdered 2 people: Norman Bashinsky, Raymond Monk" beneath. It cuts from a video of Antoine in the ring against Konitsyn to an old mug shot. Marlon turns off the TV.

"When?" Tyron says, almost unable to find his voice.

"In his dressing room after the fight. The casino owner and his head of security went in to congratulate him, and he beat them to death."

Tyron imagines the scenario. Now that he's got his head around the idea, he admits it is something Antoine could do. "Why?"

"Everyone is saying that Deco snapped. The police, the media. 'Culture of violence,' that's the phrase they keep using. 'Culture of poverty' too. They say his father was a criminal who was murdered, and that Antoine was a criminal too, before he became a boxer. They think the beating he took in the fight was what pushed him over the edge. Turned him psychotic and he killed the first people he was alone with. Bullshit, if I ever heard it."

Tyron remembers the strange things Antoine said to him yesterday. That they were brothers and Tyron should look out for him if shit went down. He knew what was coming. He planned this.

"What're you thinking?" Marlon asks.

"I saw him yesterday. Antoine. He was acting strange. Said some cryptic things."

Marlon senses his reticence and says, "Don't tell me if you don't want to. It's not my business."

Tyron begins to tell Marlon that Antoine planned the murders, but then remembers Antoine speaking about his parents and decides against it. "Maybe another time."

Marlon gives a short, sharp nod. "Sorry I asked you to

come here so early, but I need to get over to the rally point
well before everything begins, and I wanted to speak to
you in private first."

"No problem."

"Looks like you had a long night."

"Yeah."

Marlon's face sours.

"I never drink, Marlon. Last night was an aberration."

"That's good. That's good."

"What's with the saw, Marlon? You think you're bugged?"

Marlon scans the basement. "I could be. Tyron, I think
I'm being followed."

Marlon pauses for the gravity of these words to sink
in. It is a good thing he does, because Tyron needs time.
Naomi might be single, Keenan might want to fight him,
Antoine is a murderer, and now Marlon is being followed.
All this hitting him with his brain stilted and the saw ring-
ing in his ears.

"I don't know who they are," Marlon says, pre-empting
Tyron's question. "To be straight with you, there isn't
much to go on. But I can feel it. Cars lingering down the
street. Vans pulled up in front of the house. When I'm
walking, someone at the edge of my vision. I turn around
and it's too late, they're gone, but I can feel their eyes
on my back. I can feel them watching the house. I don't
want to leave 'cause then they'll break in and do whatever.
Maybe they broke in already." He juts his chin toward the
saw. "Precautions."

Tyron meets Marlon's intent gaze and nods, trying to hide his skepticism.

"You got any guns?" Marlon asks.

"Guns?"

"Yeah, I got rid of mine, so they got nothing they can use on me. You know they'll fabricate something as soon as they see an opening. We have to be perfect, 'cause they'll vilify us any way they can to delegitimize our cause. That's why I got rid of my guns. But I know something's coming, brother, and I need to be prepared when it does."

Tyron is almost certain now that the man is paranoid. "I don't have any guns, Marlon. All mine were Marine-issued. I turned them in when I was discharged."

Marlon's expression turns grim. "It's cool. I'll be all right."

"If I can help in any other way . . ."

"I know, young brother."

Marlon curls his shovel-sized hand into a fist and pounds Tyron's with it.

"There's one more thing. The rally in a few hours. I know you're concerned about betraying your boy. But I want to be clear that this is not a protest against Keenan Quinn. It's not about justice for just one or two people. It's not about blaming or punishing specific individuals for the systemic oppression that we face. You with me? This is about fighting institutionalized racism. It starts with exposing and ending police terrorism in Black

communities, but the movement has the potential to
tackle much more than that. Housing, education, employ-
ment—the things we've been fighting for, over such a
long time, now we can pursue them again. Black Lives
Matter has tapped into a level of participation and energy
that we haven't seen for decades. Its sharp focus on police
violence has given us a single issue to rally around, but
from there we can expand to a broader range of issues—
even challenge the fundamental inequalities at the heart
of capitalism itself—for all people, not just our community. We take this far enough and we could see things happen. Not lip service, not the pretense of a colour-blind
society to justify stripping away our rights, but change.
Real change. Social welfare–oriented change. The time
is now, young brother, and we need *everyone*."

Marlon's words remind Tyron of the conversations his
parents used to have when he was young. They weren't
nearly as forceful as Marlon is now, but their discussions
often ran along similar lines. When they saw Tyron listening, they would include him in the discussion, asking his
opinion. And they did the same for Antoine once he was
living with them. At first the boys were shy, intimidated
by the level of discourse. But the Shaws would coax and
encourage them, and the boys would eventually deliver
simple responses drawn from things they had heard
others say—better schools, less drugs, less guns—and
the adults would commend them for their answers. Then
Viola Shaw might ask the boys how they would bring

about such change, and the boys would awkwardly look at each other and stammer. Viola would laugh and say, "Don't worry, your father and I don't have an answer for that one either. It's what we've been working toward. The question of how hasn't been answered. Not yet, at least. But maybe one day, you two will be part of the answer."

Tyron's eyes clear from his memories and he says, "You're right, Marlon. I'll be at the rally."

★ ★ ★ ★ ★ ★ ★ ★ ★ ★ ★ ★ ★ ★ ★ ★ ★ ★ ★

8

7:19 a.m.

KEENAN RINGS THE doorbell of Sergeant Brian Fitzgerald, a friend since their days in the academy, and a reliable one at that. More reliable than Keenan ever was to him, Keenan thinks with regret. No one comes to the door and he rings the bell again. It is warm out already. And bright. A sweltering day is coming.

The blinds in the window part, a pair of eyes stare out. Seeing Keenan, the eyes narrow. The door swings open. Fitz, in a T-shirt, track pants, and bare feet, steps outside and closes the door behind him.

"Keenan, what are you doing here? Kind of early for a pop-in, dude."

"I'm sorry. You weren't answering your phone."

"That's because it's Sunday morning. My wife's losing her shit."

"Fitz, I need a favour."

"Now?"

"It can't wait."

Fitz's stocky build has grown thicker along the

waistline since Keenan saw him last. He has a trim beard and an open, affable face that can harden when it needs to. It does so now, but then, after a moment's appraisal of Keenan's ragged appearance, he opens the door behind him. With a stern yet empathetic expression, he motions with his head for Keenan to follow him inside.

After the heat of outdoors, the house feels frigid, the air conditioning turned up too high for Keenan's liking. Fitz's wife, Jessica, is hovering halfway down the stairs, arms crossed. With glossy black hair and pouty lips, she too has put on weight since their child was born fifteen months ago, yet it suits her, adding to what was already a voluptuous figure. Jess and Keenan have had a few awkward moments when they were all out drinking together. And a few not-so-awkward moments in this house while Fitz was on shift. Fitz never knew.

"Keenan," she says, arms still folded. "It's early."

"I'm sorry, Jess. I'm in a bit of a crisis."

"For a change," she says with a raised eyebrow and an ironic smile.

Keenan smiles tiredly. "It's becoming a habit."

She descends the rest of the stairs. "Coffee?"

"Please. Black."

"And you?" she asks of her husband.

Fitz looks at Keenan, estimating the level of hassle his friend is about to dump on him. "The same, hon." Apparently it's a high estimate.

She heads off to the kitchen, and Fitz again looks

Keenan up and down. "Shit, dude, did you sleep at all last night?"

"Maybe an hour."

Fitz leads Keenan into the living room where they can speak in private.

"I need the file on a murder from twenty years ago: victim's name, Raul Deco."

"I can't get you a file, Keenan. You're retired."

"Then you look at the file and tell me what's in it."

"What's this about?"

"I can't get into it now. Just trust me when I say that I have to find out who killed Raul Deco."

Fitz stares up at Keenan, holding his gaze as he assesses the situation. Then he looks around him, seeming to grow uncomfortable about having a conversation like this inside his own home. He ushers Keenan through the sliding glass doors into the backyard. The moment he is out on the red-tiled patio, Fitz seems less of a family man and more of a cop.

"Keenan, if I'm going to stick my neck out for you, you've got to give me something."

"Do you know who Antoine Deco is?"

Fitz shakes his head. "Should I?"

"You're not a boxing fan, are you?"

"No."

Keenan decides that expediency is more important than secrecy. He has to trust someone in Metro if he is going to find answers, and there is no one he's going to trust more than Brian Fitzgerald. He gives him a quick rundown of all the important points, with the exception of the Shaws being assassinated.

"Where's your father now?" Fitz asks.

"Naomi's with him and my mom. They're looking for a hotel with an available room."

"So he should be all right, for at least a couple of days, even if Antoine is after him."

"I think so. I don't know."

A stabbing headache hits Keenan behind the eyes. He grimaces and shuts his eyes against the sudden pain. It leaves as abruptly as it came; he breathes deep and rubs his eyes. Fitz looks at him with concern.

"I think you're too close to this thing. Join your wife and parents at the hotel. Get some rest. Let me look into it."

Hearing those words, recognizing how earnestly they have been spoken, Keenan almost collapses in relief, gratitude, and exhaustion. He puts a hand on Fitz's shoulder, half to thank him, half to keep standing. He experiences such a release of emotion to at last have an ally that he shares everything, as there is no point in half measures anymore. He has already divulged too much to condemn him if Fitz is with Bashinsky's people; he might as well offer him all the ammo there is and hope Fitz aims it somewhere else. "There's another murder to look into. A double homicide from sixteen years ago."

Keenan tells Fitz who the Shaws were, the work they were involved in, the reports given about their deaths, and the strange conversation he heard between his father and Terrence Shaw in the boxing gym. Jess interrupts partway through to bring them their coffees, and she says to Keenan, "Come see Anna when you guys are done. You haven't seen her since she was a newborn."

Once she is gone and Keenan has finished his story, Fitz says, "These are serious allegations. Political assassinations by active-duty police officers." Fitz rubs his beard in thought, mug of coffee in the other hand. "Did you tell anyone else about this? Fischer? Miles?"

Keenan shakes his head. "Just you."

"Good. Don't tell anyone about this, Keenan." Fitz takes a mouthful of hot coffee, gulps it down. "This might take some time."

"We don't have time. Antoine's after someone who is — or was — a cop. If not my dad, then someone else. He's going to kill again unless we can stop him."

"We'll be the ones killed if we stumble onto something we're not supposed to. I know you want to rush this, because you think it's bad right now, but it can get a whole lot worse. Not just for your old man. For you, for me, our whole families. I'll help you. But I'll help you my way. You still want my help?"

Keenan swallows. "Yes. Of course, Fitz."

"Good. 'Cause I'm interested. I don't like dirty cops."

"That's why I came to you."

"That's the reason? It's not because you had no one else?"

Fitz gives a wry smile, which Keenan returns.

"Whatever the reason, thanks, Fitz. I can't tell you how much I appreciate this."

They shake hands and Fitz says, "Don't mention it. You've always been a good friend to Jess and me."

An image springs to Keenan's mind: Fitz's naked wife in bed beneath him. Keenan shifts awkwardly and mumbles, "Right."

"I'll have to go into the station, but right now I have to check out some things on my computer. Try to relax for a couple minutes. And go say hello to my little girl. Good?"

"Good."

UPSTAIRS IN THE baby's room, Anna crawls onto Keenan's lap as he sits on the floor, while Jess, standing, watches them from above, leaning her shoulder against the baby-blue wall, arms still crossed. "She likes you," she says.

"She's a beautiful girl."

Keenan does not say it just to be polite. Anna is a lovely, plump child, with sparkling, expressive eyes the colour of the tawny Nevada plains. She reaches her chubby hand up to Keenan's mouth and tugs at his lower lip like a rock climber finding a handhold. He lifts her by the armpits and holds her against his shoulder. Her warmth and softness revive him more than the coffee, and the smoothness of her cheek against his red stubble gives him a moment's respite from thoughts of Antoine, his father, and Naomi.

He looks at Jess, his eyes content, for this moment at

least. Jess looks back at him, enjoying the sight of him with her child.

"You like her?" she asks.

"Very much."

"That's good. She's yours, you know."

Keenan's eyes pop. He stares at Jess, waiting for the joke, but there's no mirth in her face. He pulls the girl from his shoulder and holds her at arm's length, inspecting her like he would a cancerous growth. He can see no resemblance. He stares up at Jess.

Her pouty lips twitch at the corners, and she doubles over laughing.

"It's not funny," he says.

"Oh, it is," she says.

"So she's not mine?"

"Of course not. We used condoms, dummy."

"Oh yeah," he says, remembering.

He stands up and hands her the child, no longer a source of rejuvenation but just one more stress on this hellish day.

"It's not the day to mess with me like that."

She shrugs with Anna in her arms, and the baby seems to mimic her mother and half shrugs herself, which Keenan cannot deny is adorable. "It looks like you could use a laugh," Jess says.

"Does it look like I'm laughing? Holy shit, Jess."

Jess smirks and puts down the girl, who tentatively walks to her crib, holds on to the legs for support, then quickly walks the rest of the way across the room to her toys, plopping down to play with them.

"When are you and Naomi going to have a little bundle of joy of your own?"

"Never. Naomi's leaving me."

"Really?"

"Yeah. It's over."

"She finally caught you cheating?"

"No. I don't do that anymore."

Jess makes a face. Sure you don't.

"I don't."

"So if I got Fitz out of the house, you wouldn't want to join me in the bedroom?"

"Is this hypothetical or an actual possibility?"

She slaps his arm. "You see! I knew it."

"It was a joke. I was joking."

"Sure."

"I was. I really don't do that anymore." He thinks for a moment. "Not that it would be cheating anymore. Naomi's made it clear that we're done."

Jess's brow scrunches, and Keenan senses that he has missed something.

"Um, it would be cheating on Fitz," she says. "You might remember him. He's the guy whose house and family you intruded on, begging for him to help you out of a crisis."

"I didn't mean..."

He gives up and leans against the wall beside her. His body feels much too heavy to keep up without support.

"If not the cheating, then why did she end it?" Jess asks.

"The same reason I retired."

"Because of the shooting?"

He nods.

"That's a little harsh. She's part Black though, right?"

"Yeah."

Jess makes a *hmm* noise at the back of her throat, but refuses to elaborate. After a period of silence, she asks, "Are you okay?"

"Not really, no. I liked my wife. I know I didn't show it, but I liked being married."

"You know," Jess says, "if you had left Naomi when I asked you to, I would've left Fitz."

"I was already regretting every decision I ever made but I had forgotten about that one. Thanks for that, Jess. Thanks for reminding me. I can add one more to the list."

She laughs. "Come here," she says.

She reaches out her arms and he steps inside them, and they hold each other, her soft body warm against his. He closes his eyes and inhales the scent of her hair and the lush scent of her neck, mixed with the comforting smells of her child, which pervade her. "Thanks," he whispers into her ear. Then he leaves her to join Fitz downstairs.

★ ★ ★ ★ ★ ★ ★ ★ ★ ★ ★ ★ ★ ★ ★ ★ ★ ★ ★ ★

9

8:23 a.m.

"**WELL, THIS ISN'T** too bad," Naomi says upon entering their hotel room.

She lowers her in-laws' hastily packed overnight bags to the carpeted floor.

"It's the ugliest hotel room I've ever seen," says Rosie Quinn.

Naomi nods in agreement, yet smiles anyway. "Beggars can't be choosers, unfortunately."

"So I'm a beggar now as well as a coward, is that it?" Craig Quinn asks.

"Who comes to a hotel like this?" says Rosie, her eyes glued to the maroon drapes dotted with white roses, blackened with smoke stains—the smell of cigarettes in the room is inescapable.

"Gambling addicts and adulterers, I imagine," Naomi says as she unslings her own overnight bag. She checks inside the small chest of drawers beside the first of two double beds. The bed closer to the door is better, she thinks, so that Craig will have to cross in front of her if he tries to leave in the night.

"And pussies afraid of their own shadow," Craig adds.

"Craig!"

"What? She can handle it. She's a basketball player.
What do you think they talk about in the WNBA?" He gives
a lecherous wink to Naomi, which she ignores.

No matter the conditions, Naomi is simply relieved
that they have a room; it seemed every hotel in the city
was booked solid this past Saturday night. They were far
too early for Sunday check-in, so against Craig's wishes
they paid for two nights in order to hide away sooner.

Rosie gasps from the bathroom door. "The bathroom
is abysmal."

"Look at my socks," Craig says. He sits on the bed and
shows Naomi his blackened white soles. "I've only walked
across the room twice. This place is disgusting."

"We might as well keep our shoes on, then," Naomi says.

"I don't know if I can stay here." Rosie turns back into
the bedroom. "Craig, take that cover off the bed. People
have sex on those things and I heard these hotels only
wash the sheets."

Craig recoils, face twisting in revulsion, then he notices
Naomi looking at him and pretends nonchalance, rolling
his eyes at his wife's anxieties. Naomi frowns.

"Really, Naomi, I can't stay here," Rosie says. "Can't we
find another hotel?"

"Yes you can. And no we can't. You can stay here,
Rosie. We all can. It's going to be all right." Naomi runs
her hands through her hair, trying to remain composed.

"Why don't we eat something? I've brought lots of food. We can eat a little, watch some TV. Then when we're a bit more relaxed, we can have a nap and catch up on some of the sleep we've lost."

"I can't sleep in the morning," Craig grumbles.

Rosie's eyes continue to inspect every inch of the room with dismay. "I don't have much of an appetite."

"I might be retired but I'm no slob."

"I get it, Craig, you don't want a nap," Naomi says. "Why don't we talk, then? Tell me some of your stories when you were on the job."

"Keenan wants me to blab to you, huh? Subtle. I don't know how anyone so obvious could've fooled you into marrying him. Or how he thought he could be a cop either."

Staring at this grizzled, bitter, insecure man, Naomi experiences a deep sympathy for her husband, something she has not felt in a long time. "Why not just tell us what happened?" she asks, plainly.

"'Cause it's none of your damn business, that's why."

"It *is* my business, Craig. It's Keenan's business too. And Tyron's. We're all affected by what happened to the Shaws. And quite clearly, it's Antoine's business as well. He was most definitely affected. He was my friend. Maybe if someone had shared the truth with us when we were kids, we could've helped him. We could've stopped him from becoming a—"

"Murderer," Rosie says, still hovering near the bathroom door.

Naomi glumly looks from Rosie back to Craig. "It's a day for the truth to come out. We all have to face it."

Craig holds Naomi's gaze and doesn't flinch. "It's none of your business."

"Please, Craig," Naomi says. "For me."

A muscle twitches in his cheek, above the line of grey stubble. His Adam's apple dips with a loud swallow and his eyes flick away indecisively. He opens his mouth to speak, and Naomi unconsciously leans forward in anticipation.

"What's on TV?" he asks. He breaks eye contact, walks to the television, and picks up the remote. But as he flips channels there is a touch of redness to his cheeks, shame spreading beneath Naomi's scrutiny.

Naomi leaves her parents-in-law to use her phone, but goes only so far as the balcony outside their room over the parking lot. She calls Keenan first and updates him on their whereabouts. He is following Fitz to the police station.

"He's taking it seriously?" she asks.

"Very," Keenan says. "He was the right person to ask for help."

"Good. Keep me posted."

A pause. "Whatever you want."

"You get in touch with Tyron yet?"

"No. I can't get a hold of him."

"Maybe I'll give him a try."

"Sure. How are my folks handling it?"

"I have a whole new appreciation for you, let's put it

that way. They're doing fine. I haven't been able to get your dad to open up yet, but I think I'm getting to him."

"You should've been the cop."

"Keenan."

"Yeah?"

"Be careful."

"I better go."

"Okay. Talk soon."

"Talk soon."

She blurts out a sharp, urgent, "I love you," but midway through it their connection ends.

Lowering her phone, she does not know why she did that. She hadn't planned to. It saddens her that he didn't hear her say it.

It's a crazy day, she tells herself. Just get through it.

Next up: Tyron.

He is breathing heavily when he answers her call. "Hey," he says.

"Hey. You okay?"

"No. What's up?" There are plenty of voices in the background on his end.

"What's wrong?"

"I can't get into it now. What's going on?"

"Keenan's been trying to get a hold of you."

"I know. You told him we kissed?"

"*No.*" Her brow furrows, realizing what Tyron must have thought. "No, of course not. Did you hear about Antoine?"

"The murders? Yeah. Insane."

"Keenan was there. He worked security. He saw Antoine after he did it."

A loud, muffled voice erupts in the background, followed by cheers. "Crazy," Tyron says, speaking over the background noise. "I want to hear about it, but I got to go, Naomi."

"Ty, hold on, this has something to do with you. Antoine said that your parents were assassinated by the guys he killed. He said that the same corrupt cops who killed his father killed your parents."

"He said *what*?"

"That's why Keenan's been calling. He's trying to find out the truth—"

"Naomi, I can't deal with this right now. We'll speak later."

The line beeps off, and Naomi wonders what else has gone wrong.

8:28 a.m.

THERE ARE GANGS of gunmen everywhere. Firefights in the streets. They drop several of the enemy before the rest flee to entrenched positions. Miraculously, none of Tyron's men are wounded. Instead they look stronger than ever, immersed in the fight now, coated in dust, dirt, and blood.

When they concentrate their fire on the first of the buildings, squad leaders are volunteering to go in and clear it out. This time Lieutenant Lake is the one to say he'll lead them.

Tyron gives him a smile. "Aye aye, Lieutenant."

One by one they clear the buildings. He orders 2nd Platoon outside the wire too. The night wears away. Three of his men are hit by bullets: non-lethal flesh wounds. Four are hit by roadside bombs: two dead and two critical. A blood orange ribbon appears on the horizon to the east. Tyron can't even remember how the night started.

They curve around the combat outpost, to the buildings on its western flank, where fires have broken out everywhere and the remaining insurgents have dug in. On the rooftop of an abandoned low-rise, Tyron looks out at the colours of dawn. His night-vision goggles have been stowed, replaced by bullet-resistant glasses: he sees as clearly as you can in all this smoke and dust. And what he sees are the shades of damnation. If hell is real, he thinks, it must look like this. Sky and earth: red, yellow, black. A sliver of sun has risen over one horizon, while on the other the night isn't giving up without a fight. Neither are the insurgents. Bombarded from two directions, they continue to fire back from windows and rooftops.

Tyron slaps at his face. Hard. To keep fatigue from setting in.

He is not the only one battling exhaustion. All his men, who have performed so admirably, so bravely, and with such poise, look at least as tired as he feels. One more breakthrough, he thinks. One more advance and we'll bust this thing open.

He rises just above the low wall that encloses the roof, and quickly studies the lay of the battlefield. Crouches back down before a sniper can pick him off. Between his position and a darkened apartment tower, from which most of the enemy fire originates, is a market square strewn with garbage, shrapnel, bodies, and several burned-out vehicles. His men have blown open the entrance to the apartment building; they need only to cross the no man's land to get inside the stronghold and take these fuckers out at close range.

But it would take an Olympian to make it across the square unscathed. Or maybe an almost Olympian. He smiles to himself. I thought my track days were over.

Lieutenant Lake, still by his side, tries to talk him out of it. "I got the best chance," Tyron says, as cement chips rain down on them from errant enemy rounds. "And anyway, better me than one of my men."

"No sir. Not better. We need you."

"You got this, Lake. Just make sure I'm covered. And lay as much smoke as you can between me and them. If I make it, and start wreaking havoc, you send the boys in after me."

Then he is on ground level, jettisoning anything he won't need in the next ten minutes. His ruck. His food and water. Even a ceramic plate in the back of his body

armour. Fortune favours the brave, motherfucker. His
heart thumps in his chest.

His men fire smoke canisters across the square, adding
to the obscurity of the battlefield, littered with flaming
husks of metal that were once vehicles. There is a particu-
lar vehicle, a Humvee turned inferno, that lies roughly at
the halfway point between his position and the enemy's.
That is where he will go: use the blaze for cover, then
sprint the second leg. Already the twisted Humvee is lost
from view with all the smoke, but the wind is not idle, and
the cover won't last long.

Poised beside the open doorway, he thinks it is good to
feel fear again. Fear like this. He could run a world record
jacked up like this.

You better, a voice inside him says.

His men unleash a wave of covering fire, the starter's
pistol for him. He bolts, sprinting as low and as fast as he
can. He can hardly see anything through the smoke, and
his eyes are down to make sure he doesn't trip on the
uneven ground.

The gunshots are relentless, filling his ears from every
direction like he has plunged into a barrel of exploding
firecrackers. The bullets whizz by his face, blow a kiss as
they hurtle by. He pumps with the M4 assault rifle in one
hand like an oversized baton. His throat and lungs burn
from smog and exertion. The scorched carcass of a van
suddenly looms out of the coils of smoke, and he almost
crashes into it.

Where is he? Where is the burning Humvee he had
been aiming for?

There is such a cacophony, outside him, inside him,
such burning stinking fumes in his nostrils and in his
mouth, he cannot think. He sprints harder.

The smoke starts to clear. He is in an open stretch now.
The roasting Humvee is way out to his right and
already behind him. He glances at it over his shoulder as
he keeps on sprinting, while the apartment tower rises
before him, AK-47 barrels poking out its windows like
bristling thorns. Among all the windows, and the holes
blasted through the walls, Tyron somehow spots one
gunman, lining him up perfectly. He won't miss. Tyron
knows it as much as he has ever known anything. Time,
already slowed to a fraction of its speed, seems to stop
altogether, and all he can think in this frozen moment,
his final moment, is simply, This was a stupid idea

The gunman's head jerks. He tilts forward, over the sill.
The AK-47 falls from his grasp and drops slowly through
the air. Every Marine is a rifleman, Tyron thinks, thank-
ing God for his men's accuracy.

Dirt sprays up around him with wayward bullets.
He leaps into new plumes of smoke. Coughs violently
but doesn't break stride. Almost there, you fuck, let's
go. He bursts out of the smoke right at the smashed
opening of the building. Crosses the threshold into a
stairwell, and no finish line has ever given him such a
sense of triumph.

Springing over the bottom broken steps, he charges up, thunking grenades with his M203 launcher attached to the underside of his M4. As explosions rock the inside of the building and his enemies scatter, he notices that he is bleeding in three places: the outside of his lower leg, just above his boot; his left shoulder, which he now realizes aches like a knife is stuck in it; and his right side, below his ribs, where the blood is slickest. Sweat streaks onto his lips and it tastes thick and coppery: he is bleeding from his face too. The wounds occupy his thoughts for half a second at most.

He advances down the hall, launching grenades and firing bullets, a wolf loose in the sheep yard.

"TY! TY! WAKE up, you're going to make us crash! Stop punching. What's wrong with you?"

He is inside a vehicle. Not a Humvee, just some regular compact car. His arms are moving of their own accord; he pulls them into his body. Looks around. He is in the front passenger seat. Tara is driving. She keeps looking over at him like he's a rabid dog.

"I dozed off," he says.

"Dozed off? You call that a *doze*? You're lucky we didn't crash."

"What happened?"

"You were rocking and swinging and shaking the whole damn car."

"I'm sorry."

She takes a deep breath. "It's all right. You just scared me is all. No more naps in the car, okay?"

She winks and he feigns a smile, though inside he is thinking, *What the fuck is wrong with me?*

A few minutes later they arrive at the Las Vegas Convention Center Bronze parking lot, the meeting site for the rally. Tyron is surprised by the number of people already gathered, with more arriving every minute.

They find Auntie Trudy near the centre of activity, where the organizers are at work welcoming protesters, handing out signs, and giving instructions. Tyron notices that most of the people running the show are women. He hadn't expected that. He hadn't expected white people to be there in solidarity either. When he hugs Auntie Trudy, the first thing she says to him is, "Have you seen Marlon?"

He is unsure how she means the question. Has he seen him today? Has he seen him here, right now? Is she worried that Tyron hasn't spoken to Marlon yet or is she worried that Marlon isn't here yet? But what is apparent is that she is definitely worried.

"I was at his house a couple hours ago," Tyron says.

"When did you leave him?"

"About o-six-forty."

"You haven't seen him since then?"

"No. Why?"

"He hasn't shown up. And no one can get a hold of him."

A chill seizes Tyron.

Tara runs through the usual questions: When was he supposed to be here? Have you tried his cell? Has anyone else heard from him? Did someone go by his house? Who was the last person to speak to him? The answer to Tara's final question is Tyron. He was the last person to see or speak to Marlon.

Even hung over, the instincts Tyron developed overseas uncoil and worm through his body. It was gatherings like these — a large mass in an outdoor space — that always scared him over there. An obvious target, easily infiltrated. Looking out at so many people in one place he cannot help but feel that he is in another target primed to be hit.

And Marlon. He wouldn't miss this. Tyron is certain of that. What if the man wasn't being paranoid? What if people actually were following him? What if his absence now isn't a coincidence?

"I'm going to look around for him," Tyron says in a plain voice, masking his concern.

"Let us know if you find him," says Tara, who doesn't seem too worried.

Tyron weaves through the crowd, scanning faces. So many. Such a target and Marlon absent: Tyron can't quiet his racing mind. He moves faster through the crowd. The faces are unknown to him, a stranger in his hometown. And then he sees a familiar face, and is comforted a little.

"My man!" Ricky says, slapping his hand and embracing him. "What a night. *What a night.*"

"Rick, Marlon's missing. No one can reach him."

Tyron tells Ricky the full story. Ricky's expression empathizes but doesn't agree. "Ty, there could be a million reasons why Marlon isn't here and isn't answering his phone."

"Or answering the door at his house."

"Or answering the door at his house," Ricky says. "He's out, he's not answering his phone, he's not here yet. It's too soon to panic."

"I got a bad feeling, Rick. It's been building since yesterday, and I can't shake it now. By my last tour, if I got this feeling, I was always right. I knew. And the stronger the feeling, the closer it was to something going down. To people getting killed."

Ricky puts his hand on Tyron's shoulder and shakes him lightly. "You're home, Ty. You're not over there anymore."

Tyron shakes his head, frustrated. "This isn't PTSD or some shit you've seen on the news. I *know* something's wrong. And I'm *powerless*. I'm powerless to stop it. I've got no men. No guns. No intel, no rank, no contacts. No understanding of anything. No fucking nothing, man. I'm no one back here. I know something is wrong and I can't do a fucking thing about it."

"Hey hey," Ricky says. "You're cool, dude. You're cool. We'll find Marlon. And you ain't no one out here. You the last thing from that. I never met anyone as loved as you. I'd hate you with jealousy if I didn't love you so damn much myself."

Tyron laughs, just once, in spite of himself.

"And I know it's not a company of Marines, but you got me, brother," Ricky says.

"Yeah, I got you, Rick. God's looking out for me."

"Well, you don't got to be sarcastic about it."

"I wasn't."

Tyron embraces the smaller man, and the anxiety that was cresting inside him recedes. "I'm still right about Marlon, though. He's in trouble."

"Okay, so what do you want to do? I'll leave with you if you want to go look for him. But I don't know where to begin. And he might show up here anyway."

Tyron thinks it over. "Let's keep looking here for now. You're right, he might show up."

Together they scour the vast parking lot and the many people in it, while continuing to call and text Marlon's cell phone. When they come across someone they know, they ask if the person has seen or spoken to Marlon. No one has. At the edge of the parking lot, Tyron looks across a narrow road at the Las Vegas Metropolitan Police Department station. It was there that Antoine was caught breaking in all those years ago, when he was still new to the Shaws.

On Tyron and Ricky's return to Tara and Auntie Trudy, Tyron's phone rings and his heart skips a few beats. But his hope is for naught. Had Naomi called an hour earlier he would've been thrilled to hear from her; now he is disappointed and frustrated that she is not Marlon.

"Hey," he says.

"Hey. You okay?" she asks.

"No. What's up?"

While Naomi starts talking about Keenan and Antoine and the murders last night, he and Ricky move through the crowd to the front. A few women in their twenties and thirties with loudspeakers are indicating to those around them that they're about to get things under way. Naomi is still talking.

One of the women welcomes everyone, thanks them for coming, then asks if they're ready to fight injustice. The answer is unanimous.

Tyron is not sure he heard Naomi right in all the cheering, but he thinks... he thinks she just said his parents were assassinated. By the same guys that Antoine killed last night.

The woman on the loudspeaker shouts chants and questions and the crowd repeats the chants and answers the questions, all in one booming voice. He presses his ear harder against the phone but cannot hear what Naomi is saying, except that it has something to do with Keenan.

"Naomi, I can't deal with this now. We'll speak later."

He ends the call and shoves the phone in his pocket. His parents were assassinated by the guys Antoine killed, what the fuck? Who knows what is truth, what is disinformation, and what is misinterpretation. I got to get out of the desert, he thinks. I'll go north. Far north, where it's wet and cold and green, and where there's only one person I have to worry about.

He looks over at Ricky and Tara and Auntie Trudy, pumping their fists and shouting their support. Tara catches his glance and smiles at him.

I'm here, he thinks. For today at least, I'm here.

He listens to the leaders of the protest and tries to forget everything else. Everything other than that Black lives matter.

★ ★

10

9:07 a.m.

KEENAN WALKS TO the end of the police station's rooftop parking lot, so he can have a better view of the rally across the street. He grew up often being the centre of attention, at home, at school, but never has he been the focus of so many people at once. He wonders what the crowd would do if they knew that he is here, almost on top of them. He wears a black cap and sunglasses to disguise his appearance, but still stoops against the low-rise wall enclosing the rooftop to keep from being seen. Looking down on the street below, he wonders how much damage a drop like that could do. It's not a high building. A few broken bones, he imagines. Unless he dove headfirst. What would the protesters make of that? What would Naomi make of it? Maybe she'd feel responsible. He experiences a sudden morbid delight in the anguish it would cause her. A final payback for not loving him anymore.

He sniffs back tears, disgusted with himself for thinking such a thing. Looks over the edge again. Just do it, you pussy.

There are uniformed cops on the rally's perimeter. Keenan can't imagine they're the best sight for the gathered protesters, nor that the cops are looking on with impartiality. On that note, the cops in this building can't be too happy either—a rally against police violence right outside their windows. He wonders if the location was coincidence or intentional. Perhaps both. Some minutes later the cops start blocking off traffic on Sierra Vista Drive. The crowd turns and shifts and lumbers forward. Keenan stares a minute longer, then turns away, frightened of being spotted by the marching protesters.

FITZ IS INSIDE hunting for information about the Shaws' murder. Keenan didn't bother asking if he could come along.

He returns to his car and sits on the hood. The climbing sun beats down on him and sweat forces his shirt to cling to his spine. After about ten minutes, Fitz comes out with a pleased, confident waddle, flapping his notebook at Keenan like it's a winning lottery ticket. "We're in business."

"What did you find?"

"I'll tell you on the drive over. We'll take my car."

"Where are we going?"

"The Reef."

At the mention of the casino, Keenan feels immediate trepidation. "The Reef?"

"The Reef, baby." Fitz takes his keys out as he walks

around the car to the driver's side. "This is some can of worms you've opened for me, Keenan. But I'm not complaining. I love a good challenge."

Fitz beeps the doors unlocked, and he is as eager behind the wheel as he was on foot. He zooms out the building, turning east to avoid the protesters.

"Who do you suppose was first on scene when Raul Deco's body was found?"

Keenan shrugs. "My father?"

"No." Fitz glances from the speeding road to Keenan. "One Jacob Fischer."

"Fischer? You think that means something?"

"I don't know. It might, it might not. Who do you think ran the investigation of the Shaws' murder?"

"Tell me."

"The current undersheriff: Jake Fischer. And both times he came up with nothing. Just the assessment that both sets of killings were gang-related, even though there was no real evidence to support such a claim."

"Fischer," Keenan says. He wants to believe it's him. Him and not his father. But Keenan also doesn't want to jump to conclusions just to ease his mind. "It doesn't mean much, though, does it? It could all be coincidence. And what does the Reef have to do with it?"

"It definitely could be coincidence," Fitz says, "but it's something. And I've got something else for you. When Fischer was partners with Monk, they were called to the Reef all the time. Got all the collars that occurred on that property. The same thing when Monk was partners with your dad."

"But all that does is confirm that Monk was working for Bashinsky, which we already knew. Fischer and my dad could've just been along for the ride."

"True, but a lot of things are adding up. We're not trying to build a case yet, just trying to get some answers. Then we'll go from there."

"And the Reef might have them," Keenan says with a nod, understanding Fitz's line of thinking.

They turn onto Las Vegas Boulevard.

Fitz says, "Someone there must know something. And whoever it is has to be rattled with Bashinsky not twelve hours dead yet. I figure we can lean on them, see what falls out."

Keenan tilts his head to give Fitz a sideways look of approval. "I see why you got promoted faster than me."

"Let's see if I'm right first before you say anything like that again. What the *hell* is this?"

Up ahead are cops, lots of them, on the sidewalk and in the street. They look like soldiers with their automatic weapons, black bulletproof vests, and grim expressions — soldiers setting up a militarized roadblock. The two men realize simultaneously that all these uniformed cops are for the protesters who will march this way, here to block off northbound lanes of Las Vegas Boulevard and to be on hand to quell any subversive behaviour toward the protesters. Or by them.

"I can't believe the city agreed to block off traffic on the Strip," Keenan says.

"I think they figured it was better than a riot. And I know people are checking out of the hotels, but nine on a Sunday morning isn't exactly Mardi Gras." Fitz looks over at Keenan as they approach the police hot spot. "You better keep your head down. As inconspicuous as you can get. Everyone remembers the catalyst for all of this."

Keenan is exhausted of hearing about what he has done wrong. A never-ending loop. You'll never escape it, he thinks. And you don't deserve to. There's only one solution. Only one way out. Get to the bottom of this first. That is a must. And then it'll be over. It'll all be over.

So sharp is this idea in his mind, and so calming, that his vision crystallizes into pristine details. The glinting badge of the cop waving them through onto the casino grounds, the pores on Fitz's cheek above the line of facial hair, the glossy windows of the awesome structure they are approaching, all clearer than ever. His senses experience a surge in awareness: the cold artificial air of the car in his nostrils, the purr of the motor in his ears, the feel of the seatbelt against his sweat-stained shirt. He is alive in a way he hadn't been a minute earlier.

Soon, he thinks. Soon it'll be over.

9:18 a.m.

Craig has turned the television to the local news, and the three of them sit on the beds watching the march. The newsfeed alternates between an aerial view from a helicopter and handheld shots beside the protesters. "Hands up! *Don't shoot!* Hands up! *Don't shoot!*" the protesters cry, again and again, and then they chant, "No justice, no *peace!* No racist po-*lice!* No justice, no *peace!* No racist po-*lice!*" From the aerial view, the line of people stretches beyond either end of the frame.

Craig says with deadpan delivery, "Didn't I always tell you our boy would make a difference in the world?"

"Enough, Craig," Rosie says.

Naomi is subdued, the excitement and activity that ran the entirety of the night ebbing at last. She cannot sleep, but she lies on the bed, her face and body slack, her eyes dull, transfixed by the screen. It appears she has done all she can for the time being; Craig has continued to stonewall her attempts to get at the truth. But at least she tried. Tried and failed. Some way to end her marriage to Keenan—fail him in a moment of crisis.

What good is trying if it's not enough? she asks herself. Wake up, woman. Your work isn't finished.

"Craig," she says, without moving.

He twists around in his seated position at the front of his bed.

"Did you work for Norman Bashinsky?"

"Jesus Christ!" He vaults to his feet. "I've had enough of this shit."

He marches to the door but Naomi has sprung up to intercept him. She realizes, in her brief flight to the door, that she needs a new tactic, and as Craig advances on her, looking as though he'd like to hit her, she steps forward with open arms and wraps them around his shoulders. She hugs him close, and whispers into his ear, "I'm sorry. But please tell me. Just me. No one has to know. It's our secret."

His body is tense. She waits, holding her breath, refusing to let go until she has an answer. Just get the truth, she thinks. For Keenan.

Craig's arms close around her back, and she lets her breath out, breathing into his embrace, hoping this weakness for her he has always hinted at is truly there. She hears his slow exhale in her ear.

"Tell me. Did you work for him?"

"Yes," he hisses. "*Yesss.*"

He tears himself away and glares at both women.

9:32 a.m.

In a mass of people moving as one, Tyron feels that he is part of a larger whole. A similar feeling to being in the Corps. This connection to something bigger than himself is less defined, less tangible than the one he experienced as a Marine, and yet it is also more liberating, more open, more accepting, and in some ways even more inspiring. Walking among the people of his community, he is swept up in a sense of belonging he hadn't foreseen when he returned to Vegas. He believes in the mission of this cause. He couldn't say that by the end of his term with the Marines, when he feared that he was inadvertently bringing about destruction in the world.

He looks at the monolithic casinos on either side of them, a march through a valley of man-made mountains. Flashy mimicry of landmark architecture: there is a pyramid, there is the Eiffel Tower, there is the Brooklyn Bridge; and the others, those less gaudy, are nevertheless so shimmering they appear as mirages in the hazy desert heat.

Antoine almost told me about my parents, he suddenly realizes. The thought sneaks up on him. He acknowledges to himself that he does not have as much closure as he thought over his parents' deaths, so long ago now. He thinks back to yesterday in the hotel room, when Antoine asked him if he wondered what really happened to his parents. I stopped thinking about that a long time ago, Tyron had said, and Antoine almost said something. Tyron could see it.

He almost told me. What does this mean? My parents were assassinated, why? Antoine would know. It seems he's the only one who knows anything these days. But he must be long gone by now.

Tyron looks about him and sees that it is common practice for people in the march to use their phones, not just for taking pictures and videos but for texting and talking

as well. Expecting the number to be dead but hoping
anyway, he calls Antoine's right-hand man, Carlos. The
number goes to voicemail immediately. He doesn't leave
a message. Only one other person he can try.

Tyron hesitates before tapping the screen on his phone
to call Keenan. His thumb hovers, poised. He stares at
Keenan's name, brightly displayed on the small device.
He touches the screen. Makes the call. Keenan picks up
on the third ring.

"Hey man."

"Hey," Tyron says.

Someone near him shouts, "Hands up!" and a swath of
people surrounding Tyron shout back, "Don't shoot!"

"Are you in the march?" Keenan asks.

"Yeah," Tyron says. "But to support the movement, not
to protest y—"

"Don't worry about it. I mean it. I got more pressing things.
You'll be coming by me actually. I'm in the Reef right now."

Tyron sees the titanic structure in the distance. "You're
there right now?"

"Yeah. Looking for answers. Did Naomi speak to you?"

"She did. You saw him after he did it?"

"I saw him. He's nuts, Ty. A psychopath."

"So what he said about my parents, you think that's part
of him being crazy?"

"No. No, he's not crazy like that. I actually believe
everything he says."

"So my parents...you think they were..."

"Yeah. I do. You—can you ditch the march? Come into the Reef when it comes by. There's a lot I'd like to tell you, and I can't say it over the phone."

Tyron looks at those around him, at Auntie Trudy and Tara and Ricky, and he reflects that Marlon is still missing. There is no chance he would skip this unless something had gone horribly wrong. Keenan was a cop until recently. Maybe he can help.

"I'll be there," Tyron says. "See you soon."

"Sounds good. Call me when you're inside."

9:38 a.m.

THINGS ARE MOVING. His parents are safe with Naomi, Fitz is getting somewhere with the hotel desk manager, and Tyron is on his way. His old life won't return to him just because a couple of things are falling into place. But for the moment, maybe he's getting somewhere. Of course, the closer he gets to answers, the faster he hastens toward a conclusion. Toward an end. But maybe. Maybe he could turn this thing around.

He puts his phone away and returns to the front desk, where Fitz is engaged in a discussion with the manager, having already argued his way up the chain of command from the desk clerks.

"Boys, boys, boys," says a dry voice from behind Keenan and Fitz. "What are you doing here?"

They turn around.

"Detective Miles," Fitz says with a nod.

"Detective Miles," Keenan says.

The rangy detective looks like he just walked out of a sandstorm: hollows in his stubbled cheeks, coarse bronzed skin gashed by the wind, and green eyes, almost colourless as if faded by the sun, as desiccated and impenetrable as the desert itself. "What are you doing here?" he says again.

"Just trying to get some dates straight on some paper-work," Fitz says jovially.

Detective Miles stares at Fitz, while the manager waits on the other side of the long check-in desk. Miles looks past Fitz to motion with his eyes for the manager to get moving. The man complies. Miles says to Fitz, "You need Quinn with you to do that?"

"No, but coming down here on my day off, figured I might as well make the most of it. We're going to hit the tables after this."

Miles waits for Fitz to say more, then, when Fitz doesn't, appears surprised that this is the best lie Fitz can come up with.

He turns his attention to Keenan, who thinks that if Miles were a dog he'd be sniffing him right now. As it is, the detective seems to have caught the scent of every move Keenan has made. "I won't tell Fischer about you snooping around, Quinn, but you stay the fuck away from my crime scene. I won't warn you again. As for you, Fitzgerald: I'm watching you now."

Both men are struck dumb. They can do nothing but stare back at the detective like admonished children.

"Now get going, boys. I don't want you here."

They open their mouths but no words come out. So they nod their apologies as they back away. Keenan feels those arid eyes on his back, hot like the desert sun, and he quells the urge to turn around and face the searing gaze. Far down the massive hall, heading in the direction of the parking lot, Fitz says out the side of his mouth, "Miles is one tough son of a bitch. Jesus, he makes me feel like a kid."

Keenan can stand it no longer: he glances back to see if the detective is still watching them. But he is nowhere to be seen.

Keenan's phone rings. Naomi.

"Yeah?"

"Keenan, I'm sorry, okay, I'm really, really sorry."

"What happened?"

"Your dad's gone."

"What!"

"I'm so sorry."

"What do you mean, he's gone?"

"He left. I couldn't keep him here. He was—"

"Where did he go?"

"I don't know! He's turned off his phone."

"What the fuck?"

"I'm sorry."

"How did you let this happen?"

"He wasn't going to be stopped. I mean it. And he wasn't

going to have us go with him. I would've had to stop him
by force."

"So you should've, then. You could take him."

"There are limits to what I can do in this situation,
Keenan. He's a grown man. I can't imprison him. And
definitely not the way he was. I've never seen him so mad."

"Ah, fuck!" Keenan grits his teeth and bends over.
"Fuck."

He raises up and ignores Fitz's perplexed, inquiring
look.

"You assured me you could keep him safe. I wouldn't
be on this fucking goose chase if I hadn't thought that
you had it covered."

"Well, I'm sorry. I tried, Keenan. I don't know what
else I could've —"

"You should've tried harder, then. You should've chased
after him. Ah, fuck. Fuck!"

"You do know that we're both carrying guns, right?
Getting in that man's way when he was like that would
not have been safe. Not for him and not for me. Believe
me, I did what I could."

The blast of shock and anger that cracked through him
like a shotgun slug has now exited out his back, leaving
him drained of strength and blood. He continues to hold
the phone to his ear but he doesn't speak. He breathes
slowly, trying to think. Recalls through it all that he has
to tell Tyron not to meet him here anymore.

"You want me to go look for him? Tell me where he

could be and I'll find him. He should be calmer by the time I get to him. Key? Key, you still there?"

"No. Stay with my mom. I'll find him."

"I really am sorry."

"I know. It's okay. It's not your fault. I was just surprised. I shouldn't have taken it out on you."

"Thank you."

"How's my mom doing?"

"She's stressed but I don't think she's worried about Antoine doing anything. Key, there's something else I have to tell you."

"Something else? Should I get the defibrillators ready?"

"Your dad worked for Bashinsky. He told your mom and me."

"Did he commit the murders?"

"I don't know. He went nuts after admitting to working for Bashinsky. That's when he left. I pressed him too hard, Key. I'm sorry. Everything was okay until I tried to pry the truth out of him. I'm the reason he left."

He knows that he should try to assuage her guilt, so thick and sad in his ear, but he cannot bring himself to do it. For the first time he wants their marriage to end. "I have to go. I'll let you know if I find him."

Fitz asks him if he's okay. He doesn't bother giving an answer. Instead he says, "I have to find my father. He ran off."

"I'll help you look," Fitz says.

Keenan pauses and stares at Fitz, undone by his

friendship. To think that he could so fundamentally betray
a man as decent and loyal as this repulses him. He cannot fathom how he has repeatedly put himself in such
situations, how he has made so many mistakes and hurt
so many people.

"Thanks, but I'll look alone. You've helped me enough
already."

"You sure? I'm happy to do it."

"No. It has to be me who finds him."

He feels like there is a vice around his throat, time
twisting the screws with every hour until breathing
proves impossible. And yet, with circumstances so pressing, he cannot decide what to do next. He tries to think of
the best path forward but knows instinctively they will all
lead off a cliff. He is doomed. His father is doomed. Both
of them cursed, fated to pay for their sins.

Self-pity rears up in him so strong he thinks he will
break down in tears. He swallows and clenches his
teeth in an effort to keep himself composed. His eyes
flit from Fitz to the sea-coloured walls to the fake coral
to the strangers passing by — so many of them, wan-
dering around like the world isn't ending, their lives
not completely fucked. We all screwed up so bad, he
thinks. My father, me, Naomi, we all made the wrong
call at every turn. Nothing ever goes right. Nothing
will ever go right again. I've been cursed ever since I
pulled that trigger.

The faces, the walls, the coral, all of it starts to swirl

in his head. He teeters on his heels, feeling like he might faint or throw up. His tongue is thick in his mouth. Fitz is holding on to him, steadying him, but even his bearded face blends into the whirlpool. Keenan thinks he will do it. He will cry or throw up or collapse, or do all three, at last as wretched on the outside as he has been during these past months, and that is when one face sharpens out of the mash of colours.

Keenan blinks his eyes and narrows his gaze. Tries to stay centred.

Cutting across the lobby is a tall, barrel-chested man with thinning brown hair. He wears a brown suit and his eyes are down on his phone as he marches purposefully to wherever it is he's going. Undersheriff Fischer. Keenan's legs steady. Undersheriff Fischer, the only other person in all this who can give him some answers.

"I'll be back," he says to Fitz.

Fitz has caught his line of vision. "Whoa, dude, this isn't a good idea."

But Keenan is already on the move. He shifts between people in a brisk walk, and then he breaks into a jog. *Fischer. If anyone can help me it's him. He could also fuck me up worse than I am right now, but seriously, what do I have to lose? Naomi's out. I'm a waste of space. And we'll see if my father makes it through the day.*

He dashes around crowds of people, almost catching up to the undersheriff, the man's eyes still on his phone. Keenan sees that Fischer is heading for the same set of elevators he used yesterday to go to Monk's office. Feels like a lifetime ago. The glossy doors slide open and a small crowd piles in with Fischer at their centre. Keenan sprints the last of the way and springs through the closing doors, nearly barrelling over a middle-aged couple.

Fischer's eyes pop at the sight of Keenan. He heaves a sigh of exasperation, then shoves through those in front of him to press a button. The doors slide open again. "Get the—" Eyeing the people around him, Fischer turns red holding his curses in. "Get out of my sight, Quinn."

"Sir, two minutes."

"Two minutes? Two seconds is too long, you've wasted enough of my time already."

"I have new information, sir."

Fischer doesn't relent. He keeps his finger on the button, his face mottled, his eyes seething. Keenan doesn't give in either. He is sure he would've yesterday.

"Please," says Keenan. "I'm trying."

The elevator passengers look back and forth between the two large men, half disgruntled by the holdup, half entertained by their charged moment. Fischer breaks eye contact to take note of their interest, seeming more aggravated by their eavesdropping than he is by Keenan's intrusion. "That's it, everybody out." He waves his badge. "Police business, get another elevator."

The couple Keenan almost bowled over stay rooted to the spot.

"Everybody out! Police business!"

The couple scamper away. Fischer releases the button and the doors slide closed.

"You're like a fucking cockroach, Quinn."

"My father worked for Bashinsky. He told my wife. This thing is real. Deco didn't make it up."

Fischer glumly stares at Keenan. "So? And before you say anything, you've got till the seventeenth floor, so be quick."

Keenan sees that the departed passengers had hit the buttons for several floors before the seventeenth. A little extra time.

"Sir, you must know something. You were partners with Monk, just like my dad. You got called down to the Reef all the time."

"How do you know that?"

"Antoine's out there killing people because of shit that went down in this building. You know something, sir."

The doors open on a floor and Fischer jabs the button to close them.

"First, I don't have to answer to you. Second, I have no idea what you're talking about."

"I know about the Shaws. I know they were assassinated. I know my father knew about the hit beforehand. Did you know about it too?"

"Who?"

"Terrence and Viola Shaw. They were Black activists who were murdered sixteen years ago."

Fischer squints, then gives a grunt of recollection. "Them? That was a gang killing."

"A cover-up. The order came from Bashinsky. Monk and someone else pulled the trigger."

"Bullshit."

"Antoine's going to come after my dad. Or he's coming after someone else. I know it. What can I do? Except try to find out the truth. It's the only thing that could stop this. *Please*. Do you know something?"

The undersheriff stares back at him. The elevator stops and the doors slide open. "Seventeenth floor," he says, walking out and looking at his phone.

Keenan goes after him. Puts his hand on the man's shoulder. Fischer turns with a fist curled.

"I ought to knock your teeth out, Quinn. Or throw you in jail for tampering with an investigation."

"What difference would that make to me now? I've got nothing left."

For the first time Fischer's eyes soften. "Ah hell, Quinn, don't get all mushy on me."

"Sorry, sir."

Fischer scratches at his unshaven cheek. "I do take all this seriously."

"There's no one else to turn to, sir. I need help. I wish I didn't, but I need help."

Fischer checks his phone and winces. He looks back at Keenan, debating something in his mind. Hesitantly, he says, "I might know something." He hands Keenan his card. "This is my direct line. Call me later today."

Keenan is afraid to reveal the gratitude overwhelming him, for fear it might upset the precarious balance he has attained with Fischer. So he quietly nods and slips the card in his pocket. Fischer turns and lumbers down the hall, checking his phone once more.

Keenan stands there, gathering himself, recovering from the intensity of the exchange. He watches Fischer, a distance away, stop outside a room and knock. He appears in too much of a hurry to care that Keenan can still see him.

In the midst of all his swirling thoughts, Keenan vaguely wonders who Fischer is meeting. The door opens and Fischer goes inside. Keenan turns and heads back toward the elevators.

He's still got to find his father as soon as possible, but maybe with Fischer's help he — maybe with the truth he can save . . . someone. Anyone. Do one fucking thing right.

He pushes the button to recall the elevator. Waits. Hangs his head and closes his eyes. Feels the bruise on his shoulder blade. Feels the lump at the back of his head. Wishes he could fall asleep on the carpeted floor.

His eyes open. He sees his reflection in the elevator doors. He looks five, maybe ten years older than he did yesterday. Has it not been five, ten years since yesterday? And still not over.

The doors slide open, the reflection gone. He takes one step inside and his heart stops.

A gunshot. Muffled, but unmistakably, a gunshot from down the hall.

9:47 a.m.

TYRON RECALLS MARCHES in the Corps, heavy boots hitting the ground in unison, a firm sound composed of confident notes. It made him think of the power, the physical power, humans possess when unified. In this march the patter of so many feet is chaotic and mostly drowned out by chatter and chanting. But the feeling is similar. He feels powerful. It is the first time since he left the Corps that he has felt this way.

But to say it's *he* who feels powerful is not exactly right. It is all of them, together. He feels a part of something powerful.

The people around him walk tall. Some have their kids with them, and the kids walk tall too. Some groups are holding hands. Others have fists raised. Signs nearby read JUSTICE FOR REGGIE HARRISON, END POLICE TERROR, #BLACKLIVESMATTER. Marlon was right, he thinks. Something big is going down. It pervades the air: something is building. Every one of them can feel it. Today is important but something is growing beyond today.

The Reef looms vast as his section of the march approaches it, and he feels a burst of shame that he is about to abandon the protesters to meet with the man who precipitated all this outrage. He wonders if he really is betraying his community to consort with a killer cop. Even if it is to enlist his help to look for Marlon. That could be even worse, asking the killer cop to help save his friend.

Maybe he should abandon Keenan for what he has done. Maybe that's the right thing to do. But the notion of it stabs Tyron with shame too. It's not like he hasn't killed people. Far more than Keenan has. And this thought brings the deepest shame of all, the thought that keeps returning to him: those men whose lives he stole, whether terrorists or insurgents or extremists or whatever else the Western world labels them, they were home.

He can say that these men were trying to kill him and his Marines, that they were trying to detonate bombs intended to murder as many people as possible, that he was often on patrol when he came across them and not after them specifically, but he cannot escape the fact that he came, from continents and an ocean away, to *their* home and put them down. Places he has no connection to. Places even now he does not understand. Populated by peoples whose languages he does not speak, whose religions he does not practise, whose histories and traditions he has little or no knowledge of. And he left his home so many thousands of miles away and trained with utmost concentration, effort, and discipline, to develop himself into a killer of extreme proficiency, into a leader of proficient killers, so he could come to their home and hunt them. Maybe it was the right thing to do. Maybe so. But then why would it wreak such torment in him now? I'm always trying to do the right thing, he thinks, but somehow it always turns out wrong.

The blue glass windows of the Reef shimmer in the sunlight like the ocean on a cloudless day. It's now or never: he leaves the march or he keeps on walking. Either way he's letting someone down.

He looks at the protesters around him, and at Auntie Trudy, Tara, and Ricky beside him, and he wonders if he has a right to count himself among these people. So determined, so hopeful and good. He has been gone too long. Seen and done too much. If they knew . . . would they still want him to be a part of this?

Perhaps he belongs with guilt-ridden Keenan, a man with innocent blood on his hands. The blood Tyron spilled directly came from enemy combatants, but what about the mistakes he made? He was lauded and decorated as an officer, but with that much time in the desert it was impossible not to make any mistakes. Impossible to pick the safest route every time, impossible to be everywhere, protecting his men and civilians always. He never spilled innocent blood, but he would often lie awake at night thinking of how he could have saved it, what he could have done differently. Years of that and it began to feel like not preventing death was the same as causing it.

Tyron doesn't know, rent as he is, how he can live up to the faith Marlon has put in him. How he can contribute, here, to this cause or any other.

Marlon's still missing, he reminds himself. That's how you contribute. You find Marlon. Worry about the rest later. Do your duty, Marine. Loyalty to your brothers and sisters in arms. Your brothers and sisters in struggle. That's how he rationalized his role in the Middle East. That's how he'll rationalize his role now. Honour, courage, commitment. He's still a soldier. He's still a Marine. Only instead of the Corps, this community is his family now.

Your service doesn't end, he tells himself. You'll go mad if you try to live for yourself. Your service never ends. It evolves, but it never ends. Whatever I'm needed for, wherever I can help, that will be my mission.

Right now, Marlon needs my help. And Keenan does too. He committed a terrible crime, but I won't abandon him. I won't abandon anyone.

With that, Tyron turns to Trudy, Tara, and Ricky, hugs each of them in his strong embrace, and says, "I'll catch up with you later. There's something I have to do."

9:48 a.m.

FROZEN IN THE threshold of the elevator, Keenan knows instinctively where the gunshot came from. Terror seizes him. He cannot move. Cannot turn to face this latest threat. Until the elevator doors close on him. Jolt him into action.

He seems to skip moments in time: suddenly he is loping down the hall. His gun is out. Oh Christ, Fischer, are you dead too?

Don't stop. You stop — doubt, fear, common sense, they're going to catch up to you.

But Keenan does stop, just outside the door Fischer went into, and the menace closes in around him. He wishes his hands weren't so sweaty. He wishes they were steadier. He wishes his heart would quit pounding for a fucking second so he could focus.

Another gunshot. So much louder than before. Undoubtedly fired from inside this room.

Keenan experiences a split second's hesitation, a fractional moment of horror at what lies beyond this door. He doesn't overcome it, merely doesn't act on it, doesn't try to halt his police training kicking in, compelling him to literally kick in the door. He throws his full weight behind his outstretched foot. Jabs his heel as hard as he can. Wood splinters with a crack. A lock snaps off and the door crashes open.

Keenan advances, weapon poised. He sees a familiar face at the back of the room. Standing over the legs of a motionless body, recovering from his surprise, pivoting toward the door with a smoking pistol in his hands, is Thompkins, Fischer's right-hand suck-up. Fucking Thompkins, what the fuck is he doing here?

Thompkins lines Keenan up. He's going to kill me, Keenan thinks. What the fuck is going on?

Even as Keenan registers all this, he is pulling the trigger of his own gun. He is aiming and squeezing and exhaling as he fires his own pistol, blasts deafening in the enclosed space. He pulls again. And again.

Thompkins lets off an errant round as he jolts backward. Blood sprays out the side of his neck and from the centre of his chest. Keenan keeps pulling the trigger, advancing as he does, until Thompkins is lying spread-eagled on the ground, pistol still in his hand but cast limply out, blood seeping into the carpet all around him.

Keenan distantly recognizes that he has ended the life of a second human being; nevertheless, his training has him swiftly scanning the rest of the room. He sees Fischer's brains spattered on the floor-to-ceiling windows, marring the view of the Vegas skyline. He sees Fischer's stretched-out body on the floor, immobile but for the blood leaking out the back of his skull and the front of his belly. Then he sees, huddled in the corner, a large, thickly built, bald man, bound and gagged, staring at him with wide eyes. Keenan sees all this and what his mind is consumed by is his own heart and its pummelling contractions. He never knew it could beat so loud.

By the time he has cleared the bathroom his heart's beating has begun to slow, and he starts to hear the thoughts in his head. By the time he is back in the bedroom, fatigue is already hitting him. He moves to ungag the man in the corner, then drops to one knee. Tries to catch his breath. He shifts his gun to his left hand and dries his right against his pants. Then wipes away the perspiration he hadn't realized had beaded on his forehead and upper lip.

What the hell is going on?

He looks up. The man is still staring at him. His skull looks like a shiny dome. His eyes are set deep. There is recognition in them. Probably knows who I am, Keenan thinks. Probably hates me.

Keenan heaves himself up. Lungs sucking in big gulps of air. He can rest when all this is over. Rest for good.

He puts his gun in its holster and removes the gag from the man's mouth. The man grimaces and topples over with his wrists and ankles bound behind him by zip cuffs. Keenan helps him upright.

"Argh, that motherfucker," the man growls. "That motherfucker! He set me up. That *punk*. He set me up. Stuck a suicide note in my pocket. Thank God you got him. I'm glad you did. I know who you are. I know..." The man's fury has him out of breath. He slows his panting. Grimly sets his jaw. His eyes narrow, conflicted.

"What happened?" Keenan asks.

"That motherfucker set both of us up. A murder-suicide, that's how it was supposed to —"

"Police! Everybody down!"

Keenan dives into the prone position, hands over his head. He hears a flashbang grenade bounce into the room. The explosion rocks his ears like somebody cuffed them, and sears his eyes even though his lids are closed. Smoke

fills his mouth and nostrils and then his lungs, which con-
tract with deep coughs. His head is swimming. He tries
to resist the animal urge to bolt. The stomp of rushing
boots is muted beneath the whine in his ears, and then
he feels a knee in his spine and strong hands wrenching
his wrists down to his lower back to cuff them. Multiple
voices yell at him not to move.

At last he opens his eyes. The tactical officers are everywhere. They fill the hotel room, each one looking vast
in all-black ballistic body armour. Helmets, automatic
weapons, tactical gear, they are huge. They are terrifying. Lying on the ground, Keenan wonders if they might
shoot him, execution style.

One of them removes Keenan's gun and another pulls
him to his feet. They are doing the same to the man in
the corner, whom they cut loose of his bonds, then cuff
again with their own.

Keenan's skin prickles all over. His hands are shaking.
They would be shaking more if they weren't cuffed behind
his back. He can't stop blinking his eyes. It is the first time
in his life that he has been at the mercy of the police. His
mind retrieves the sight of that boy on the ground after
he shot him. Keenan keeps blinking, although now it is
to hold back tears.

One of the cops gets out of the way of someone new
entering the room. He wears no tactical gear, just a plain
grey suit. Detective Miles. He quickly surveys the crime
scene, then lets his eyes rest on Keenan. His thin, parched

lips pull into a sneer. A sneer not of anger or horror but annoyance. Annoyance so potent it has grown into disgust. Disgust for Keenan Quinn.

"What the fuck did you do?" he asks in a withering tone, and all Keenan can manage in response is to drop his head and weep.

★ ★

11

10:09 a.m.

TYRON PACES IN the entrance lobby of the Reef. Keenan is nowhere to be seen, nor is he responding to his calls or texts. What is more, there is a surprising amount of police activity. No public alerts have been given, and patrons of the resort continue to go about their business, but everyone is staring at the variety of police officers — uniform, plainclothes, and tactical — hustling back and forth, in and out of doors, elevators, and stairwells.

Tyron recedes far out of the way, against a side wall over the flowing image of a diving dolphin. He wonders if this still has to do with Antoine's murders, but no, the action has a liveliness and uncertainty to it that suggests something more immediate. There is even a look of shock and horror in the police ranks that gives Tyron a sense of foreboding. He watches closely, but can't pick up any additional information until a SWAT team marches through the lobby in a convoy, surrounding a few plainclothes officers and a pair of handcuffed prisoners. Tyron's breath stays. Trudging along in the midst of all the commotion are Keenan and Marlon. Tyron looks to the heavens and says a quick prayer of gratitude, then pushes off the wall to intercept the convoy.

Both Keenan and Marlon look physically intact, but they are clearly dazed and exhausted. Marlon looks unbroken, stooped but unbowed. He acquiesces to the authority of the police, but otherwise he plods along with a steady stoicism. Keenan, meanwhile, looks lost. His head hangs heavily, eyes on the ground, face emptied of any hope or fight. Whatever happened has broken him, Tyron thinks, as he hurries toward them.

"Marlon," he says as he gets close, and the entire convoy, except Keenan, rotate to face him.

The look on the cops' faces makes Tyron hold his hands up and shout, "I'm a veteran"; it is the look people give when they want to shoot someone. The information dilutes, but doesn't vanquish, their contemptuous stares. Tyron moves closer anyway.

"You all right?" he says loudly, through the men in his way.

"Yeah," Marlon says, his voice gruffer than usual. He glances at Keenan shuffling ahead of him, who still hasn't looked up. "Look out for your boy," Marlon says to Tyron. "He saved my life."

One of the SWAT police advances on Tyron. "Back up."

Tyron takes a step back. "What are they being arrested for, officer?"

"You know them?" the cop asks. He is as big as Tyron,

but looks bigger with his gear and body armour. Both hands are on his submachine gun, pointed down—for now. The man seems dangerously jacked up and he keeps inching closer like he wants an excuse to bring some pain.

Tyron looks from the cop's tense grip on his weapon up to his face. "I'm unarmed," he says.

"I asked you a question."

"Yes, I know them. I'm a captain in the Marines. Honourable discharge a few days ago. That man is a friend of mine. He went missing earlier today."

The cop stares at him, seeming unsure how to process Tyron's statements. He looks back at the convoy, moving on without him, and an older plainclothes officer in a grey suit, who walks beside Keenan, motions for him to rejoin the group.

The cop looks back at Tyron. "Back up, I said."

Tyron backs away slowly. "Where are you taking them?"

"You ain't in Baghdad anymore...*captain*."

The cop turns away and catches up to the convoy, exiting out the Reef's main doors. Tyron whips out his phone and calls Tara.

"Get out of the march," he says, "and get your car. I found Marlon."

10:17 a.m.

BREAKING NEWS. BREAKING NEWS.

The words keep flashing on the screen in gigantic letters. Two more dead—the reporters seem to relish saying it—killed in the Reef just half a day after the murders of Norman Bashinsky and Raymond Monk by Antoine Deco. It's almost too delicious for the reporters to maintain their practised air of sobriety. All the crews covering the march have abandoned it to swarm the casino.

Naomi and Rosie watch in silence. There is a sense, unspoken but palpable between them, that the world has spun off its axis.

"At this time, we still don't know if today's shooting is connected to the Bashinsky-Monk murders, but we do know that the police have two men in custody."

Naomi stands and paces to the window. The parking lot tarmac shimmers like water in the heat. Cars whisk by on the street beyond. The city is careening out of control, and where is she in all this? Holed up, hiding, no use to anyone.

"This just in, the police are coming out now with the apprehended men. We should have a visual momentarily."

Naomi turns to Rosie and asks, "Should we try him again?"

"When Craig wants to be alone, it's best to leave him alone," Rosie says, glancing away from the television, then fixing her gaze back on the screen.

"What about Antoine?"

Rosie leaves her eyes on the TV this time. "I know Antoine. He was a good kid. He's not after Craig."

Naomi frowns. Nowhere to go. No one she can get a hold of. Just the television incessantly reminding her that the planet these days is just one crisis after another. And that she can't do anything about it but tune in for the conflagration.

Cops start coming out of the Reef's shiny double doors. SWAT officers surrounding a couple of plainclothes cops and—

Rosie lets out a moan, like she will be sick. Naomi rushes to the TV. Keenan. One of the handcuffed men is Keenan. Naomi unconsciously places her hand on Rosie's shoulder. And Rosie places her hand overtop, neither of them looking away from the newsfeed.

The reporters' words fade away. Keenan. What has he gotten himself into now? He wears a listless expression as he stumbles along to the convoy of police vehicles.

Naomi spots Brian Fitzgerald among the cops, talking animatedly to someone in a grey suit. Fitz can help her.

Naomi grabs her keys.

"Where are you going?" Rosie asks.

"The Reef. I have to do something."

"But he'll be gone by the time you get there. They'll take him in for processing."

Naomi looks at the screen. "I have to do something!"

"I'm also scared," Rosie says. "But—"

"If Keenan's detained, then he can't look for Craig. I can do that." Naomi nods to herself. "I can do that."

"Naomi, please! Don't go."

But she is already rushing to the door, flinging it open. She looks back one last time. Rosie's forlorn face halts her on the threshold. Naomi opens her mouth to speak. There is no comfort she can offer. Not for Rosie, not for herself. She walks back. Leans down. Kisses her mother-in-law on the forehead. Hugs her. "It'll be okay," Naomi says.

With that she is gone, and she doesn't look back this time.

10:47 a.m.

KEENAN JOLTS AWAKE to the migraine waiting for him. He shivers. Tries to rub his temples but his hands are cuffed behind him, wrists and shoulders sore. All he can see is blinding light. His back is stiff. He arches his spine and shifts up in his seat, blinking. The light begins to split into shapes and colours, shades of red, beige, and brown.

He is in the back of an unmarked police cruiser. A metal grate divides him from the front. The only other person in the car is the driver: Miles. Outside he sees mountains and the desert. He cranes his neck around, but there is no Vegas skyline behind him, just the black road disappearing into the horizon, a thin pencil line drawn into the craggy landscape.

He catches Miles's eyes in the rear-view mirror, roving

up to stare at him, then sliding back to the road.

Keenan starts to speak, but his throat is so dry that his words catch. He swallows and says, "Where are you taking me?"

Again Miles's faded green eyes in the rear-view mirror.

Keenan feels a chill in his shoulders. He hunches them in. What is Miles up to?

"You're really not going to tell me where we're going?"

No answer.

There's only one reason to take a bound man into the desert, and it's not to let him go. What Keenan can't figure out is why Miles would want to kill him. Then it comes to him: Thompkins killing Fischer; Miles showing up with a SWAT team immediately after; his look of disgust, like Keenan had ruined his plans. Miles was working with Thompkins. Keenan knows too much.

He strains at his cuffs for a moment, just long enough to confirm the futility of the action, then wonders if he can kick through the grate — or if he should try to smash a window with his heels. But he's doubtful he could throw himself out the window of a speeding car with his hands cuffed. Even more doubtful that he could survive it.

Keenan is surprised that his heart is not pounding. Nothing like it had in that hotel corridor. It should be, though. It should be pounding, but he just doesn't care anymore. Not about himself, at least. The truth, though, he cares about that.

"Why?" he asks.

The green eyes study him in the mirror, then shift back to the road, no answer given.

"Why did Thompkins kill Fischer?"

Miles ignores him.

"Why did Thompkins kidnap that guy?"

No response.

Though the engine purrs and the tires rumble, the scenery, so open and monotonous, seems almost still out the window, and though the air-conditioned interior is cool, the auburn sand outside looks ready to combust beneath the scorching sun.

Keenan's eyes pop wide. *My father.* He leans up to the grate.

"Let me call my father. Please. Antoine Deco is coming for him. I won't tell my dad anything, I just need to —"

"He's not after Craig."

"What?"

"He's not gunning for your father."

"How do you know?"

"Because your father didn't kill Raul Deco. I did."

Keenan stares at Miles. "Why?"

"What difference does that make?"

"Look, I know where we're headed. I know what you're going to do. I don't care anymore. But tell me. Tell me why. Tell me all of it. Raul Deco. Bashinsky. The Shaws. Fischer and Thompkins. That man he kidnapped. Why? What possible reason do you have for fucking up so many lives?"

Miles purses his lips and keeps on driving. Keenan

waits, crouched forward on the seat, his face an inch from the grate. Minutes pass. The yellow-brown mountains are in sharp relief against the cloudless sky. Keenan leans back in his seat. So, no answers, he thinks. A fitting end for a wasted fucking life.

"Raul Deco was a thief. We had him run jobs for Bashinsky. He pulled a big one for us; Bashinsky didn't want the loose end."

Miles's dry, deadpan voice, confiding these past crimes, awakens Keenan. His back straightens as he leans forward, unsure why Miles would reveal the past to him but grateful that at last he may get some answers.

"What was the big job?"

In the mirror Keenan spots the tiniest of smiles on Miles's thin lips.

"Bashinsky had worked in the casinos a long time, but he couldn't get his own resort. Especially not on the Strip. So he planted a woman in the life of an old man who owned a casino, and he paid off the people around that man to encourage him to marry the girl and to wedge conflict between him and his kids. The old man married the girl and left her controlling shares of his casino in his will. Someone must've snitched, or maybe he started investigating, but he found out that the girl was working for Bashinsky. He had a new will drawn up fast, giving the casino back to his kids. That's where Raul Deco came in. He cleaned out all the copies of the new will. Monk and me took care of him. Then we took care of the old man. Made it look natural, though.

The girl got the casino. She handed it to Bashinsky and got a fat payout. Bashinsky tore it down and built the Reef." Miles's eyes flick to the mirror, amused at the story. "No one ever knew how to get his way like Norman Bashinsky."

Keenan swallows. He flexes his shoulders and pulls at his cuffs. "And the Shaws? Why did they have to die?"

"How do you know about the Shaws?"

"Antoine told me about them too. I didn't trust you or Fischer enough to tell you about it. One of the few good decisions I've made."

"The Shaws were warned. They should've known better."

"Warned about what? What did they do?"

"They were a threat."

"The Shaws?"

"They were agitators, making us look bad in the media and the public. And their following was significant. They wanted the casinos to pay higher taxes and hire more minorities. That's not how this town works. That's not how this country works."

Keenan remembers the Shaws' funeral. Tyron's tears. His own tears. Antoine's too.

"You're not worried about Antoine?" he asks.

"I'll find him before he finds me."

Miles pulls at the wheel and they bounce off the highway onto a dirt road.

"Anything else?" Miles asks. "Now's the time."

"The shit today, what was that all about?"

"I told you to get out of my crime scene, didn't I? Now you have to pay the price."

"How the fuck could you kill Fischer? Why do something so—"

"Fischer had to go. He was sticking his nose in places it didn't belong. And long-term, Black Lives Matter isn't good for business. Marlon Joseph, the man you found, isn't good for business. We faked texts from him to Fischer with info on a Black power extremist cell. All bullshit. A well-known Black activist kills Fischer, then kills himself: it gets Fischer out of the picture and defames the movement. Two birds, one stone."

"Two birds, one stone, you—" Keenan shakes his head. "It's sick. You're sick. Bashinsky's dead, what the fuck do you care about business anymore?"

Miles gives him a look through the rear-view mirror that seems to ask, How stupid are you? "Is the Reef dead? Is the Strip dead? Business is business. It keeps rolling. Someone falls off, someone else takes his place." His faded eyes flash. "It's the natural order of things."

Keenan glances left and right, his breath quickening. The road curves around the base of a rocky hill and descends into a valley between tawny peaks.

"But your plan didn't work. Marlon Joseph's alive. You're fucked."

"Wrong again, Quinn. Thompkins takes the fall for everything. I can thank you for that."

"What are you going to tell them, huh?" Keenan leans

back and kicks hard at the grate. It rattles but holds fast. "You take a man into custody and he disappears? Pretty fucking obvious what happened."

Miles doesn't bother looking in the mirror. "I'll think of something," he mumbles.

"They'll put you away for this."

"You'd be surprised."

Keenan lies back and slams his feet into the glass window. Other than a scuffed thud, the window is unmarked. He pulls his knees in again for another savage kick, when the car swerves and he slides across the seat to bump headfirst into the far door. He sits up and sees that they have left the dirt road for a track through the sandy brush, winding deeper into the hills. The car bounces over striations in the ground. He looks out the back window, but there is no visibility through the cloud of dust kicking up in their wake.

He stares at the back of Miles's leathery brown neck. Contemplates begging for his life. No, he thinks. Not to this scumbag. This corrupt hitman. Fuck him. Antoine wouldn't make a mistake, he must know that Miles is his guy. My dad'll be okay. And with any luck, Antoine will finish off this motherfucker.

The car slows, then eases to a stop in a shadowed basin surrounded by mountains.

Miles opens his door. His leather boots crunch the dirt with each step. He opens Keenan's door, gun drawn.

"Get out."

"Fuck you. Shoot me in here."

Miles's dry eyes don't blink.

"Splatter my brains all over this fucking car. Explain that to Metro."

"*Out.*"

"No."

Miles lunges inside the vehicle. Keenan leans back and kicks at him; the quarters are too close, no room to unload. Miles shoves his legs aside and pounds the butt of his pistol into Keenan's unprotected solar plexus. He gasps. His breath, his soul, his life sweep out his mouth. He doubles over, unable to breathe, the pain through his abdomen and chest unbearable. He feels Miles dragging him out of the car, and thinks the man won't have to shoot him; the blow might do the trick.

He falls into the dirt, still gasping, wriggling like a worm. His starved lungs strain at his ribcage. Miles drags him further from the car.

At last he sucks some breath back in, and then he is a man quenching himself, inhaling air as fast as he can. Focused on his breathing, Keenan doesn't immediately register the whining of a second car engine. He looks up, still gasping. Miles stands a few paces from him, pistol pointed at his face, head turned in the direction they came. The roaring engine grows louder. Miles shifts his stance to meet the interruption, raises his pistol with both hands, and braces to fire.

An old green sedan, long and wide, skids around the

outstretched arm of one of the mountains, clouds of dust swirling around it. The engine revs furiously and the vehicle charges down the track.

Miles pulls the trigger. Keenan recoils from the gunshot. He tries to stand and staggers back to the ground, his knees, shoulders, and face hitting the hard earth without his hands to protect him. Miles keeps firing. Keenan spits the bitter sand from his mouth. Cranes his neck.

The heavy car bounces a foot off the ground over a divot and continues rumbling. Its windshield shatters. Miles fires again and again. Keenan's feet slide in the dirt as he tries to push himself away.

The vehicle is almost on them, a huge hurtling thing, its engine screaming.

Miles takes one last shot and Keenan cringes.

10:48 a.m.

TYRON SITS BEHIND the wheel of Auntie Trudy's two-decade-old beast of a sedan: ancient and sturdy, engine stout, she's kept it in fine condition. He glides over the asphalt, across the desert, hanging back out of sight, with Tara and Ricky far ahead, in front of the target. Running a rotating tail was one of the many useful things he picked up in the Middle East. His phone is in the cup holder, on speaker, Tara and Ricky's updates coming in and his orders going out.

After he told them to leave the march they cabbed back to the Convention Center parking lot to pick up Tara's car, and she drove to Las Vegas Boulevard. Tyron remained at the Reef to watch Marlon and Keenan get taken away. There was a lot of commotion outside the resort, with the police trying to keep the public and the press at bay. There was also a short, plainclothes cop accosting a rangy guy in a suit, who seemed to be running the operation; it looked like they were arguing over Keenan, as the young cop with a beard kept pointing at him. All in all, it took a while before Marlon and Keenan were loaded up and sent on their way, which gave Tara and Ricky time to get into position. Marlon was put in the back of a police van while the rangy cop took Keenan alone in an unmarked car. Tyron didn't know who to track, but Marlon had told him to look out for Keenan so that is what he did. He relayed the colour, make, and licence plate to Tara and Ricky, who picked up the vehicle as it passed them by. Then he cabbed to the Convention Center where Auntie Trudy was waiting for him with her keys. She wanted to come along, but the moment he heard from Ricky that the unmarked car had not gone to a police station but was instead on the highway heading out of the city, he knew something was up.

"I got to be alone for this," he told her. The further they go, the more certain he is of that fact.

Ricky's voice comes through over the phone: "Ty, they turned off onto a dirt road. What do we do?"

Tyron hammers the gas. The car picks up speed and then it soars.

"Which dirt road?"

"You'll hit it soon. There's a big grey rock in front of it. What do we do now? Should we turn around?"

He tears past intermittent cars. Pulse steady. Sees the grey rock up ahead.

"Go straight for another minute, then turn around. Turn onto the dirt road but pull over. Wait there for further instructions. I'm out."

He picks up the phone, taps the call closed with his thumb, and drops it onto the passenger seat. No civilians chattering in his ear for this.

He skids onto the dirt road, gravel shooting out from beneath his tires. Vehicle handles better than he expected.

He rumbles along at a speed he is barely able to control, taut arms keeping the wheel steady. His lips peel back in a grimace, so intense is the exertion. It is worth it. Up ahead a trail of dust leads into a cluster of hills and mountains. He gains on the sandy cloud.

Around a hill and down into the shadows between slopes, the shark chases the wisp of blood, evaporating as he inhales it, and so he cannot slow down, he cannot rest a moment, he can only speed up, only pursue harder. The scent leads him off-road altogether, and he almost spins out skidding onto the tracks his prey left behind. The blood is thick in his nostrils now. The scent of sweat too. Perspiration beads on his face and across his arms straining to navigate the desert scrub.

He pulls around the thrust-out ridge of a mountain, and there, up ahead, what he has been searching for: a stationary car and two men, one on his knees, one standing with a pistol. He slams the pedal to its limit.

The gunman opens fire. A shriek as the bullet pierces the windshield. Tyron holds his course. Fortune favours the brave, motherfucker.

More bullets. An excellent shot: the windshield is pockmarked. Tyron ducks low in his seat. The vehicle hits a hole and pops off the ground. Lands with a screech. The wheels want to spin out. Tyron fights them straight. Don't hit Keenan, he thinks.

Crack. The windshield shatters. Glass cascades into Tyron's face. But he is on them. Only a moment now.

Keenan's too close. Fuck, he's too close.

And the gunman has Tyron lined up. Time freezes, like that morning in Baghdad.

This is the one. The bullet with your name on it. And there are no Marine snipers to save you this time.

He leans low into the steering wheel. A burst from the barrel, a whistle by his ear; a searing gash across his cheekbone. Tyron doesn't flinch.

The gunman dives out of the way, but Tyron wrenches the wheel.

A crunch of metal and a fleshy thud. Another crunch as a body disappears under the wheels.

He crushes the brake. Skids to a stop.

Pops the seatbelt. Throws open the door. Sprints.

Keenan is on the ground throwing up, sand scattered over him but seemingly unscathed. A short distance away is the gunman's mangled body, splayed at grotesque angles.

Tyron slides onto his knees and checks Keenan for injuries. Keenan keeps retching, even though all he brings up is clear fluid, and that gives way to dry heaving. Tyron holds his hands to Keenan's head, his neck, his jaw, shoulders, arms, torso, legs. Tyron realizes, while he is at work, that he is bleeding from his own cheek. He lifts his shirt up from the collar and presses it against the wound, then continues his examination of Keenan.

"This bump from now?" he asks, returning to the large lump at the back of Keenan's head.

Keenan's heaving has been replaced by huge, heavy breaths. At the end of an exhale, he gasps, "From last night."

Tyron lifts him onto his knees. "You're okay," he says with a weary smile.

Keenan nods, eyelids drooping almost closed. He falls forward into Tyron's arms.

Tyron embraces his friend. Holds him. Supports him. "I thought I'd lost you, brother."

Keenan, still huffing like he hasn't taken a breath in a month, says in a raspy voice, "Me too."

"You okay to stand?"

"I think so. Just...just stay close."

Tyron helps Keenan to his feet and keeps an arm around his shoulders.

"Naomi's leaving me." Keenan shakes his head. "Don't know why I'd say that now."

Tyron stares at his friend. "I'm sorry, man."

Keenan looks at him, his eyes open now. They fill with tears. "You saved my life, Ty." Tears streak down his face. "After everything I've done. You still saved my life."

Tyron embraces him again. "Always, brother."

When he feels that Keenan can stand on his own, he says, "Let me get these cuffs off. Think the keys are on him?"

"I don't know."

Together they appraise the sprawled, pulpy body.

"He killed your parents," Keenan says.

"Him?"

"He told me in the car."

"He say why?"

"It was political. They were—" Keenan sighs. "I'm sorry. I'll tell you everything in a minute. I should call my dad. Make sure he's okay. Let him know that Antoine's not after him."

Tyron studies the corpse in the dirt. He thinks a revelation like this should have him shocked and bewildered, his parents' killer before him, but he is in operation mode. The new intel is stored away to be dealt with at a later date. For now, complete the mission.

He approaches the body and crouches to search its

pockets. His hands on a corpse is nothing new for him. As he finds the keys, he takes note of the pistol cast a few feet away. He won't touch it: best to leave the crime scene as is, and he definitely won't be putting his fingerprints on the gun.

He walks back to Keenan. The cuffs come off. Keenan pulls his hands in front of him, massages his wrists and rotates each of them. Then he turns and hobbles to the unmarked police cruiser. He searches the dead man's suit jacket on the passenger seat. Comes back with a phone in his hands.

Tyron looks up at the sun-scorched peaks above them. Looks back at Keenan holding the phone to his ear. Watches as relief washes over his face.

"Dad. Thank God," says Keenan.

10:49 a.m.

ANTOINE WATCHES THE alley behind the sports bar from the passenger seat of a grey compact with tinted windows. Carlos sits behind the wheel. They don't talk. Every so often Antoine's eyes flick down to his phone. One of his people is inside.

Antoine is a legend in the Latin Knights now. Not only did he raise the profile of the gang by shocking the boxing world and assassinating the most powerful man in Las Vegas, he pushed for them to wager as much capital as they could raise on him winning the fight. The gang made a fortune. So did he. Every dollar he owned, every dollar he could borrow, every dollar he was paid upfront for the fight — and he negotiated less money but a larger advance — he had Carlos bet for him. He determined that either he beat Konitsyn and got his shot at Bashinsky, or he failed in his life's purpose. Since he didn't plan on failing, he risked everything that he would succeed.

He will have enough to live like a king in Venezuela. Or Bolivia. Not that he cares about living like a king. Not that he cares even about getting south of the border, where he will fly from Mexico City to Caracas. They can catch him. They can lock him up or kill him. He doesn't care so long as he finishes what he started. It's all he has. And he's almost there.

But he *will* make it out of this country — this country that has never been a home to him despite living his entire life within its borders. He has no doubt he will make it out. His people know what they are doing, and they will lay their lives down for him now.

His phone flashes with a text. Ahora, the message reads.

He glances up at Carlos, who nods. Antoine gets out of the car.

He walks stiffly across the street to the alley, a baseball cap pulled low on his brow, his shades hiding his swollen, blackened, and bloodshot eyes. He wears a starched white shirt and black pants, and except for his battered knuckles, he could be any other Latino man on his way to bus

tables, wash dishes, mop floors. The locked back door
of the sports bar opens from the inside and his associate,
Tulio, leans out, a large, serious man with buzzed hair
and a goatee. Antoine slips inside without a word. Tulio
closes the door behind him.

Antoine takes off his shades, which saves him from
having to adjust his eyes from the desert sun to the darkened passage. He passes the door to a storage room and
hears the bustle of the kitchen up ahead, but it is only a
few steps from the back door to the men's washroom and
he makes them quickly. Out of the corner of his eye, he
catches Tulio returning up the corridor to the bar floor.

The dimly lit washroom, with four urinals and two
stalls, is empty, scouted already. He crosses the filthy tiled
floor to the far stall. Locks the door, lowers the lid, and
sits on it. He pulls up his pant leg and pulls his knife from
the sheath at his ankle. He rolls the linen back down over
the top of his shoe. He takes his phone from his pocket
and holds it in his left hand, his knife in his right. He waits.

There are no nerves. They have been burned out
of him over the past twenty-four hours, his adrenaline
drained empty.

His phone flashes. Vienen 2. No es el.

Half a minute later Antoine hears the door whine open.
Footsteps of two men entering. The splash of their urine.
A few mumbled words between them and some chuckling.
One of them farts. The door whines again, then shushes
to a close.

He waits.

He wonders if he could have done things differently. Not today, or last night—he has executed his plan perfectly—but twenty years ago. Could he have done things differently twenty years ago? Could he have picked a different path through life?

But how could I have survived without such a purpose? he thinks. I would've been broken a thousand times over.

He supposes it makes no difference. He has become what he has become. The past won't return.

But there were times he tried to do things differently. Even after Terrence and Viola Shaw were killed, he tried. He wanted a normal life. He was ready to relinquish his mission.

Viene otro. No es el.

But normality never wanted him. No one wanted him. Not until he had crafted himself into something they could benefit from. A soldier for a gang. A prizefighter for businessmen. A wallet for women. And by then it was too late. No turning from the path then.

The door opens. New footsteps. The customer opens the door to the stall beside him. Sits down with a heavy sigh. Antoine sees beneath the divider brown shoes and slacks bunched over them. He listens to the man's bowels at work. Smells what they have to offer. The man keeps sighing, as though he is in the midst of great exertion.

Hurry up, *hombre*. I don't like witnesses.

The man's stench is so foul, and his strained sighing

so annoying, that Antoine hopes his mark has to relieve himself before this *pendejo* is finished. Such a humiliating way to die. Worthy of a bitch like this.

The man finally does finish, before anyone else comes inside. The door whines open and shushes closed.

Antoine waits.

What does it matter if people care about you when you're an asset to them? It doesn't. It doesn't matter. They still don't care about you. Only what you can do. And they'll dump you as soon as you're no longer of service to them.

I made the right choice.

Ya viene. Solo.

His grip tightens around the knife handle. Relaxes and tightens again. He slips his phone back in his pocket. Stretches the fingers of his left hand.

The door whines open. Heavy steps on the tiles. Antoine silently rises. Slides the lock open. Hears a stream of piss hitting the urinal. He slowly pulls the stall door inward, not a sound from the door or his feet.

In the mirror he sees the tall man standing over the urinal, his head down. His piss still streaming.

Antoine takes his time. The man has drunk much beer.

A boxer's feet must be light. A murderer's feet must be lighter. Silent as a python slithering out of a tree, he creeps behind the tall man.

The piss slows to a trickle.

Antoine wrenches the man's head back. Jabs the knife

into his throat. Rips it across his gullet. Blood spatters the graffiti above the urinal.

Antoine pulls the knife free and stabs his victim four, five, six times in the stomach. The man gurgles and feebly reaches for his severed throat and his punctured intestines. Antoine lowers him to the ground. He stands above him. Watches the puddle of blood grow into a pool.

The man's eyes are bugged halfway out of their sockets. Antoine stares into them. Sees the recognition. The shock. The horror before death.

The eyes turn glassy. The blood keeps flowing.

Antoine drops the knife and washes his hands. Scrubbing, he hears a phone ring. He turns. It's coming from the body. Half the floor is awash in blood now. Antoine steps into it and crouches to retrieve the ringing phone from the man's pocket.

He stares at the screen. Keenan, it reads.

He stands. Slides his thumb across the screen to answer the call. Holds it to his ear as he walks to the door.

"Dad. Thank God."

His associate is standing on guard in the corridor. He leads the way to the exit, and Antoine glides after him.

"Dad. Dad, you there?"

Tulio pushes open the door. Sunlight streams in. Carlos has the car pulled up in the alley outside. Antoine and Tulio get in. Carlos pulls away.

"Dad! Dad!"

"He can't make it to the phone."

10:55 a.m.

NAOMI DRIVES FAST down the wide, quiet boulevards. She has to find Craig.

When she left Rosie at the hotel, she didn't know where she was headed. She feared for Keenan, not knowing what he'd gotten himself into, but she knew that Fitz was with him. Fitz could do more for him right now than she could.

But she's not going to be a bystander in all this while a hurricane rips her people apart. Keenan wanted to look for his father, but he can't now that he's in police custody. So she will look for his father. She'll track him down, make sure he's safe. She doesn't think Antoine is actually after Craig, but she wants to put Keenan's mind at ease. She cares for him, regardless of anything else.

What a day it's been. She faintly remembers giving that speech to her girls in the locker room after the game. Was that really yesterday? Not a month ago? A year? Perhaps another lifetime because everything has changed since then. She used to dream about the four of them being back in town together again, never thinking they were each combustible ingredients in a fireball that would scorch the city. And the day isn't even over. It keeps on rolling. Rolling over each of them, crushing them beneath its wheels. She wonders what new surprise is lurking around the next bend.

The first place she checked was Craig and Rosie's house. No sign that anyone had been there since they left earlier that morning. She then remembered a sports bar where she and Keenan had watched games with Craig on Sunday afternoons during football season. They always had pretty waitresses in skimpy clothes. Craig was positively giddy when he flirted with them. And the servers, they humoured him. He was a regular, and it *is* Vegas.

She wonders if Craig, stressed and looking for comfort, would gravitate there by force of habit, even if it isn't football season. And so she drives rapidly and smoothly to the bar.

She pulls up on the street in a no-parking zone right in front of the doors. Gets out into a blast of hot air and jogs inside to a blast of air conditioning. It's a large space, with numerous flat-screen TVs all tuned to sports, and busy enough, with people loading up on breakfast: heaps of eggs, sausages, bacon, ham, home fries, washed down with pints of beer.

"I'm looking for Craig, tall, middle-aged guy, have you seen him?" she says to the hostess, who shrugs and looks about the place ineffectively. Naomi strides past her.

She scans every table but doesn't see him. She accosts one of the bartenders: "You seen a guy this tall, greying hair, Craig, he been here?"

The bartender nods. "He was sitting over there," she says, pointing to a stool at the bar with a half-finished mug of beer in front of it. "I think he went to the bathroom."

Naomi takes off to the back of the bar, turns right down a dim hall, at the end of which someone is leaving out a back exit. The shaft of light through the closing door is dazzling, and it silhouettes the exiting figure, who has a phone to his ear. The door swings shut and clicks closed. Naomi pauses. It was only a glimpse from behind with the light coming from the wrong direction, but it looked like...

She sprints to the men's washroom. Bursts through. Takes two long steps and halts in her tracks. She gasps. The floor is awash with blood. She steps back from the edge of the crimson liquid. Craig's eyes, utterly vacant, are still open. Blood bubbles out of his throat and leaks from his torso. Tears spring from her eyes like someone has cracked a water main. So much blood. She has never seen anything like it.

She has one more moment of shock and then registers that it *was* Antoine in the doorway. Making his getaway. She bolts, grabbing for Keenan's handgun, which she has holstered at the small of her back, beneath her shirt. Out one door, dashing down the hall, out the other, into a flood of heat and light. She is blinded for a moment, and then the alley comes into focus; at the end of it a car is turning right into a back street.

She runs, pistol in hand, tears up the alley like she's on a breakaway. She hits the street in a flash, but the car is already a block away, turning onto a main street. She plants her feet and points the gun with both hands. Her finger presses the trigger but doesn't pull. The car is too far away, and a second later it is gone from view. She lowers the gun. Clicks the safety back on.

My God, Antoine. She stares at the ground. What have you done?

★ ★ ★ ★ ★ ★ ★ ★ ★ ★ ★ ★ ★ ★ ★ ★ ★ ★ ★

12

11:00 a.m.

KEENAN STUMBLES ON a rock in the dirt. His head spins. The mountains swirl.

"Antoine?"

"Yes. It's me."

"Where's my father?"

He glances at Tyron, who is staring at him, looking like he wants to save him from this too. Keenan turns away, to the dry, scraggy slopes before him.

"Antoine. Where is he?"

"He's gone."

"No." Keenan shakes his head. His eyes sting. "No, no, no, no, no. Where is he?"

"He's dead. I made sure of it."

Keenan's eyes flood. He blinks and tears stream. "It wasn't him." He gulps back a sob. "It wasn't him. It was Miles."

His face contorts. "You hear me, you fuck!" The mountains echo his words back to him. "It wasn't him! Miles confessed to me, you worthless punk! *He* did it! Not my dad! *He* killed your father!"

307

"Miles confessed to you?"

Keenan folds to his knees. "Oh God. Oh fuck. You bastard. You piece of shit, Antoine."

"Where's Miles?"

"He's *dead*! Tyron killed him. You psychopath... My father... it wasn't him." His tears overwhelm him. "It wasn't... it wasn't..."

"I know."

Keenan wipes at his eyes. Takes deep breaths. "You got the wrong man. It wasn't him. You got the wrong man."

"I know."

Keenan hears crunching footsteps and looks up to see that Tyron has joined him. He looks away, unable to face his friend. "What?"

"I know about Miles. I know it was him."

Keenan gets to his feet. "What?"

"Miles killed my father. With Monk. At Bashinsky's orders. My foster parents too. I know."

"You know?" Keenan strides up the mountainside. "You sick, fucking—I don't even know what to call you. I don't know what you are. Why? Why my father, then?"

"You could've saved him, Keenan."

"Fuck you."

"You could've saved him when we were sixteen."

"You're insane. When we were sixteen—listen to yourself—what the fuck is wrong with you?"

"You took in Tyron, my only family, and you turned me away. Your father turned me away. *You* turned me away. I know you had a choice, Keenan. You made the wrong one."

Keenan screams. His entire body contracts. The mountains echo. "I'm gonna kill you. I'm gonna kill you, you fuck."

"You'll never see me again."

"You pathetic, worthless shit. You give Miles a pass and you kill my father."

"I've had a team at Miles's house since last night. As soon as he went home he was gone. But thank you...you and Tyron...for doing my work for me. Goodbye, Keenan. You see what life is like without a father."

The line beeps off.

Keenan crumples to the ground, his face in his hands.

11:19 a.m.

A STEP TOO late. Like she had been on the basketball court. Always a step too late.

The police ask her questions, and she can answer the specifics. Coming to the bar, seeing Antoine down the hall, entering the bathroom, seeing the body, the blood, chasing after Antoine.

"What kind of car?"

"Grey. Small."

"Make?"

"I didn't see."

"Licence plate?"

"I didn't see."

"Why do you think he did this?"

Here she stumbles. The deeper questions, the why, she cannot explain. Keenan told her not to let anyone know that he had been at the Reef last night or that he had seen Antoine. Keenan is in police custody; he can tell them everything when he's ready. So she does not tell the cops what Antoine said about avenging his father's death. Even if she were to divulge this, she still wouldn't be able to explain how Antoine could do such a thing. She would have to recount the entire history of the four of them to begin to make sense of the last twenty-four hours, and she is not ready to do that. Especially not in front of a bunch of strangers.

At last the police give her some space. She sits on the curb outside the bar, not wanting to be in the same building as that body and its endless blood. Calling Rosie was even worse than finding Craig. Hearing that sweet woman's heart break.

Naomi knew Craig was dead the moment she saw him. That's why she went after Antoine instead of calling an ambulance right away. If she had just gone after Antoine first, as soon as she caught a glimpse of him, she would've caught him. She wonders if he would've tried to kill her too.

I let him down, she thinks. He wasn't a monster when I knew him. I shouldn't have listened when he said to stop visiting him in prison.

But really, what difference would it have made? How do you save someone from all the horrible things that have befallen them? How do you save them if they don't want to be saved?

You try, she tells herself in an admonishing tone.

She thinks back to when they were kids. She wants to say, How could we have known? But the truth is they did know. All three of them knew that something sinister was ripening in Antoine, and they left him to fend for himself, each of them consumed by their own ambitions.

She gives a snort of self-reproach. Where have their ambitions taken them?

If this is it, it wasn't worth it.

She hangs her head. Runs her hands through her hair. Feels like she could cry again if she wasn't emptied of tears.

For some reason, at that moment, the smiling faces of her girls yesterday, as she high-fived and shoulder-bumped them, return to her. Fill her mind with their radiant exuberance. They make her smile, in spite of everything since then.

You wouldn't be a coach now, she thinks, if you hadn't tried so hard to be a baller.

She stands up. Paces like it is the fourth quarter and she, on the sidelines, is in support of her players.

She has lost Antoine. No doubt of that. He is gone. Become something worse than if he were dead. But she is alive. She's still here. And she's not going to lose Tyron and Keenan. She's not going to divide them anymore. She'll be there for both of them, and they'll be there for her. But she's not going to be *with* either of them ever again. That time has passed. They are her brothers. Her family. She understands that now. For the time being at least, she will be on her own. And yet she can feel, as sure as she can feel the sun warming her skin, that she will be less lonely than before.

Her phone rings. It's Tyron.

"Hey," she says.

"Naomi." The gravity in his voice is evident in that one word.

"What's up?"

"I'm in the desert. I'm with Keenan."

"What happened?"

She listens. Learns of Detective Miles and his gruesome end. Learns of Antoine's phone call with Keenan. Learns of Keenan's shootout in the Reef. And when he is finished, she tells him all that has transpired with her.

"So Antoine was telling the truth," he says. "I was holding out hope that he was lying about Craig."

"I fucked it all up, Ty. I promised Key I'd keep his father safe. Instead I'm the one who sent him into Antoine's hands."

"None of this is your fault. Believe me. Antoine made his choice. Nothing that happened to him excuses what he's done."

"We should've never turned our backs on him. He needed a family and we were it."

"I've had that thought too. But the truth is we had our own issues, Naomi. Who we are now? Yeah, we could've been there for him. Who we were then? We weren't ready for it."

"So he knew Craig wasn't involved in killing his dad. Or your parents. He knew it and he still killed him."

"That's right."

She takes a moment. The viciousness and vindictiveness, the extent of it. "How'd you turn out so different, Ty? Your parents got murdered when you were a kid too. How come you're not filled with hate?"

She waits for his answer. Can almost hear Tyron thinking it over.

"I'm not sure," he finally says. "It's not because I'm naturally good, I know that much. Antoine lost his dad at a younger age than I lost my parents. Also, I had my parents a lot longer than he did, and *they* were good people." He pauses. "And the Quinns took me in. He was left on his own."

No matter what he said about them dealing with their own issues in the past, not being equipped to support Antoine, she can hear it in his voice: he blames himself too.

"You're wrong, Ty," she says. "You are good. You always have been."

"Thanks, Naomi." She can't be sure, but she thinks there is less guilt in his voice. She hopes so.

"How's Key?" she asks.

"Bad."

"I should be there. You guys coming back or staying put?"

"We're staying. Key says we shouldn't leave the crime scene. So we can explain how everything went down. He had me get a hold of a cop friend of his. Fitzgerald. I told him everything. He's on his way out here with the rest."

"Fitz. I know him. His wife's too flirty for my liking, but he's solid. He should help us."

They are silent a while, nothing to say, yet taking comfort in their connection over the phone. She wanders away from the bar and the surrounding commotion of emergency workers, witnesses, and bystanders.

"Naomi."

"Yeah?"

"About us..."

"Yes?"

"Whether you're leaving Keenan or not, he loves you. I can't—"

She laughs. Nothing jovial, just a gentle release of tension. "I can't either. We're family. You, me, Keenan. I know that now."

"Good," he says.

She feels like he is going to say more. She wants him to say more. But he just says "Good" one more time.

It is enough for her.

11:28 a.m.

TYRON LOWERS THE phone and looks at it. He takes a deep breath. Then he puts it away.

He raises his eyes to Tara and Ricky—he called them in after he got off the phone with Fitzgerald. For once Ricky is speechless. Tara, never overly demonstrative, looks composed, but he can spot the tension along her jaw-line and around her eyes, the protectiveness with which she carries herself. Civilians, he thinks, glancing at the corpse in the dirt.

Ricky, staring at the body, reaches out his hand to Tara. She looks down, contemplates it, then takes it in her own. Their eyes meet. They smile briefly. Look away, as though they might ruin the moment by drawing too much atten-tion to it. But they continue holding hands. Tyron is glad that they do.

He turns and looks at the slope behind him. Keenan is nowhere to be seen. Must've hiked around to another face of the mountain. For the best. He needs his space.

Tyron follows the tire tracks toward Auntie Trudy's car, which takes him past the body. It does nothing to him. If anything, he feels calmer looking at it, its limbs bent unnaturally, its clothes torn, its face broken and bloody. He is not a civilian, no matter that his uniform hangs in a closet or that his rifle is in the hands of someone else. He comes around the sedan to inspect its blood-smeared hood and dented bumper. He fingers the broken glass at the edges of the smashed windshield. He will pay for the repairs. Or perhaps a new car.

He understands that Vegas PD will most likely come after him. Even with Keenan's friend Fitzgerald on their side, the cops won't hold back on someone who ran over a decorated detective.

But this doesn't bother him either. Enemies, adversity, danger, death, it's what Tyron is equipped for. Built for it, one piece at a time.

Marlon was right, he thinks. I can be of use. It's not everyone who can keep their head when the world goes to hell.

But no more fighting and killing for men I would never vote for. No more fighting and killing for economic interests I will never benefit from. No more fighting and killing poor people. I decide who I fight. And who I fight for.

A breeze stirs and is a moment's respite from the oven-like heat. It is cool on his cheek. One corner of his mouth tugs upward. Maybe the desert is where I belong. Where else would a breeze like this feel so good?

"Ty," Tara calls to him. "Where's Keenan?"

He walks over to her and Ricky, and notes that they drop hands when he gets close. Glancing back, he says, "He went up there somewhere."

"Do you think you should go after him?"

"Why?"

"I think you should check on him."

"The man's pops just died," Ricky says. "That could

push anyone over the edge." He looks up at the mountain. "Bad pun. Unintentional."

Tyron turns and looks up. Suicide. He didn't think of that.

"You think?" he asks.

Tara shrugs. "It's been a long day for everyone. He shouldn't be alone, though. Not up there. Find him, Ty. He needs you."

Tyron nods. He jogs across the valley and onto the low slopes of the mountain. At first, suicide struck him as an unlikely concern. It's not something Tyron would ever contemplate, and so it didn't come to mind. But Tara has put the idea in his head, and the sight of Keenan weeping on his knees, clawing at the dirt with his fingernails, makes Tyron think that any outcome is possible.

He hoists himself up over rocks and continues on a small footpath between the thorny brush, winding his way up and around the mountain. The world drops away and stretches out to the horizon, a flat sea of reddish brown, but for a peak here and there in the distance. Tyron's shirt clings to his back, perspiring with each step higher. He stops, breathes deep, looks up from his footing, and sees Keenan above him, standing on a ledge.

"Key!" he shouts.

Keenan looks down at him.

"Hang on, I'm coming!"

Tyron bounds up the stony path.

11:49 a.m.

AS FAST AS Tyron can run, Keenan knows he can jump ten times over before his friend will reach him. It's a long drop onto the sand and rocks. Not the worst way to go, he thinks. A fine view, a final rush, dead before you can feel a thing.

"Key!"

Keenan looks down. Even now Tyron is trying to save him. The man is indefatigable. Keenan cannot deny that it is inspiring.

He has learned a lot these past twenty-four hours. He has learned that the world is a brutal place when you're not sitting on top of it. Learned that he can endure. Endure his own failings and those of others. Endure pain like he couldn't have imagined. Endure loss. Most of all, he has learned that more death solves nothing. It's just more death. It doesn't bring back Raul Deco, or Terrence and Viola Shaw. It doesn't bring back Craig Quinn.

Tyron is a few yards away. Now or never. Keenan leans over the edge. Studies the drop. He closes his eyes.

It doesn't bring back Reggie Harrison. It won't bring him back. It won't.

"Key!"

Eyes open.

Tyron is panting as he clambers up onto the ledge. "You all right?"

Keenan helps him to his feet. "Not all right. But I'm not going to jump, if that's what you were wondering."

"I wasn't but... my cousin, she..."

Keenan shakes his head. He looks out over the ledge. The desert blurs as fresh tears come to his eyes. He feels Tyron's strong hand on his shoulder. Looks to his friend, grateful.

"We can never escape the wrongs we've done. Can we?"

"No," Tyron says. "We can't. But that doesn't stop us from doing right with the time we've got left."

Keenan stares at Tyron. At last he nods.

"Let's go back. I'm ready to face whatever comes."

Tyron smiles. "Me too."

Keenan embraces his brother, and they begin their descent down the mountain.

11:56 a.m.

ANTOINE, IN THE backseat of a car with tinted windows and clean plates, speeds westward toward California and the Pacific coast. Another of his associates sits behind the wheel and Carlos sits in the front passenger seat. Carlos will accompany Antoine throughout his journey by ship to Mexico and by plane to Venezuela, and will most likely be with him long after. A loyal ally. A proficient employee. A fearless soldier. But not a friend. Definitely not a brother. Antoine has no need for either of those.

At this point he is more content alone. He is stronger alone. People are resources, assets, and none is more valuable to him than Carlos, but all are expendable. There's no shortage of people in this world. That's what he never understood as a boy. You lose one person, you replace them with another. People let you down, you find new people. All expendable, all interchangeable.

The men he killed are replaceable. No doubt of that. They won't be missed long. And if anyone does, they're a fool. Those men were meant for the grave.

Thirty-two years old, he reflects, and my life's work complete. What now, Antoine Deco? I like making things happen. Being a player. My game is over, but maybe I could compete in someone else's. Rent my services out.

Maybe Venezuela or Bolivia can use a man like me. You would like that, *padre*, wouldn't you? Is that why you never told me where you or my mother came from? So that I would think all Latinos are my brethren?

Are you sleeping easier, *padre*? Your son is no coward. He has set right your wrongs. He is no coward.

Antoine stares out the front window. The land is open.

Yes, he thinks, I would like to play in another game. I will need a long rest, but when I am strong, I would like to hunt again. Perhaps that is what fate had in mind for me. Perhaps that is why fate took you, *padre*. To give me a purpose that would prepare me for something larger. There is much out there.

I would like to hunt again.

Acknowledgements

First and foremost, I have to thank my family: my parents, Chris and Debra, and my sister, Ruth — not only for their endless love, support, and encouragement, but also for being with me on this long journey to publication. Listening to my ideas, sharing their opinions, and editing my early drafts, they have helped make me the writer I am.

I must thank my agent, Michael Levine. I never dreamed that I would have such a staunch supporter in my corner, and I will forever be indebted to him for the generosity he has shown me and my family, and for the doors he has opened for me.

Thanks to my editor, Doug Richmond, who has provided me with the incredible opportunity of publication, and whose insights have taken this book to new heights. I will always be grateful.

I'd like to thank Sarah MacLachlan, Janie Yoon, Maria Golikova, Holley Corfield, Sonya Lalli, Joshua Greenspon, and everyone else at House of Anansi Press. It has been a dream to be associated with their reputable publishing house, and I could not be happier with the finished product we have put together. Especial thanks to Anansi's senior designer, Alysia Shewchuk, for creating such an incredible cover, a significant component in the experience of reading this book. I could not have asked for anything better. Thanks also to my copyeditor, Tilman Lewis, and my proofreader, Gemma Wain. Their excellent work ensured that the book reached its full potential.

Thanks go to Donna Morrissey, my advisor in the Humber School for Writers program. Her guidance took this book and my writing to new levels, and I will never forget it.

Thanks also to David Bezmozgis and everyone involved in the Humber School for Writers for being such a valuable resource and support network for me.

Thanks to everyone at Westwood Creative Artists, especially Maxine Quigley, for all the work done on my behalf. I greatly appreciate it.

Thanks to my Queen's University Creative Writing professor, Carolyn Smart, whose teachings and encouragement helped make me the writer I am today (hopefully that's a compliment).

A huge thanks to my web designer, Louis Wong, for doing such an incredible job on my website. I could not be happier with the outcome.

Thanks to Jacobo Romo and the Spanish Centre in Toronto for their assistance in correcting the Spanish.

Thanks to all the readers of my early drafts (not just of this book but of my previous unpublished works too), far too many to name, but whose comments and edits have shaped my stories, forever teaching me what works and what doesn't. Thanks also to family, friends, and acquaintances who had a kind or encouraging word for me during the seemingly endless and difficult road to get to this point. It helped.

Lastly, thank *you* for reading this book (and its acknowledgements). All my life I have wanted to write stories that people could enjoy. I hope you have enjoyed this one.

Born in Durban, South Africa, **DAVID ALBERTYN** immigrated to Canada with his family when he was ten years old. Since 2005, Albertyn has been a competitive tennis player and coach. A graduate of Queen's University and the Humber School for Writers, Albertyn lives in Toronto. *Undercard* is his first novel.